The Dark

13 Days

K.Lippi

ISBN 978-1-936352-98-2
1-936352-98-2

Published by Mirror Publishing
Milwaukee, WI 53214
www.pagesofwonder.com

Printed in the USA

Meet the cast

Seth and Selene Holloway

Seth, eighteen years old entered the show with his younger sister, Selene, in order to save their parents ranch.
Seth is very good-looking and outgoing unlike his little sister who is quiet and reserved but not without courage and loyalty.

Jennifer and Joanna Johnson

Jennifer and Joanna are sisters from Seattle, WA. They entered the contest to repay some of their parent's debts.

Wayne and Warren Jones

William and Warren are nineteen year old twins from Austin, TX and freshmen at Texas Culinary Academy.
With the winning money they wish to open a restaurant – so they say.

Carmen Skylark and William Hawthorn

Carmen Skylark and William Hawthorn are small TV actors and have been together since the start of their career. With the game they hope to regain their status of fame.
Carmen is hoping to rekindle William's love but he is entwined in Selene's puzzling secret and at the same time, William is trying to find pieces of his past in St. Clara Asylum with the help of his dead little sister, Alice.

Yolanda Perez and Raul Ramirez

Yolanda and Raul are cousins from Miami, FL and they want to invest a big part of the winning money in their education and the rest for traveling around the world. Everything seemed fine until Yolanda's prior life hunts her down.

Pricilla Long and Ivy Woo

Pricilla Long and Ivy Woo are the daughters of rich tycoon dads from San Francisco, CA. They applied for the show just for fun and hoping to be the next London Holton and Nicky Rich but the show it turn out to be more than they bargain for.

Phillip Stewart and Maria Sanchez

Phillip and Maria are eighteen years old and a couple from Tucson, AZ. They are high school sweet hearts and determined to win the money for a breath taking wedding followed by the purchase of a house for the start of their new life – but Maria has a dark secret, this secret could cause the destruction of her and Phillip's relationship.

Matthew and Anthony Roma

Matt and Tony are two gifted brothers from Boston, MA. Matt is nineteen and Tony is seventeen years old. They are two well-known young writers and already have three bestselling books out in the market and one of their books is being made into a movie. The talented brothers embarked upon this journey to write about the many dark secrets of the place and hope to solve the massacre that had happened many years ago that caused the asylum to be shut down.

Part One

The Cast

Day One

Friday, August 13, 2010

Selene

It is a beautiful warm August day filled with the tenderness of the summer season. The sky is clear and sunny. The Ocean is calm and peaceful. Not like I pictured it to be. I imagined it mighty and angry.

I always wanted to see the Ocean, and being on the water is not as exciting as I anticipated it to be. It is not as unique or breathtaking as I had hoped; it is a rather strange and uneasy experience. The constant rocking of the boat tenses me and I find myself shoulder to shoulder with my older brother, Seth.

Not wanting to let anyone know about my delicate state, I continue to look out of the porthole and think to myself how bizarre life can be. Who would have known that one day I would be sitting in a fishing boat gliding along the Pacific Ocean with fourteen other contestants for the latest Reality TV show, "13 Days".

The show was created by YTV, a young and hip channel for young and hip teenagers.

Advertisements for the new reality show ran on the YTV channel 24/7 and producers of the show traveled all over the country in search of unique and quirky contestants who could make their show a hit amongst the young population.

Out of thousands of people hoping to be the latest Reality TV star and have the chance to win one-million dollars, my brother and I were fortunate enough to be selected.

We applied for the show out of desperation. It is our last and only hope to help our parents and, thanks to our lucky star, we were selected to be on the premiere of "13 Days".

I look over to my side and stare at my big brother who was always, and still is, my idol.

Seth is eighteen years old and has my mother's stunning look. He is tall, well-built with fine sandy hair, and chocolate brown eyes. He is a typical young cowboy with a straight 4.0 GPA at Montana State University. Over all he is perfect and has trails of girls wishing to be his girlfriend. But in the last few months his only preoccupation has been how to save our ranch.

I, on the other hand, am the ugly duckling in our family. Sometimes I think when my parents created my brother they gave him all their best qualities and I was stuck with the leftovers. I'm slim with no curves. I have long fine hair but unlike my brother, my hair is black-blue like the feathers of ravens, and my eyes are bright green, like cat's eyes. To top it all off, my skin is as white as snow. I tried to tan, but all I got was heavy sunburn after lying under the warm rays for only twenty minutes. I couldn't sit, lay, or sleep for days, and in the end I looked like a lobster on two legs. Seth was laughing at me for days, especially when I had to spend the first night underneath the shower with cold water running down my body.

My sixteen years of age makes me the youngest contestant on the show, and probably in the eyes of the others competitors, the least threatening to their chances. But they are wrong. Unlike many of them looking for a quick and easy way to gain success and fame or fulfill their dream that requires a lot of money, my brother and I came into this game in order to save our family's ranch, which is just weeks away from being lost.

He smiles at me and I smile back at him. Then he goes back to his conversation. He is animatedly talking to Yolanda Ramirez and Raul Flores about random stuff. For some strange reason all three of them became quite good friends in less than 24 hours. I think it is useless, because it doesn't really matter how much we like the other contestants. Sooner or later we will start stabbing each other in the back for that one-million dollar prize.

Yolanda and Raul are cousins from Miami, and their parents are originally from the Dominican Republic. Yolanda's mother sent her to live with her aunt, uncle and Raul in the US a few years ago. She wanted a better life for her daughter.

The two cousins are both seventeen years old and have very exotic features: hazel brown skin, dark hair, and beautiful olive green eyes. They look more like siblings then cousins.

Yolanda and Raul are participating in the show in order to invest some of the money into their education and their childhood dream – traveling the world.

I shift my attention away from my group and begin to observe the other competitors. I only know about them from their Bio Video running through the channel two weeks ago in between the commercials. I am not too excited and don't know how to interact with others, especially with people around my age. My brother and I were home schooled and grew up on a small horse ranch with our parents in the middle of nowhere in Montana. Seth was, and still is, my best friend, but since he left our ranch at the age of thirteen for Mauston Academy, a boarding school, our relationship has suffered. It is not as strong as it used to be. He has distanced himself from me.

Behind me I can hear Phillip Steward and Maria Sanchez whispering sweet and soft words to each other. Both are eighteen years old and from Tucson, AZ. They are high school sweet hearts and determined to win the money for a breath taking wedding followed by the purchase of a house for the start of their new life.

I do have to admit, they make quite a stunning couple; they are both quite attractive. Phillip has a well-proportioned body, shaggy brilliant blond hair with piercing blue eyes. I read he does some modeling from time to time.

His fiancée Maria looks like a Latino sex goddess with her long, dark, curly hair, chocolate colored eyes, bronze skin, and an hourglass figure that evokes jealousy and envy from every woman she comes in contact with.

Sitting in front of them are the two gifted brothers from Boston, MA. Their names are Matthew and Anthony Roma. Matt is nineteen and Tony is seventeen years old. They are two well-known young writers and already have three bestselling books to their credit. One of their books is being made into a movie.

The talented brothers embarked on this journey out of

curiosity and hoped to write their experiences in another bestselling book. By the sounds coming from behind me, I guess they have already started. The tapping of the laptop keys bounces from bulkhead to bulkhead of the boat.

On the other side of the ship are the twin brothers, Wayne and Warren Jones, joyfully talking to the two best friends from San Francisco, CA, Pricilla Long and Ivy Woo. The girls are attractive seventeen and eighteen year olds with long, silky black hair and dark eyes.

Wayne and Warren are from Austin, TX and are freshmen at Texas Culinary Academy. Their goal, as with most of us, is to win the prize to achieve their dreams, of opening a restaurant. They discovered their passion for cooking at a very early age through their grandmother Cecile.

Pricilla Long and Ivy Woo are the daughters of rich tycoon dads. Their families own property all around the world and they applied for the show just for fun. They hope to be the next London Holton and Nicky Rich.

As we were about to embark upon the boat, I discovered an attraction, or the beginning of a romance sparking into life, among the four of them. The Jones brothers aren't too bad either.

They are muscular with mocha brown skin and sparkling eyes that look like shining stars. Every time they smile their white teeth dazzle in the sunshine.

I can expect more romance or drama blooming among our group. TV Producers make sure to cast people who are somewhat attractive and can bring drama, romance, shock and tension to their show in order to entertain the audience.

Behind the twins and the two best friends are the last two groups made up of the two sisters from Seattle, WA, Jennifer and Joanna Johnson and Carmen Skylark and William Hawthorn from Los Angeles, CA, two TV show stars from Beesney Channels.

Jennifer, age eighteen, has long brown hair and eyes with a well built body, while her sister Joanna, age seventeen, has short black hair, brown eyes, and a lean body. Both sisters are completely mesmerized by the two small celebrities among us. They are constantly asking stupid questions about their lives in Hollywood among the other stars. They are absolutely gaga for the two stars, especially for Carmen Skylark.

I, on the other hand, am all gaga for William Hawthorn, even though Carmen and William have been a couple since the beginning of their careers and have been inseparable since then. Carmen isn't ugly – actually she is quite pretty with her long red hair and green eyes and ivory skin. She is flawless – unlike me.

I remembered at age eleven how crazy and addicted I became when I saw William Hawthorn for the first time appearing on a TV show called "Jack and I". I had my bedroom walls plastered with his posters and collected everything about him. I can say I was his first fan and still am number one. William was, and still is, in my book *the* hottest and coolest guy my eyes had ever laid on. His dark brown hair and deep blue eyes make my heart melt every time I look into them, not to mention his cool British accent. I'm a sap when it comes to accents, especially on good looking guys like William Hawthorn.

He wasn't always seen as attractive. Most of the teen girls thought he was kind of a troll and they revolted against him and the movie director when he was cast to play the part of the handsome Devon.

After the movie came out, William became the new teen sex idol, and I can't believe he is standing a few feet away from me. This is a great opportunity for us to get to know one another. Perhaps he might fall in love with me too and….

I stop dreaming, take a deep breath, smile, shake my head and think how childish I am.

All of a sudden William Hawthorn places his book aside and stares straight at me, causing my heart to jump a few beats and my face to turn red. I can feel my ears and cheeks burning. He smiles at me and I return the gesture, my face getting redder and redder by the second.

"Keep your eyes on the prize and not on boys," Seth whispers in my ear. "You know how important it is for us."

"I know that," I snap at him. He didn't need to remind me how important the prize money is for all of us. I know how badly my brother wants to save our ranch and how long he's been yearning to take over the ranch from our parents.

Feeling cross, I stand up needing some fresh air. I didn't realize how uneasy the ocean makes me. I always found an attraction to the sea, but now that I'm on a boat and gliding on the surface of the ocean – I'm terrified.

Cold, salty, fresh air greets me on deck. Strange sounds from beneath the boat startle me. I look down and to my amazement I find a school of dolphins riding side by side with the boat. I smile and I can feel my body fill with joy. They are so striking, and I consider myself very lucky for experiencing something this beautiful.

"They are Pacific White Side Dolphins."

I tense my upper body and quickly look toward the voice.

I start and my eyes widen at the sight of William Hawthorn standing next to me. Our shoulders touch. I can feel a swarm of butterflies building up in my stomach.

He smiles at me once again. He is waiting for a response but all I can do is nod and give him a shy smile.

Out of the blue William takes a step back. He looks curiously at me. I have to admit, I feel a bit uncomfortable by the way his eyes wander over me. No one ever stared so intently at me before. My heart is palpitating, my hands are moist and I can feel my face warming.

A raven squawks loudly, drawing William's attention away from me. I follow his gaze and spot the silhouette of Black Bird Island slowly forming on the horizon.

"Black Bird Island," he announces, and by his tone of voice I have the feeling he doesn't want to go there.

After a long pause he asks, "Do you know the history behind the island?" I shake my head. "In the late eighteen hundreds a small group of people moved onto the island. They made their living by fishing, and donated a lot of their fortune to their surrounding communities." He smirks. "Some said that the donations were more of a pay off to keep the locals silent about their true identities, you see," and he moves closer to me with a smile that makes my heart skip a few more beats. "They were notorious criminals. They made their living by robbing banks and trains, and when they got enough money to retire, they moved to Black Bird Island.

"Months passed and slowly the small group of criminals vanished, one by one. The remaining five began to accuse one another of the disappearance of their companions and in the end, they killed each other.

"Local stories say that seventeen ravens emerged from the island's rotten soil. The exact number of criminals that moved to the island decades ago is unknown." He points ahead at the swarm of black birds circling the citadel. Chills run through my body. I wrap my arms around me and start to rub my hands up and down my upper arms. "And that's where the island got its name," he quickly adds with a heart melting smile. "The locals proclaimed the island to be one of hell's gates.

"Years later a man named John Kane bought the island. He and his brother were partners in an oil company and made a fortune.

"During one of his business travels he purchased an old English castle and transported it stone by stone to Black Bird Island. It took over ten years and many lives were lost during the rebuilding of the castle.

"John Kane and his wife moved in soon after their wedding but their welcome didn't last long," William says with his narrative voice. He gives me the creeps. "According to the story, John Kane's wife was a Creole woman and John created a sanctuary on the island for himself and his wife where their love wouldn't be judged or hated. Some say she was a black priestess," he adds with a wink in my direction. "James Kane, John Kane's older brother, wouldn't have a Creole in his family and so, on their wedding day, he poisoned his brother and his new bride.

"It didn't take long for James Kane to move to Black Bird Island along with his wife and three children. A month later his three children vanished from the house. They were nowhere to be found. His wife hung herself in the library and soon after her death Mr. Kane's staff committed suicide too. They jumped off the west wing tower after cutting their throats.

"A year after Kane's wife's death, Mr. Kane walked into the library with a loaded pistol and shot himself." William places his index finger on his right temple, bends his thumb down. "Bang," he says with a sadistic smile. "Twenty years passed and the stronghold was converted into an asylum for the insane. In 1992 the asylum was closed and in a few hours we will be on that haunted island, awakening what should remain dormant."

Cold chills run up my spine, stiffing my back. "Did you say haunted?"

William smiles, "Did I scare you? I'm sorry," and he leans his upper body upon the banister ogling me once again from top to bottom and once again my cheeks feel warm and my heart is about to jump out of my chest.

"No," I state timidly, but in reality my bones are shaking underneath my flesh. William grins lightheartedly. "How do you know so much about Black Bird Island?" I ask.

"A few nights ago, as I was flipping through the channels, I saw one of those ghost tracker shows and Black Bird Island was their destination."

"And – is it – haunted?" I gulp.

"According to them – it's very haunted." My heart stops. "They brought a medium with them and......" William pauses, shifts his head to one side and his expression transforms before my eyes. "Are you OK?"

I frantically nod, "Yes – I'm great – fine," I tensely smile at him.

I find myself uneasily rubbing my hands within my long light cotton black and white striped gloves. William takes one step forward and is about to touch my exposed arms. Immediately, I take two steps back and swiftly grab his hands. I feel awful especially when I look at his confused expression. He wants to comfort me and I rudely interrupted him.

"I – have to go," I mutter, and leave, feeling terrible for my impolite behavior. But I can't help that I'm different from most of the other people.

I give one last quick peek to William before I descend the ship's ladder and see him staring at me confused and perplexed. It makes me feel even worse than I did a few seconds ago but as I said, I can't change what I am – an atrocity.

William

"You scared her away," Alice, my departed little sister moped.

Don't worry. I'll have the next thirteen days to know her, I reply with a smile.

Alice walks next to me. "William," she whispers. "Are you sure – you want to do this?"

"There's no turning back," I say. "I want to find out who I really am and why our mother gave me away."

"If you really insist," Alice quickly states as she watches the island move closer. She seems distressed.

"You don't have to come with me."

"No," she shakes her head. "I promise to stay by your side until you find yourself. Until you're happy and safe."

"Until I'm happy," I repeat her words aloud not believing that I could ever be happy. Until now, life hasn't been too kind to me and I haven't tried to change it either. I did pretty much everything I could do to destroy myself until Alice came to me one night while I was hanging on by a thread after a car crash. I was wasted and sped down LA's streets over 80 miles per hour. I took a wrong turn and drove into a building. I was in a coma for three weeks and when I finally woke up a little girl around the age of ten with a big smile on her face, pretty blue eyes, and long dark curly hair welcomed me back to the world of the living.

"Hi, I'm Alice – your sister," she smiled and gave me a kiss. I still remember how cold her lips felt on my forehead and how confused I was. From that day on, she's been at my side, keeping me company and looking after me.

"William!" Alice calls for my attention. I turn around and watch her balancing on the handrail of the boat.

Come down from there before…

"Before I fall and die," she interrupts me with a smile, "I guess you haven't noticed, but I'm already dead."

I shake my head in disappointment and keep thinking how much my life has changed since I met Alice.

"Beautiful – isn't it," I hear Carmen's voice next to me. I turn and see her lovely face smiling at me. She embraces me and gives me a gentle kiss on my neck.

"Not here," I tell her moving away from her arms. "Not now."

"Don't worry our plan is still safe," she smiles. I take a deep breath and think how someone as beautiful as she is could be so rotten.

"This is the last time. After this I'm done – we are done. I'm moving back to England."

"And what will you do?" she laughs at me. "Marry, have a few bastards in the world, and wait until death comes to collect you from your boring and insignificant life." She laughs some more. "You could start with that cowgirl."

"I can't believe I once loved you," I tell her and watch her gleeful face become preoccupied. I walk around her, back to my seat.

Selene

I look out of the portal and up into the sky. Above the island I discover the large, group of black ravens flying and cawing around the massive fort, built on the island's dark walls.

The closer we get to the island, the harder we are shaken from side to side by the constant rocking of the boat. The Ocean is uneasy and makes it hard for the captain to dock his "lady of the sea", as I heard him call his ship several times.

The boat tosses violently against the black rocky walls of the island and finally, after much cursing and yelling, the captain is able to dock his vessel without any further complications.

Finally, we descend from the boat. Some of us are pale, others green, ready to vomit at any moment. It was a rough and frightening experience.

The captain, along with his two older sons, begins to offload the boat by throwing our luggage onto the sand. While still in shock, we stand close to each other and stare straight ahead at the menacing colossal black stoned fortification with ten camera men aiming their lenses right at us.

Above, the sky is a clear, bright blue, and the sun is warm and welcoming. But the asylum at the peak of the island emanates danger, death and despair.

Unable to examine the building further, I turn my head and observe Carmen's finger tracing William's ear down to his neck and underneath his black T-shirt.

Something is disturbing my stomach, as is a load of bricks had fallen on it. Depressed and ready to leave the two love birds alone, I turn my eyes away when I suddenly hear Carmen.

"What's the matter with you?" she asks through her tightly clenched white teeth. She looks around making sure no one has seen them. Her gaze stops on my face. Automatically, I look away for two or three seconds, and then turn my attention back to them.

I watch William moving his upper body closer to hers and his lips touching her ear lobe. Carmen's body shudders with pleasure. He whispers something to her, and by the look on her face his words aren't sweet. Her happy and carefree expression transforms into rage in a matter of seconds, and her charming smile is replaced by a macabre one. She whispers something back to him. And at this moment William's features harden, his lips tighten, and his hands fasten upon Carmen's upper arm.

"You – are – hurting me!" She says aloud, attracting the attention of all of us. William releases her but his gaze is still locked on her. He looks dangerous – menacing. "I call the shots – not you," Carmen snaps at him.

Seth smirks, "Actors," he mutters dismissively.

I stare at my brother and then back to William. My heart is aching. His body is so tense and his eyes are filled with agony and anger. This is the one time I wish to use my extra sense to know what's going on with them, but that would be wrong. I would be breaking their privacy barrier. Everyone deserves to have secrets.

Unexpectedly my brother takes my hand and pulls me in the direction of my newly discovered torture chamber on earth for the next thirteen days.

The rest of the group follows our lead.

In the background I hear Carmen complaining about the drenched, narrow, broken stairs cut in the rock. She keeps sliding in her new Proda stiletto shoes.

"Shit!" All of a sudden Carmen shouts. Everyone stops and watches her standing heatedly to the side as she takes her left shoe off. Its heel dangles from side to side. "My shoes are ruined," she whines, and stomps her bare foot on the ground like a spoiled little girl. Seth sneers and keeps pulling me onward. I have a feeling he doesn't like them very much. I think it has something to do with their profession.

The rest of the group proceeds to follow us, as do nine of the cameramen. The tenth stays behind with Carmen as her two new minions stand besides her trying to comfort her while the cameraman films each and every movement they make and records their conversations down.

In the meantime, the building, with its pointed roofs and steeples, seems larger and more imposing, and looms above us in a very intimidating manner.

"Quite charming," Raul says with a hint of sarcasm in his voice as he rests his hand on the building's frame entrance door. "The perfect place to raise a family."

I smile.

Matt

"We're finally here," I tell my brother.

"Yep, we are," Tony agrees with me. How long we've researched the haunted history of this place and how long we've yearned to be here; to discover its deadly secrets.

As soon as Tony and I found out about the opportunity to come to this island, we hired lawyers, had our agent contact the station manager, and finally, after long negotiations, we were allowed to participate in this Reality TV Show.

Tony and I don't really care if we win or not. We have enough money. We only want to find out for ourselves if the rumors and the haunting are real or not.

With Tony at my side, we cross the threshold of the asylum and I begin to stroke the building like a long lost lover. I start to study the structure and feel the castle calling me – wanting me.

"I'm here," I whisper as I feel her cold, rough surface under my hands while I'm going over her history in my mind.

St. Clara, also known as Seapeak Castle, was built by Sir David Seapeak in 1402 on the shores of South England, and there are many macabre tales about it. One involves Sir Seapeak and his trusted servant, George.

George had a macabre sense of humor, and supposedly killed anyone who disrespected him. Word is that he practiced sorcery and introduced Sir Seapeak to black magic.

One night Sir David Seapeak and George had a violent argument. George lost his temper and stabbed his master. Soon after, George realized what he had done and slit his own throat.

Sir David Seapeak died three days later from infections of his wounds. Supposedly moans of agony can occasionally be heard in the west wing of the castle.

Another story concerns Sir John Seapeak, son of Sir David. John had two daughters, Elisabeth and Eleanor.

Eleanor was his favorite daughter, while Elisabeth was the troubled child. She caused him a lot of pain and grief.

Elisabeth was not only inhuman, she was also very vain, and often performed black magic to preserve her youth with the help of her servants who were mostly witches.

During that time, many young girls from the surrounding villages mysteriously vanished, forcing Sir John to conduct an investigation. In late November, an underground chamber was found beneath his castle. The crypt walls were drenched in blood. Body parts with clothing and belongings of the missing girls were found piled up in a corner.

Elisabeth was found guilty and her father locked her in the same chamber where she killed all those poor girls.

Eventually, Elisabeth died but it was not a quick and kind death, but rather slow and painful.

Shortly after her death, a black dog stalked the castle. There followed the mysterious disappearance of family and staff members. It is believed that the demonic dog was Elisabeth haunting the grounds, looking for revenge.

"Matt. Come," Tony calls my name, "They are waiting for us," and he points to the center of the courtyard were Jay Owen, the host and creator of "13 Days", patiently stands.

Jay Owen is a well-know and beloved singer from Australia. He is in his early thirties with jet-black hair and brown eyes. Since the day I met him, I have never seen him wearing anything other than expensive Italian business suits.

"Welcome to Black Bird Island," he says cheerfully, and starts to give us details about some of the historical facts of the island and the castle. My brother and I already know its history – even better then most historians.

"The asylum was closed down nineteen years ago after the massacre. Nurses, doctors, staff members, and patients were found with their throats cut. The culprit was never found," Mr. Owen continues. "Black Bird Island is now under the control of the US Cost Guard, and once a year they open the gates of St. Clara Asylum to the public. This year they opened the gates for us – for the next thirteen days." He begins to clap his hands. We start to clap ours as well. "Now to the rules of the game." We stand still. No one has any clue as to the rules or what the show is about other than that it's a cross between "Big Watcher" and "Clues", with an YTV twist, and the channel is very well-known for its outrageous shows with many twists. "The rules of the game are simple," Owen continues. "You'll be spending the next thirteen days on this deserted island and supposedly (haunted) mansion, interacting with one another.

"The money is hidden in the mansion and each day you'll receive a clue to its whereabouts. But the clues will not be easy to find.

"Remember, if you find the money, it doesn't mean you win. The ultimate goal of the show is to leave the house with the money and not without it.

"The best advice I can give you is this: if you do find the money or clues, hide them well. Also, choose your allies carefully. You are allowed to steal the money and the clues from each other.

"I wish you all good luck," he smiles, and once again we all cheer. "Your bags are waiting for you in your rooms. Have a pleasant time on Black Bird Island and I'll see you in thirteen days." Jay Owen raises his glass and swallows the contents in one gulp. The cameras shut down and he disappears from sight.

Some of the contestants begin to mingle, others look around as Tony and I start to explore the grounds.

Raul

"Hey! You two," I call for the Holloways' attention. "Let us check our rooms."

Seth and Selene turn around and give me their full attention. I motion for them to follow us. Seth seems agitated and Selene aggravated. I wonder what's bothering them.

"Sure," they say in unison, and we walk together through the large oak dungeon door.

The inside of the asylum is the complete opposite of the outside – at least on the surface. It is warm and welcoming. The lobby has four double doors on each side with dark wall to wall wood panels. Panoramic oil paintings hang on the walls, and a large crystal chandelier is suspended above a beautiful majestic staircase that is located in the center of the entrance hall, welcoming us inside. Medieval suits of armor stand on each side of the staircase, and a long golden-red Persian rug on the concrete floor leads into the residence.

All four of us stand with our mouths open. We have never seen a place this beautiful. It's majestic and most of all, elegant. It is impossible to believe that this was once a mental institution.

"What's wrong with you?" I hear a loud female voice. It sounds like Carmen. We turn our attention to our right. One of the double doors is open and leads into an entertaining room. Carmen is barefoot glaring, down at William who is comfortably sitting on one of the dark leather couches. "You've been acting strange ever since you had that car crash. Is this one of your rebellious phases?" William doesn't respond, instead he stands up and walks away.

Carmen's confused gaze follows her companion. "William Hawthorn, be aware of your choices!" she yells after him. "They might destroy your career or worse – your LIFE!!!!" and she slams the door behind him.

William smirks, quickly straightens his shoulders, and ascends the stairs, happily whistling to himself.

"Trouble in Paradise," Yolanda grins. I agree and feel sorry for Carmen, even though I don't like her very much. I can hear her crying behind the closed doors.

"Raul," I hear Yolanda calling me. I look up and see the three of them walking up the stairs. "Are you coming?"

I nod and quickly follow after them.

We reach the first floor and stroll down to the left side of a long hall with walls white as snow and a thick black stripe running horizontally down the middle. The other side of the hall is blocked by a metal door as are the stairs leading to the upper floors. I'm wondering why the upper floor is blocked but I don't give any further thought to it. My main goal at this moment is to find my room. I turn to the other side of the corridor and discover twenty black metal doors on each side. This is where the patients were housed, and we are now about to sleep in their rooms. I gulp and notice I'm not the only one who feels uncomfortable. Something evil is here with us. The castle is awakening.

Together with Yolanda, I start scanning the hallway, reading aloud the nametags beside each door. I read the names to the left side while Yolanda does the same with the ones on the right. To nobody's surprise, Jennifer and Joanna are sharing one bedroom as are the Jones's. Pricilla is sharing the same room with her best friend, Ivy and the two Roma brothers are also roommates. They are the only ones staying together, unlike the rest who are disappointed to be separated from their teammate.

"Selene, you and I are roommates," Yolanda smiles and raises her hand up high, "Give me a five."

"That's mean. Carmen and Maria are sharing one room," I say.

"Good for them," Yolanda replies. "They can now talk about fashion and their disturbed relationship with their boyfriends."

25

"Phillip and Maria's relationships isn't troubled," Selene replies.

Yolanda raises her eyes up at her, "Oh! Please. They pretend to be in love and all that gooey stuff, but when they're alone, they fight like two cats in heat."

"How do you know?" Selene asks. I notice how interested Seth seems to be in our conversation.

"I heard them fighting last night. Their room was directly next to mine and....." Yolanda looks around. "He can't stay away from other women. He's cheated on her for quite sometime with models, strippers, and some of her friends."

"No – Way"

"Way.....he is a sex addict," she whispers and Selene's face blushes. She is very sweet with a heart-shaped face, cute little nose, full red lips, and almond-shaped eyes. But there is something strange about her. For some reason she reminds me of a black cat – a witch's cat, only she seems too innocent and pure to be the pet of an evil creature.

"I'm with Phillip," Seth utters, interrupting our conversation.

A smile crosses my face. "This means, I'm with Mr. *Gorgeoooouuus*!" I sing the last word. They all smile at me except Yolanda. She raises her eyes and shakes her head.

"What? He is very attractive – you have no taste when it comes to men," I state, waving my hand at her.

"Whatever," she says and walks into her room. Selene follows her.

"I'll see you later," Seth says and we march into our rooms.

I open the bedroom door and discover Mr. Hot Guy, AKA William Hawthorn, lying on the first bed. He is pretending to sleep. I scan the room and notice how dark blue my new sleeping quarters are. Two hospital beds sit to the right each with different shades of blue bedspreads. Next to the beds are two small, white, night stands and on the opposite side are two white, double door closets behind our luggage. Straight ahead is a wide open average sized window with thick bars.

White translucent curtains ripple in the breeze and I can smell the cold, salty sea air. In between the two closets is a door partially ajar. I turn to the side and discover a very white and depressing hospital bathroom.

Oh, Well, I think to myself and walk to my closet. I start putting my clothes away and hope that William wakes up soon. I can't wait to get to know him better.

Carmen

The knock on the door startles me.

"Come in," I call in a voice much too loud. My high hopes of seeing William walk in quickly dissolve. It is Phillip collecting his fiancé.

"Wow," he gasps as he spots his sex goddess.

Seeing Phillip admiring Maria the same way William used to look at me gives me pain. He used to worship me and we were inseparable, unlike now. He is different. He has changed. He used to be fun and easygoing. No matter – I'll make him fall in love with me once again. I'll make him want me, and this dress will push me a step closer to his heart.

With high hopes, I stare at my stunning image in the mirror. I keep thinking how perfect the dress is. The black silk material brings out my red hair and green eyes.

I think I'm stunning, and Phillip confirms my intuition. I see his reflection in the mirror observing me with glee and desire. My ego is growing. I love it when men desire me. I smile within.

"Do you want us to wait for you?" Maria asks as she grabs her purse.

"No, thanks. I'm waiting for William," I reply, and spray Charnel # 5 in my hair.

"Ok, then. I'll see you soon." she leaves.

Minutes pass and I'm still wondering where my partner

could be. Tired of waiting any longer, I grab my purse and stroll into his room. It's empty and I notice it is identical to my room except for the colors. Mine is pink. I hate pink.

"William," I call, hoping he might be in the bathroom.

Unexpectedly the bathroom door opens and my hopes quickly fade away as I see Raul emerge with a towel wrapped around his lower body.

He's a bit on the flabby side, I smile at his love handles protruding from the top of his towel.

"Hey," I say with a forced grin. I don't like him or his cousin. It has something to do with their friendship with the Holloways. For some reason I can't stand that little country girl, not to mention her brother. I don't like the way he looks at me. He can't stand me and it bothers me. Normally, I don't care what people think of me but for some reason his opinion is important to me. "Have you seen William?" I continue.

"He already left."

"Alone?"

"He left the room alone – if that's what you mean," he replies with a confused expression.

"Thanks," I tell him and before I open the door, I quickly ask, "Do you know where Selene is?"

"None of your business," says another masculine voice from behind me. I turn and stand face to face with Seth. He glares at me and my heart gives a small flutter. I stay cool and glare back at him.

"I was just curious….."

"If she was with William?" Seth rudely cuts me off. "No. She and Yolanda are waiting for us in their rooms. You can soothe your nerves and your paranoia."

I nod and I leave the room without further explanation.

Generally I would let no one disrespect me that way, but at the moment I'm in a secluded set with fourteen strangers, and my partner seems indifferent of my well-being.

I enter the dining room and William is sitting by the table conversing with the two Roma brothers about the island. I do not know why he is so interested in this God-forsaken place. It gives me the creeps. It is old, stuffy, and smells of mold and death.

To my surprise, the dinning room is wide open with a long oak table in the center of the room. A red table cloth with exquisite silverware sits on top along with many mouth watering foods. Three large arched balcony windows dominate the left side of the wall, and animal heads hang on the opposite side. I wrinkle my nose at the vulgar hunting trophies. I can't understand how people find it amusing or tasteful to hang the heads of dead animal on walls or, as a matter of fact, killing them in the first place. Unable to look at them I walk closer to the table and notice nametags sitting in front of each plate.

"Hey, there," I smile at William, placing my hand on his shoulder. He looks up and gives me a quick greeting with a head bob. I bite my lower lip and try to keep my temper under control.

Demoralized, I sit in my designated place and contemplate my next move. The Holloways and the two cousins from Miami walk in. William stops talking and directs his attention to Selene. I sink my fingernails into my knees. He is supposed to look at me that way, not her! Why is he so attracted to her? She is not his type and she cannot give him the lifestyle I can provide. Look at what she's wearing! A hand me down dress that was in style five years ago. What's happening? I'm losing him. I can't lose him. He is my best friend, partner and soul mate.

"Hey!" he smiles at her as she sits next to him. Meanwhile, I'm forced to sit next to her brutish brother on the other side of the table, watching my man flirting with that cowgirl. She blushes and gives him a timid smile. William smiles and the way he is staring at her makes my blood run cold. He never looked at me that way. He can't be – he couldn't be – in love with her. No way – not him.

I stand up and leave the room. I need some fresh air and cannot bear for anyone to see me in this state. Cameras are positioned around the house and I do not want my fans to see me like this.

I walk up and down the hall, trying to convince myself that I'm just imagining things. There is no way he is in love with her. He loves me – not her. He is just sticking to the plan.

Yes, he is sticking to our plan. I smile, take a deep breath, and before I walk back into the room, I take a quick glance in the mirror to make sure my appearance is as flawless as always. Satisfied with myself, I join the others with my spirits high.

"I love old black and white movies," that dimwit of a cowgirl says to William.

"Me too," he smiles back at her. His eyes seem filled with sparks.

I sit back in my chair and begin to eat. I turn to the side and begin to converse with Joanna while William is still flirting with that naive little cowgirl.

All of sudden a voice interrupts our conversations, "Fifteen little trespassers are dining. One little trespasser is not." It is the voice of a little girl echoing through the room.

All of us start to look around, confused and curious.

Then the lights turn off and the loud sounds of metal gates sliding and locking can be heard. Lightning is flashing outside of the windows and the booming reverberations of thunder echo through the fortress. Everyone begins to scream. My heart is in my throat and my stomach turns upside down. None of us knows what is happening.

Everybody is panicking, chairs crash to the floor as people shove me from side to side, calling for their partners and friends. I do the same and William is immediately at my side.

"What's happening?" I ask, taking deep breaths. I'm claustrophobic and darkness makes me feel like I'm being shut up in a small box. I start hyperventilating and William gently kisses my cheek and massages my neck. I start to relax until I hear Matt scream, followed by a loud thud.

"And now there are fifteen little trespassers left," concludes the voice. As the lights turn back on, I find everyone scattered throughout the room. William is by my side – as it should be.

"Is everyone all right?" William asks. They stupidly nod and at the same time glance around with wide eyes, inspecting the room to make sure their partners are fine.

"Matt!!!" Tony calls for his brother. "Did anyone see Matt?" He frantically glances around the room.

We search for Tony's brother everywhere but he is gone. We only find a chess piece lying on Matt's chair. A rook.

We wonder what it means. Is this part of the show or not? The way Matt disappeared took our breath away. It was so abrupt, unpredictable, and terrifying. I just hope it won't be the beginning of a horrific experience.

Priscilla

Shaken and confused, I follow the group to the entertainment room. It is quite large and has a lot of equipment. There is a large flat screen TV connected to a DVD player, and a video game console. To the side of the room there is a pool table next to a small stage with a karaoke machine connected to another large flat screen TV on the wall. In the center of the room, in a comfortable semi-circle around the fireplace, is a large U-shaped leather couch.

I sit down on the couch and observe Raul and Seth playing pool as they discuss the frightening event. I just hope it won't be typical of the show. I was right next to Matt when it happened. Matt's screams still ring in my head and I can still feel his hand grip around my ankle when he tried to pull himself up from the opening that magically appeared beneath his chair. I haven't told that part to anyone and I don't intend to.

In the background, I hear Ivy and Wayne's voices. They are singing one of the Black Beans songs on the small stage.

Everyone stops what ever they were doing and begin

watching them. Ivy has a strong and beautiful voice. I was always jealous of her artistic gift. I wish I had her talent.

Our concern begins to lift away as we watch Wayne goof around. He is trying to cheer us up and by the look of the faces around me, it seems to be working. Most are smiling now, and others can't wait to jump on stage and sing one or two songs.

To the side of the room I notice Phillip and Jennifer slipping away from the group. Odd.

Jennifer

"Want one?" Phillip asks me as he places a piece of gum in his mouth.

I shake my head and continue to look out of the window. I have never seen a sky filled with so many beautiful stars as tonight. I never knew the sky had so many stars.

In the distance, I watch a falling star disappear below the dark horizon of the Pacific Ocean. I close my eyes and make a wish.

Unexpectedly, Phillip grabs my hand and pulls me to his chest. I feel my heart beating against him and his heart against mine. He leans forward and I do the same. I know I shouldn't, but I never felt so comfortable – so secure – in my life.

We kiss and it is fantastic. I don't want this moment to end.

"What a show." I hear and we quickly pull apart. Maria is standing in front of us with an expression that brings cold shivers to my body. I don't know if I should stay or run.

"Maria," Phillip says, and gives me a gentle push signaling me to leave.

Thankfully, I depart while keeping my eyes on Maria, just in case she decides to jump me and rip my hair off.

Once out of the room, I hear Maria shouting and slamming things around. I feel sorry for Phillip, that he has to deal with her, but I don't feel sorry for what we did. I'm happy we kissed.

Wayne

"Wakey, wakey," I tell Warren as I shake his body from side to side. "Wake up!!!" I yell and shove him hard to one side. Warren jumps straight up.

"What the hell!!!!" he shouts back at me.

"It's three in the morning and you know what we have to do," I tell him, and shake my U-Touch in front his face. He yawns and goes back to sleep. "Get up."

"I want to sleep," he yawns. "Why this early?"

"Because," I snap at him.

"I don't want to get up. It's cold and I'm tired and…"

"Shut up. You sound like a broken siren," I jump at him. "Get up."

"Fine. Have it your way," Warren gripes and gruffly puts his morning robe on. "Let's get up in the middle of the night and prank the others," he says sarcastically.

"Are you finished?" I ask him. Warren glares at me and says nothing. He knows we could go on forever and at the end one of us will lose his temper and start to pound the other. We made a promise not to fight during the course of our stay and we're trying very hard to live up to that.

Warren stands up and takes a deep breath, "Finished and ready," he announces in an annoyed tone of voice.

I nod and we walk out of our bedroom. I raise the volume on my U-Touch and click the play button. Screaming women, crying children, and whispers radiate through the hall. In the meantime, Warren scratched each bedroom door with a screwdriver.

Suddenly three bedroom doors open. Warren and I jump back into our.

"What was that?" I say followed by a yawn. Warren scratches his head and yawns as well.

"I heard screaming," Maria says and I notice how shaken she is. From behind her, Carmen sticks her head around the corner.

Yuck! She is pretty scary without make-up.

"Someone was scratching on my door," Tony explains and Warren and I have to bite our lips, not wanting to laugh.

"Whoever it is cut it out or I'll stick my foot up your ass!!!" Phillip shouts and slams the door.

Warren and I walk back into our room and start to laugh.

"Who ever it is cut it out or," Warren starts.

"I'll stick my foot up your ass," I finish the sentence and jump on my bed laughing out loud. "In a few days this place will be ours. They'll lose their minds and we will win the title and the money," I state. Satisfied with my daily job well-done I go back to sleep.

15 contenders remaining

Day Two

Saturday, August 14, 2010

Phillip

I enter the kitchen in need of a strong cup of coffee. What a night! Maria caught me flirting with one of the two sisters from Seattle. I think her name is Juliana or Jessica or Jenny. No. I think her name is Jennifer. Yes – Jennifer. Anyway – she threw everything she could grab while I dodged and, as usual, I waited for her to calm down. Then we made up. I hate fighting with her. It can be dangerous but I love the part after that. She is so passionate and hot. It turns me on.

Our relationship has always been rocky. We've spent more time off then on, and a few months ago I was forced into the engagement. To be honest, I don't even want to get married. I'm not the type of man anyone would want to be married to. I know I'll be a horrible husband. I love women too much to settle myself down with just one, not to mention with someone like Maria. I do know that I love her but her temper is awful. Anything can set her off, and it then takes a long time for her to calm down. I can't deal with that.

"Hey!" I say to one of the twins. I don't know which is which. They look so much alike.

"Horrible night," he smiles back at me.

"You can say that again."

He chuckles, "We heard."

"Actually, the whole house heard you – even the dead," the other brother steps in.

I give them a small smile, "Do you have some coffee. I have a terrible headache."

"Over there," he says, pointing to the coffee machine. The carafe is filled with fresh, hot coffee. I thank them and pour some into one of the mugs.

"Say, is there a way to recognize who's who?" I ask gesturing toward them with my mug.

"I'm Wayne. You can identify me by my exceptional good

looks," and he flexes his upper body muscles.

"No, no, no," laughs his sibling. "My brother is delusional. I'm the one born with the exceptional good looks in our family. I have the entire package." He turns to one of the camera placed in the left corner of the kitchen. He shows off his muscles and tells the female viewers to give him a call. One thing for sure, they are both quite entertaining.

I decide to leave them alone. I have a horrible headache and need to be alone somewhere in a deep, dark room. "See you later," I tell them and walk away down the hallway. I look for a small secluded area. To be honest, I want to be alone and do not whish to see Maria or any of the other women – at least today. I'm taking a day off from temptation.

Behind a pair of red thick curtains I find a door. I open it and stumble upon William sitting on a chair reading a file. He glances up at me and doesn't look too happy to see me. I guess we share the same desire to be left alone for a few hours.

"You have found my hiding spot," he says to me.

"I guess I did," and motion toward a recliner, "May I?"

"Be my guest," he motions and closes the file.

"What are you reading?"

"Nothing important or interesting. Something I found lying around."

I nod in understanding and observe the small room cluttered with file cabinets, chairs, and decades of dirt.

"What's with this room?"

"It was a file room. I guess it held the patient records." William smiles, "To think how much money the Roma's brothers spent to gather the St. Clara Asylum's assets. If only they knew everything was sitting in here, waiting to be discovered."

I begin to smile too. According to them, they spent a small fortune collecting old photographs, patient files, news articles, and so on. They even paid visits to some of the relatives. They went all the way. I guess writing books demands a lot of research.

"Are you hiding from Carmen?" I ask.

William smiles and shakes his head, "I just want to be alone for a few hours. That's all."

"Why?"

"I don't like to be bombarded with questions about my life or career. I'm very protective when it comes to my private life, unlike Carmen who loves to be in the center of everything."

I have to laugh, "It reminds me of someone else too. Maria."

William nods, "What's with you two?"

"What's with you and Carmen?" I answer his question with another question. I don't want to talk about Maria – not today.

William understands and says nothing. The room turns silent – maybe too silent. I look around the small space pondering if I should tell him or not; if I can trust him. Hell, why not? I need to talk to someone about my crisis. I didn't tell anyone and William seems like a trustworthy person. I take a deep breath and start, "She wants to get married and I don't. She wants to have a large family and I don't." I move closer to him. "You see," and I look around for cameras or any other devices, "she is pregnant and to be honest I don't know how – well – I know how and I know I was very careful. I used protection." I continue and William remains silent. He just nods in understanding. "I'm thinking that she might have cheated on me and is trying to push somebody else's baby on me, or she isn't pregnant and she is just trying to push me into marriage." I punch the armrest of the chair. I'm so frustrated. "Supposedly Maria is in her fourth month and I don't see a bump or any strange pregnancy behavior. I confronted her and as always, she either dismisses me or calls me delusional," and once again I slam my fists on the armrest of the chair. "Please – don't tell anyone about – this."

"I won't."

"Thanks."

He nods and says, "Carmen entered us in this contest to resurrect our career – you know – after…"

"The incident," I interrupt him. I notice how hard it is for him to talk about it.

"She also wants us to be a couple again but I have other plan."

"What plans?"

"I want to quit acting and become a movie director. I was always fascinated by movies and at a very young age I decided to write and direct my own films."

"What stopped you?"

"Carmen," he puffs, "she's always wanted to be an actress and her stepfather is a big shot Hollywood producer. He does everything for her…"

"As do you," I interject.

William nods, "I did, but not anymore. Like I said before, I have other plans."

"Selene," I say with a smile and take a few sips of coffee. He stares at me. "I saw the way you look at her." I move closer. "To be honest everyone knows how bad you want to get in her pants and Carmen doesn't look too happy. If I were you, I would watch out for her brother. He doesn't seem too pleased about it either." William nods. "That's why I stay away from girls with older brothers. They can be a pain in the ass. Older sisters too, but I can deal with them. If you know what I mean?" I raise my mug toward him. William smiles. He knows what I mean.

"She is cute but she is not my priority – at the moment." He states.

"She's ok. She's too innocent for my taste," I explain. "I like my women with a lot of experience in the love department," and wink at him. William chuckles.

We stay silent a minute or two until William stands up and says, "I have to go," and slowly walks out.

"I'll see you later," I yell after him and place my mug on the floor and close my eyes. I can finally relax.

Maria

Phillip is nowhere to be found as are the two sisters. Fine. He wants to play? I can play too, and I'll be spending my time with......I look around the breakfast table. Hmm! Tony is too dorky. Besides, it seems Yolanda has a crush on him. Yuck! I think she needs a new pair of eyes.

I keep looking down the table and observe the Jones brothers. Nope – too annoying. Maybe William. I smile. What am I thinking? It's already too crowded. Carmen is after William.

William is after Selene and Selene – well – she is definitely after William. How marvelous – a love triangle. That will be fun. This journey won't be boring after all.

I turn my search to the other side of the table and see Raul talking to Seth. Perfect. Seth Holloway you are the winner.

Seth looks up at me. I smile and he smiles back at me. Oh, Yeah! He is already in my web. Phillip, watch out. Soon you'll taste the same bitter medicine you've been forcing me to swallow all these years. Now, all I have to do is to wait for the chance to make my move.

I sit calmly in my chair and start to eat. Once in a while I give Seth my most sensual smile. He seems very interested in me and I know he'll be mine by dinner – at the latest.

Breakfast is coming to an end and I'm tolerantly waiting for my chance to be alone with Seth, but to my dislike he is too deeply involved in his little sister's affairs.

William and Selene are sitting across from Seth. William seems genuinely interested in Selene. He is curious about her and he is intently listening to her stories about her life on her family's farm. This is bad for Carmen. When a man starts to listen to a woman, he is usually interested in her.

Swiftly, yet in an unobtrusive manner, I turn my attention to Carmen. Her face shows indifference but her eyes – they show fear, jealousy, and solitude. I feel for her. I know what it's like. How many nights, I've lain on my bed, crying my soul out and at the same time imagining Phillip in the arms of another woman. What's wrong with me always wanting someone who doesn't desire me?

"Selene," Seth interrupts their conversation. Selene looks at her brother with mixed emotions. I guess Seth must have told her about his dislike of William's attention to her. "Why don't you go and play your violin?" he asks and she blushes. She didn't like the tone Seth used to speak to her. It was commanding and controlling. They glare at each other – neither of them speaks and everyone in the room is watching them.

"Please. I promised Mom to make sure you would practice on your violin daily. It's not everyday that Julliard offers a full scholarship, especially to people like us," Seth softly pleads.

Selene says nothing and without any further argument she stands up and before she walks away she gives her brother a discontented glare.

William stays seated. He is watching Selene walking up the stairs and then he turns to Seth. They glare silently at each other. I have a strong hunch that something has happened between them in the past. They are no strangers and my hunches are always right. I'm wondering what could have taken place.

William stands up, leaves the room, turns left, and he is gone. Carmen quickly rushes after him. As I said before, I feel for her. I've been in the same situation many, many times before.

"Don't worry," I tell Seth, "it will pass soon." Seth looks up at me, confused. "Selene and William," I clarify. "Carmen thinks he is trying to get back at her for cheating on him…."

"I know that," he says aloud while slamming his fist on the table, rattling the dinnerware.

I press my lips together. Seth is very intimidating and very attractive – for a cowboy –of course. I'm not into country and nature. Too green and too far away from civilization, but I wouldn't mind spending a weekend in a log cabin alone with him. He is buff and strong, compared to my shrimp of a fiancé. I take a quick breath and think how much I still love Phillip no matter how many times he has cheated on me. We have a love hate relationship. We can't get along and we can't be apart. We are addicted to each other.

"Do you know what I think?" I ask with my sexiest smile as he looks up at me once again. "I think William's feelings for your sister are genuine."

Without a word he stands up. "You are so naïve, just like my sister," and leaves too. I'm grinding my teeth. I don't like his tone of voice nor that he called me naïve, because I'm not. I also never had a man walk out on me especially when I put myself out like I did with Seth. I have to go to the extremes.

I stand up, grab two mugs filled with coffee and search for Seth. I'm determined to make him want me, not only because I want to make Phillip jealous but because I never had a man deny me. My ego is badly hurt.

I walk down the long hallway, look into each room. Selene's violin melody grows louder. I open the last door and finally find Seth – not alone, to my dislike. Selene is standing next to the window, facing the ocean while playing classical music. I'm not familiar with the tune. I got a B- in music appreciation. It was an easy class and very boring too. I could barely keep my eyes open.

Seth is sitting on the couch with his legs crossed. His arms are wide open resting on the back of the couch with his eyes drilling holes into William's skull. The only thing Seth is missing is a gun.

William is on the opposite couch with Carmen at his side. He is agitated. Carmen is talking to him about something. It looks more like she is pleading with him. William looks aggravated and when I walk towards Seth, he stands up and leaves.

"William!!!" Carmen yells for him but he has already left and it doesn't look like he is going to come back. The three of us stare at her.

Then she turns and vents all her frustration and anger toward Selene, who stopped playing her violin as soon she heard Carmen pleadingly call for William.

"It's all your fault," she spits out at Selene. Seth moves forward ready to protect his sister. "STOP FOLLOWING HIM!!!" and she starts smashing objects, ripping the pillows open, and kicks the furniture down. I thought no one could surpass my fits but I was wrong – Carmen is the queen of temper tantrums.

We leave her alone.

"She is right at home," Seth smirks and in the background I hear Carmen screaming, shouting, and objects being smashed again.

"She fits perfectly in this place," I agree and wrap my arms around his. At first he looks shocked and when I smile at him, his face shows confusion.

"What will your fiancé say when he sees you wrapped in my arms?"

I quickly raise my shoulder up. "What fiancé?" I ask, and he smiles. He has a very beautiful, sensual smile.

"It's fine with me," Seth replies and pulls me into an empty room. I flash a gleeful and evil smile. I have him now. He's mine.

Yolanda

I'm standing in the center of a large oval room with Tony by my side. He is babbling something about the history of this place while I'm admiring the area and start to imagine the room in its prime. The room has a large, heavy, honey colored wooden bookcase running from wall to wall, with an arch window snuggled inside every five feet. There are exactly five windows facing the Ocean. Beneath my feet is a shabby round red carpet with golden flower designs imprinted on it.

Suddenly, images of two nice black leather couches with two reading chairs beside them situated around the fire start to

43

form in my mind. There is also a large desk sitting at the other end of the room.

"This is where Kate Kane hung herself," Tony explains as he terminates my day dream and points up to the metal spiral stair case set in the back left corner of the room. Tony tells me that this was Mr. Kane's treasure room. He collected first editions books from around the world, and when the castle was purchased by the asylum all of Mr. Kane's possessions were either sold or given away. What a pity.

"Soon after the disappearance of her three children, Kate became very ill and delusional. She was convinced that the house was malevolent, and she constantly talked about a black dog with red eyes visiting her every night in her room. She believed that she and her three children were cursed, and were the castle's prisoners.

"Mrs. Kane spent endless hours searching the castle walls for her lost children but it was useless. All she found were the bones of Elisabeth Seapeak."

I gasp and my body starts to shake uncontrollably.

"Mrs. Kane didn't know about the island's history or the castle's history – you know, the convicts practicing black magic, Hell's gate…." He soon stops and stares down at me.

I shake my head, "I don't."

"Oh!" he says and joyfully adds, "I will keep this part of the history tour to myself until we reach the basement. You'll love it."

I give him an anxious smile. I can feel the muscles of my face tensing and my lips quivering. I'm a big chicken. I don't like horror movies and I was unable to finish the first chapter of "Thing". It took me days before I could go back to the bathroom at night without imagining red glowing eyes popping out from the thick dark night and pulling me down the drains. My fear for the supernatural world is due to the gift that was given to me. That's what my mother and grandmother keeps telling me, but I don't see anything special being a retrocognition. Constantly seeing the past and the deceased; it doesn't bring me joy or pride, like it does my grandmother.

My grandmother used to be my mentor until I begged my mother to send me to the US. I wanted to leave that life behind but it didn't work out the way I hoped. Death continues to find me.

"The next morning servants discovered Mrs. Kane's dead body swinging left and right above them," Tony continues, and I start to picture the scene. Mrs. Kane, barefoot, wearing a long black Victorian dress climbing the stairs with a rope in her hands. Her hair, wild, dark, and long. Dark bags beneath her grey eyes stand out on her pale, sickly skin.

"Her husband walked in and, according, to the stories, he collapsed crying on the floor at the site of his beloved Kate."

I look to the roof and the vision of Kate begins to form in front of me. She is exactly how I imagined her, except that she is weaker than I had first assumed. Mrs. Kane's body is rocking back and forth. I'm entranced by the movement of her limp body.

Unexpectedly her eyes open and she says, "He is awakening."

I scream and dash from the room. Tony follows me and grabs my hand.

"What's wrong?"

I shake my head. Tears are running down my face. "Fantasma," I tell him. When I'm in panic, angry, or under a lot of stress, I tend to speak in Spanish.

"A ghost?" he states and I nod. "Who? Where?"

"Kate," I say and try to calm down. "I saw her dead body." I told him about my vision.

He smiles. "This is great!!!"

"Great?" I whisper, and he nods. "What are you LOCO?" I yell at him.

"No – not crazy – happy. This is what my brother and I came here for. We wanted to tell their stories and hoped for their help and – here they are." He hugs me. "You'll be my muse."

"Your what?"

"Muse. You know from the Greek and Roman mythology.

45

They used to sing and dance and inspire poetry and music. You'll be my muse."

"No, thanks," and I turn away from him ready to leave but he stops me.

"Please. I need you," Tony begs me. "I need your help. I think the house is trying to communicate through you. Please."

"No – thank you," and I try to free myself from his grip. Then he pulls me closer into his chest and starts to whispers in my ear, "Please. I really, really need you." His hot minty breath tickles the base of my neck and in mater of seconds the surface of my entire body is covered in goose bumps. I'm melting in his arms. I've always had a soft spot for dorky guys but I stay strong and keep turning him down while he keeps begging me until I give in.

"Thank you. Thank you. Thank you," and he squeezes me. "Shall we?"

"Shall we what?"

"Go back to the library."

I shake my head, "I'm not going back in there. It's evil."

"I promise to stay by your side," he says, looks deep into my eyes and stretches his hand forward. "Please. I really need you."

I take a deep breath, "Fine," I tell him as I place my hand in his. "But if I see more ghosts I'll leave." He wanted to protest, but when he saw my unyielding expression he gave up.

"Fine. As you wish."

We walk back into the library. I look to my left and see a robust man sitting on a red and gold arm chair. He has black short hair and a thick mustache. He looks sad.

"You'll be next," he whispers to me and points a gun to his temple and squeezes the trigger. Blood spurts from his head and his body collapses to the left side of the chair.

Once again I scream and run away from the room. Never again will I set a foot in that room.

I keep running down the hall to get as far away as possible from that room. Tony is right behind me calling my name but I don't stop. I hear the voices of Selene and Seth. They are arguing loudly. I don't pay much attention to their words, only to their tone. I look for people who I can trust.

I open the door to the living room and find the two of them standing face to face with their bodies tense. Seth looks worried and Selene angry.

"I'm glad you're here," I gasp and rush into Selene's arms as if she were a comfort blanket. She is a bit shocked. So am I. Selene hadn't expected me to do that like a little girl with tears running down my face, but neither did I.

She places her arms around me, "What happened?" she asks, but I can't stop crying. Tony enters the room and approaches me. He tries to comfort me but I push him away.

From the corner of my eye I see Tony sit on the couch, and he starts to explain what happened in the library. The more he talks the more I feel like a delusional old lady.

"You really saw them?" Seth asks with a skeptical smile. I stare at him.

"You need something warm to drink," Selene tells me and I keep holding her. I do not know what's wrong with me. I'm acting like a fool.

"I'm sorry," Tony says in a concerned tone of voice.

I continue to ignore him.

Seth steps up to me, "Let me get you a cup of coffee or tea."

"Hmm, no – thanks," I tell him.

"I don't mind."

"No. Thanks. I'm not in the mood for anything at the moment."

"Ok, but if you need anything let me know. I'll be in the kitchen making myself something to eat." He turns to the others. "Do any of you want something from the kitchen?" Tony shakes his head. "Selene?"

"No, thank you," she replies and before he leaves us, Seth gives Selene a very disapproving glare. I wonder why.

"What were you two doing in the library?" Selene asks. I look down and feel uncomfortable.

"I thought of checking the library, and since my brother is out of the game I considered pulling Yolanda to my side," Tony explains and I feel even worse than a few minutes ago. I glance up and study Selene's facial expression. She doesn't look angry or upset.

"But," Selene starts. "I thought the west wing was barricaded?"

"Not for me," Tony explains and pulls a large pair of garden scissors out of his backpack.

Selene looks over to me in shock.

"I know," I start, "I shouldn't have but," and I point with my eyes in Tony's direction. "I couldn't resist."

Selene smiles and moves her lips closer to my ear, "you couldn't resist exploring the house or – Tony?"

I blush.

"What did you say?" Tony asks and I panic. I don't want to give myself away – at least not at the moment.

"I asked if you found some clues," Selene replies with a smile and winks at me.

"No," Tony sighs. "The room is a mess and I'm not sure where to look."

"We've searched everywhere and everything in that room with no results," I conclude, and nod at Selene in gratitude for not giving me away.

Joanna

"Lucy Kane was just seven years old when she vanished," Tony is talking to the Holloways and Yolanda as I'm walking in to look for my sister.

"Who's Lucy Kane?" I ask.

"She was the youngest child of Mr. and Mrs. Kane, the

48

owners of this cursed island." Tony explains. "According to a news article Matt and I found, Lucy was the first to vanish."

"What do you mean, vanish?" Carmen says as she enters the room with William standing behind her. He has a soda can in his hand.

"Adults die in these walls while children mysteriously disappear," Tony says and stares at the walls. "Lucy was in this room, playing on her piano." He points to a corner where a chic, slick, black grand piano stands. "That's her piano," he says and everyone in the room gasps. "Her father was in his beloved library, reading. Her mother was taking an afternoon walk. The twins where playing outside, and the rest of the household was very busy with their daily routine until the high pitched scream of a little girl stopped everyone for a few second?

"Another scream came and everyone ran into this room, only to find it empty.

"Soon after the police arrived and searched for the little girl for days without finding her. Many were accused but none got charged. They had no evidence, no clues, nothing.

"A year later Geoffrey and George, the twins, vanished as well," Tony walks to the window and stares at the grounds. "They were playing outside and never came back, and just like Lucy, the police had no evidence, no clues, no motives, not even a lead.

"A month after the twin's disappearance, reports of a black dog roaming the grounds circulated among the servants and everyone who saw the black dog committed suicide. They walked up to the west tower and, just like lemmings, jumped out the window.

"A few days after, Mrs. Kane hung herself and a year later, after his beloved wife's suicide, Mr. Kane shot himself in the head. The last eight surviving staff members ran away from this island and never came back.

"The castle was secluded for decades until a private company bought the island and transformed it into an asylum for crazy people," Tony concludes as he turns around to face us all.

Suddenly the piano begins to play. We jump and stare at the keys moving up and down. Some of us gasp, others are too scared to make a sound, but we all respond the same way. We run out of the room and hope to never again return.

"What was that?" Seth gasps.

"That was the house, contacting us," Tony says with a thrill in his voice. "The spirits are awakening. They are welcoming us...."

"Or warning us," Yolanda cries out. "This is not fantastic or great. We believe spirits who don't cross over are bad – dangerous."

Tony laughs, "And this is your professional opinion?"

Yolanda glares at him and walks closer to him. Their noses are an inch or two apart, "Yes. Spirits who don't cross over are afraid of the consequences of their actions while in the living world.

"Back home – in the Dominican Republic – I saw people possessed by evil spirits. I saw with my own eyes what poltergeists can do, and let me tell you, it's not some cute or spooky fairy-tale. They are real and very dangerous, and it isn't wise talking about the dead." She steps back. The two of them glare at each other for a while until Seth steps in and suggests that everyone should follow him to another room.

I decide to look for my sister. I'm worried about her and run up the stairs calling her name. Maybe she is with Phillip. I hadn't seen him all day either.

I enter our room and she's not there. Everything is exactly as I left it except for the window. It's open. I walk over to the window and before I close it I look up at the swarm of ravens. I've never liked birds. They are dirty and spread diseases and my distaste for them has escalated since I came back from Italy ten years ago. It was another "cultural" vacation on which my parents insisted on dragging us. My mother is a painter and my father teaches history at Emerald Bay High. They love to travel and experience culture, and at the age of seven I got a taste of culture that I will never forget.

We were in Venice and my mother wanted pictures of me feeding the pigeons. Bad idea. Imagine cute little me marching into the center of Piazza San Marco with a bag of seeds, and soon after I started to feed a few pigeons a cloud of birds attacked me. My father and mother quickly came to my rescue but it wasn't soon enough. I was covered from top to bottom in bird scratches, bites and poop. If that wasn't enough humiliation, I had tourists and locals laughing at me and taking pictures. From that day on I have had a deep dark hatred of birds.

I huff, close the window and decide to join the others. I have to admit that for someone like me, who doesn't believe in ghosts or afterlife or magic, I'm pretty frightened by the stories Tony has just told us, and by the piano playing by itself.

"Get a grip," I whisper to myself and walk out of the room.

Halfway down the corridor, I hear a girl's giggle. I turn around and look down the hall. I see nothing – just rows of doors. I look to the other side of the hall and see two boys between the ages of eight and ten in early 1900's clothes standing shoulder to shoulder. Their black eyes lock onto mine, and I can feel my legs giving out on me. I collapse on my hands and knees.

"Fourteen little trespassers are chatting away. One little trespasser is not," the boys sing. A strange white mist slowly approaches me. I can't move or take my gaze away from the two of them.

"And now there are fourteen little trespassers left," a girl's voice whispers in my ear. I jump and look around but I see no one, just the white mist taking over the entire hall.

Something is crawling up my legs, I look down and see an eight foot long albino python slowly wrapping itself around me. I scream.

Warren

"Hurry up!!!" I tell my brother. "What are you looking for?" I look from the empty hall to where my brother is searching through Maria and Carmen's stuff.

"I told you," he says as he admires their underwear. "Catch!!!"

I turn around and a pair of red thongs flies across the room and into my face. "Will you stop that?" I snap at him.

"Bingo!!!" Wayne smiles and shakes a bag containing make-up and creams.

"What are you now – into make-up?"

"Ha, ha! Very funny," and he opens the window. "I told you about my plans. I want to make their lives miserable and day by day we'll destroy their possessions." He drops the bag into the ocean. "We will watch them destroy each other while we win the game."

"By disposing of their make-up?"

"Today their make-up and tomorrow their sanity." Wayne smiles as he continues to dump more of their belongings out the window. "I know those spoiled rich women. They can't live without their beauty products." He throws their razors out the window with a vindictive smirk. "They will be going all natural," and I see pairs of push-up bras disappear out the window. "I have to give the casting director two thumbs up for their choices. The house will go down in a matter of days."

"How stupid are they?" I smile and Wayne looks at me. "How could they actually believe that we are culinary students?"

"I know, and do you know what it is even funnier?"

"They actually love our food," Wayne and I say in unison.

"And we don't even know how to cook." I add.

"They believe every story we tell them."

"I love the story you told them about our imaginary dog that we had to put down because we didn't have enough money....."

52

Wayne burst into laugher. "And all the girls were in tears."

"We are GOOD!"

"We are better than good, and I always told you we should become actors instead of following in dad's footsteps."

I smile, "If they only knew that we are actually rich and that our dad owns food chains all over the US, and that we live like kings."

Wayne nods and we both start to laugh out loud. We give each other a knuckle touch.

"They would probably lynch us."

"Yeah." Wayne promptly stops talking as we hear steps coming closer. I glance out the door and see Joanna walking into her room.

"It's Joanna," I whisper to my brother. He nods and walks around the room. He is not satisfied. Wayne is still looking for more material to damage.

A door opens and once again I peek. It's Joanna leaving her room. She looks agitated.

"Psssst," Wayne calls me over and lifts up a journal. "Maria's diary," and a grin spreads across his face.

I close the door and step toward him. We both stand over her diary and start to read:

May 13, 2010 – Phoenix

Dear Diary:

I find myself in a very difficult situation. I did something horrible and I do not know how to resolve it. I tried to confess my sins to my friends, family and Phillip, but I couldn't. I'm too ashamed and so I find myself writing instead into your pages.

A few weeks ago I decided to go down to San Diego for my spring break with a couple of good friends.

Phillip and I had just broken up our long relationship. It wasn't devastating or unusual to me or to Phillip, or to anybody who knew us since the beginning of our relationship. We constantly break up

53

and then mend our relationship. But this time was different. I met someone. He was a good-looking native surfer. His name was Ernesto. Yeah, I know. Not an attractive name but his good-looks make up for it.

Wayne and I stop reading and stare at each other with big fat smiles plastered on our faces.

It was the best time I ever had and very short too. I didn't expect Ernesto to give me a souvenir. A child.

I'm desperate. I don't know what to do. Only one thought comes to mind and it is to lie to Phillip and tell him that he is going to be a Dad. I feel horrible but I have no other choice.

I looked for Ernesto and I couldn't find him. I feel terrible about doing this to him but I can't think of another way.

I have to go. Phillip is here. Wish me good luck.

"Man, this is – awesome!" I smile at Wayne and watch as he flips through the pages. He stops.

July 3, 2010 – Phoenix

Dear Diary:

Two days ago I lost the baby. I was sad but I'm starting to feel a lot better now. No one knows about the miscarriage and I'll keep it a secret, at least until after my wedding.

Phillip is so loving and caring and I'm afraid he'll postpone our wedding down the road.

You must think that I'm horrible but I love him so much and......

A scream from outside the door startles us. We glance at each other and then run out of the room. Down the hall, right before the staircase is a black leather boot, lying on its side. Next to it is a solitary chess piece.

"It's Joanna's boot," I tell Wayne. I pick up the pawn and see the rest of the crew coming up the stairs. Quickly, I place the pawn in my pants pocket.

"What happened?" Seth asks and my brother and I shake our heads. We have no idea.

"We were in our room when all of a sudden we heard a loud scream and….."

"And we ran out here and found this." Wayne steps in and points to the boot.

"It's Joanna's boot," Jennifer cries. "Where is my sister?" She grabs the boot, holding it in her arms as if it were a small, fragile infant. She looks up at something behind us. Her face turns white. Her eyes widen and her mouth starts to tremble.

Wayne and I turn around. On the white wall, in red ink is written:

You'll be next

"Is this part of the show? If it is, it's pretty macabre," Jennifer snaps and walks down the stairs.

Seth

"Seth!" Selene whispers my name and pulls my hand. I stop and watch the rest of the group descending the stairs. Jennifer looks angry at the loss of her sister and keeps complaining to the other contestants that there are more appropriate candidates to leave the castle before her sister. She continues looking over to Selene. I take a deep breath and try to control my anger. I never like it when people judge my sister before they get a chance to really know her. Sure, she is different than most people, but she is authentic and kind and has a heart of gold, and it pains me when people are mean to her. I just wish I could protect her, or put her underneath a glass top, shielding her from all those people.

Since the day she decided to accept Julliard's offer and move to New York City, away from our parent's ranch, a sanctuary built just to protect her from the evil psyche of the human race, I haven't been able to stop worrying about her. I won't always be there to protect or comfort her. She'll be all alone and that troubles me.

I smile at Selene and hope that she hasn't learned of Jennifer's comments, even though she is pretty good at disguising her emotions. She's learned at a very young age how to protect herself.

"Follow me," she whispers.

"Where?"

"To the library." She drags me down the stairs and through the long hall. We enter an oval room that must have been an impressive library once. It was later transformed into a therapy group room by the asylum. What a pity. Chairs used in the therapy sessions are still here, piled up at the end of the room covered with dust and cobwebs.

"What are we doing in here?" I finally ask her.

"Looking for clues, of course," she says. Not wanting to upset her even more, I start searching the room even though I believe it is a waste of time.

In the background I hear Selene humming.

"Don't," I snap at her. She turns around and looks quizzically at me. "You know how much I hate that melody."

"Not to mention the curse," she adds with a smile but I know her too well not to understand how much she suffers. How much she wishes to be normal. We come from a very long line of witches, and according to our grandmother my father and I are the only males to be have been born into the Holloway family for centuries. My father and I are supposedly excluded from the curse, and until Selene was born my grandmother thought that she had finally managed to break the spell. But she was wrong.

"I don't believe in the curse," I reply.

Selene says nothing. She knows how upset I get when we discuss that topic. There is so much I want to tell her but I can't. Cameras and microphones placed all around us prevent us to from continuing our conversation.

Ivy

"Who would have thought this game could be so intense?" I'm nervous. Priscilla says nothing. She continues to apply lipstick. "I just hope when our times comes, it won't be so dramatic."

"Who says we'll be next?" she snaps.

"No one. I just stated a fact. After all, only one can win. I just hope to leave the show quietly – peacefully."

"And who says that you'll be leaving," she glares at me. I stare back at her reflection in the mirror.

"Between us, I know it won't be me, and that's fine by me. You are the one who wanted to come here and I'm glad to help you with your dream…."

"Stop talking." She raises her voice. I stop and watch her place the lipstick back in her purse. She turns around.

"What's wrong?"

"Nothing. I'm just tired. I couldn't sleep. You know – horrible mattresses and the loud commotion this morning."

"Yeah, what was that?"

"Someone was pulling a prank, that's all." She walks toward the door. "Shall we?"

I smile. "We shall." We walk out of the bathroom and encounter Jennifer surrounded by a large group of people. Jennifer has a boot in her hands and looks upset.

"What happened?" Priscilla asks.

"Joanna is gone," Warren says and Wayne starts to go through the facts.

"How horrible." Priscilla and I gasp at the same time.

"Do you believe these disappearances are part of the show?" I ask. When I see their bewildered expressions, I wish I hadn't asked.

"Of course it is," Priscilla snaps at me.

"Who do you think would take us one by one out of the castle?" Wayne smiles at me.

"You're right. Silly of me to think otherwise." Without any further argument I follow the three of them to the game room.

Tony

I take my research papers out of my bag and place them on the bed. I'll have a lot on my plate. Without Matt, I'm not sure if I'll be able to complete my task. One thing is for sure – the house is starting to awaken and I've recorded some great sounds.

I reach for my EVP recorder and press play. I hear Yolanda and me talking in the library. In the background I can hear unfamiliar voices. I place the recorder closer to my ear and start to write down what I think they are saying:

Have you seen my mommy?
I'm not crazy. I'm not crazy.
I am the devil and you shall be my prey.
TONY!!!

I drop everything. My pencil and the recorder bounce on the floor. I'm in shock, or at least, freaked out.

I pick up the recorder from the floor and rewind it. I hit the play bottom again.

"TONY!!!" whispers a cold, groggy voice. Quickly, I stop the recorder. The voice panics me. I don't know what to think or what to do.

Then my bedroom door opens and someone calls my name. Startle, I turn and see Yolanda standing at the threshold, holding her hands over her chest.

"What's the matter with you?" she snaps, and looks like she is about to strangle me.

"I'm sorry," I tell her and take quick breaths. I try to calm down. "I was listening to the EVP and one of them called my name and when you came…."

"Didn't I tell you not to mingle with the dead?" she scolds me.

"But I...."

"Never mind. I don't want to hear it. I just came to inform you that dinner is ready and Joanna is gone."

"What? Joanna?" I'm stupefied. Yolanda nods. "What happened?" I ask.

14 contenders remaining

Day Three

Sunday, August 15, 2010

Jennifer

I can't sleep. I'm constantly thinking of my poor little sister already out of the game. I'm all alone now. I can't stop wondering why they chose her to leave. Why didn't they choose that weird Holloway girl with her pale skin and frightening green eyes? She gives me the creeps every time I see her. She reminds me of a character from a horror movie or an evil creature from Greek mythology.

Frustrated and unable to sleep I decide to get up and clean the bedroom. I always clean when I'm worried or upset. It calms me down.

I start with our beds, then begin to pick up Joanna's clothes spread all over her half of the floor. I open her closet and start to fold her clothes. She is a bit messy – well – very messy actually, while I'm the neat freak. I need to have everything clean and in its proper place.

Joanna used to come in my room and turn it upside down. It brought me to the boiling point. She knew that and every time I did something to her she would take her revenge on my orderly room. Since Joanna and I became closer she stopped doing that.

A giant knot forms in my throat. I miss her a lot and I never felt so lonely in my life. I barely know these people and I came to this show just for fun, but mostly for our parents. A few years ago my mother was diagnosed with breast cancer. She is doing fine now, but my parents are stuck with thousands of dollars worth of medical bills. They were forced to take a second loan on their house, and now I see how they're struggling to pay it off.

"God!" I shout in frustration. I feel like such a failure. I've let down my parents and my sister as well. How could I be so selfish? I always put my needs before anybody else's. My mother keeps warning me that one day it will bite me back, and it just did. Flirting with Phillip was the right decision. Not only because I find him very attractive but, it will also put tension into the game

61

and make the viewers want to see more. But I hadn't thought of Joanna. How could I not think of that?

"God!" I say once again. I slam the closet door shut and turn around. The alarm clock reads two in the morning. I take a deep breath and sit on Joanna's bed. I grab her pillow and lay there staring into the emptiness.

"Why did Joanna have to go?" I ask myself, and I start to punch the pillow out of frustration at my stupidity and selfishness.

Next, I stand up and glare at the camera. "Why not Selene or Yolanda or Maria or Tony. Anybody but her," I shout and for a few seconds I stay still, staring down the camera. Then, out of the blue, I jump up, rip it off the wall and smash it on the floor. I start to calm down. It feels so good to release all of that anger and frustration.

Feeling much better, I start to clean up my mess. I collect the camera pieces from across the room and toss them into the wastebasket. Then I replace Joanna's pillow back beneath her blankets. I glance at her side table and notice a picture of Joanna and me in our homecoming dresses. She looks so beautiful. I remember how nervous she was. James Forester asked her out. She'd had a crush on him since seventh grade and finally, after four years, he had the courage to ask her out.

I smile and stare at the picture. My vision begins to blur. I'm about to cry again.

Mom was more excited than Joanna. She hadn't seen Joanna in a dress since first grade. Joanna has changed a lot since then. She became more independent and more fascinated with the Goth world. The walls of her room are pitch black, and she has dark wood furniture and red curtains and blankets. Stacks of horror DVDs sit in a corner together with some bloody mannequin body part. Gargoyle statuettes sit on each corner of her furniture, and posters of her favorite emo groups are plastered on her walls. It looks like a shabby-chic version of Dracula's cottage.

Anyway, our mom spent weeks finding the perfect dress that

they would both like. It was a nice black spaghetti strapped dress, and I still remember how she left the house in a nice pair of flats. When I met her back at our high school, I found her wearing knee-high leather boots. She smiled and winked at me. She had changed her shoes in James's car. I nodded knowingly, and walked off with my date and friends.

I place the picture back on the night stand and march down to the kitchen. I'm in need of a strong cup of black coffee.

The house is deserted. Everyone is asleep and I start to imagine things. I hear voices and see dark shadows out of the corner of my eyes. Stupid Tony and his bonfire stories. My mind is starting to play tricks on me.

Finally I reach the kitchen, turn all the lights on and start to prepare the coffee. I'm very noisy. I try to keep myself occupied and the noises I create make me feel more comfortable – not alone.

While the coffee is brewing, I sit patiently on the kitchen counter singing to myself like a lunatic. I look once again out the kitchen window and see nothing but darkness.

"Jennifer!!!!" a voice whispers at the base of my ear. I jump from the chair, sending it crashing to the floor. "Jennifer!!!!" continues the voice.

"Who is there?" I ask, badly shaken.

"Help me!!!" I recognize the voice.

"Joanna – is that you?"

"Help me."

"Where are you?" I yell out loud into the empty kitchen. "Where are you?"

"Follow my voice."

Promptly, I open a small drawer and remove a flashlight I find in there.

"Keep talking," I tell my sister. "Keep talking," and begin to follow her voice which leads me to the door of the basement, even though – according to Tony, it's more or less a dungeon and was used to conduct horrible experiments on the inmates. Shivers run down my spine.

"Don't be such a coward," I tell myself. "Your little sister needs you." I try to push the door open. To my surprise the door is unlocked. I remember this particular door was closed a few hours ago. Phillip and I tried to open it. We wanted to be alone and made sure no one would catch us making out, especially his fiancé.

My sister is singing one of her favorite song from the group 'Ponder', and it spurs me on down the stairs.

"Joanna, I'm here!" I keep moving the flashlight left and right. I hate dark, wet, and dirty places and this basement is all of them. Also narrow. It isn't an open space as I had imagined. It has a long corridor with doors on both sides only a few inches apart. On top of each door is a red roman number.

"Jennifer!" my sister calls me. "Over here."

I turn my light to her voice and notice one of the doors is open. I run and enter the room.

"Joanna, where are you?" I say as I flash the light around the room looking for her. But I can't find her. "Joanna!!!" I keep calling her name but she doesn't respond. A thin white vapor is slowly seeping into the room and strange scratching sounds emanate from the mist.

"Thirteen little trespassers are slumbering. One little trespasser is not," says a bone-chilling voice. I quickly move the light around the room and at the bottom of the haze I see an army of different colored spiders crawling forward. I scream and withdraw to a corner of the room. I'm terrified of spiders – always have been and always will be.

I feel them crawling up my shoes and legs. Hysterically, I start to scream, cry, shove them away. I begin to stomp on them, but when I see a tarantula the size of a Chihuahua, I start to panic. I begin to sweat and the perspiration causes my eyes to sting and water until I can see nothing. In the distance I hear, "And now there are thirteen little trespassers left," and I'm gone.

Selene

I open my eyes and observe the morning light intruding through the curtains. I sit upright on the bed and look to my left. Yolanda is still sleeping. I heard her moaning, screaming and talking to herself in Spanish throughout the night. Fortunately for her, I don't speak Spanish, so whatever she said is still private. I guess the unexpected way Matt and Joanna have disappeared from the game is a bit of a shock to her, not to mention the crazy stories Tony has been telling about this place. I wonder if they are all true? Well – it doesn't matter now. I'll find out soon enough.

I stand up and before I walk to the bathroom, I stop in front of the window. Straight ahead lies a large body of blue water and below the window bound by the asylum walls is a lawn studded with hundreds of graves. They have no names, just numbers carved on white stone. They were patients who died here within these cold walls and were never claimed by anyone. Maybe their families were ashamed of having a lunatic for a relative, and left them here to rot.

I tiptoe to the bathroom trying not to make any noise. I'm an early riser. Normally by this time, back in Montana, I'd already fed the animals and prepared and eaten breakfast while Mom and Dad...... my stomach tightens a bit at the thought of my parents, the ranch, and my pets. I sit on the edge of the bathtub, looking down at the white tiled floor while tears fill my eyes. I've never been invited to a sleepover or even left my parents for more then a few hours. This is the first time I've been away from my comfort zone, and it is very hard for me. I'm wondering how I'll be able to live in New York City.

From Carmen and Maria's room, I hear footsteps gently tapping on the floor, followed by the squeaking sound of a door opening and closing. I wipe the tears from my face, and quickly step out of the bathroom, cautiously opening my bedroom door. I see Maria cross the hallway in a white silk nightgown.

I follow her. And there, hidden in the shadows, I watch Maria enter the small reading room.

As soon as Maria closes the door, I enter the living room. The two rooms are separated by a wall of bookcases and in the center of the wall there's an arch with thick dark green velvet curtains.

I position myself next to the arch and shift the curtains an inch or two to observe Maria. She is taking her robe off, and I can see her red-hot and very revealing lingerie.

The door of the reading room opens and my heart stops as my brother enters the room. Seth rushes to her, and within a matter of seconds, he is all over her. His lips on her skin, his hands touching her body. Maria's hands begin removing his clothes.

I'm shocked and embarrassed seeing Seth so – passionate. I look away and slide down to the floor, unable to believe what I have just witnessed. In the meantime, their kisses are becoming more and more passionate.

I choose to leave not wanting to know more about my brother's love life. Deep in my own thoughts, I find myself back in my room. Yolanda is up and ready to enter the bathroom.

"What's wrong, chica?" I look up at her and shake my head biting my lower lip. I try not to show my disappointment. "You look horrible. Did something happen to you?" she continues.

"No, nothing happened." I give her a faint smile and sit on my bed.

Promptly, the door of our bedroom opens.

"Oh, my God – my God," Raul says entering the room with his cell phone in hand. Excitement emanates from every pore of his body. "You've got to see this." He pushes the screen of his cell phone toward my face. There is a picture of a naked man's backside. The figure has a tattoo of a black dog or possibly a jackal on his right shoulder blade. I blush at the sight of an exposed butt.

Yolanda grabs the phone from her cousin's hand, "Don't tell me this is who I think he is," she exclaims Raul just smiles.

"Who is he?" I ask.

66

"You don't know who HE is?" I shake my head and Yolanda gives me the phone. "Look closely at the back of his head."

I stare intently at the man's head and my heart leaps as I recognize him.

"William? William Hawthorn?" Both Raul and Yolanda simultaneously nod their heads and grin broadly. "How?" My face feels hot.

"Let me tell you the entire story," Raul begins as he sits down on Yolanda's bed, staring straight into our eyes. His words project excitement and amusement. "Last night I was calmly and peacefully reading my gossip magazine 'The Fabulous', trying to calm my nerves after the pandemonium of last night, when all of a sudden the bathroom door opened, steam shot out into the room, and there he was, William Hawthorn, walking across the room in God's given clothes.

"I was composed and indifferent but little me, Raulitto, was joyfully dancing the meringue on the inside." Raul's upper body swings left and right. Yolanda and I laugh. I really needed some distraction and some mood lifting. "Once I saw William leaping into the bed naked – I had to take a little souvenir. I placed my phone on mute, prepared the camera and patiently waited until he got up. And," Raul's smile grows wider, "this morning when he re-entered the bathroom I took a quick picture of his cute, adorable behind. Rrrrrrr," and he starts to bite in mid-air after the picture. "He has such a cute little baby butt," he adds and I continue laughing. Raul is quite funny.

A knock on the door interrupts our gathering. It is Seth with a smile brighter than the morning light in our room. He got lucky. My joyful mood is dissolving and I'm doing something I've rarely done before. I look away from my brother sight. I don't know why, but I can't meet his gaze. There are so many questions I want him to answer. For example, how could he start a relationship with someone who is engaged with somebody else, and how could he be so passionate with a person he barely knows?

67

"Not dressed yet?" Asks Seth with a smile. I shake my head and start to make my bed. "I was going to have breakfast. Do you want me to wait?"

"No, go ahead. It will take a while," I reply. The image in my head of Seth and Maria making out makes me cringe and shake my body in disgust.

"Is everything all right with you?"

"Sure – I'm fine – great," I snap. "Just go and I'll see you in a few."

Seth shifts his head to one side and squints at me. He is assessing my mood. Raul stands up and opens the door. "Why don't we go down and have some breakfast? Yolanda and Selene will meet us downstairs once they are ready." Seth nods still with his gaze locked on me. He doesn't ask any further questions and leaves.

"Selene," Yolanda calls and I look up at her. "What do you think about the show so far?" I stare at her in confusion. Her question caught me off guard. For the last few minutes I had completely forgotten that we are in a show. "You know – the disappearance of Matt and Joanna," she explains and I smile.

"I have to admit that it took me by surprise. I tried to figure out the game but never this. I never could have imagined that the game would be so suspenseful."

"Yeah, me too, and Tony said…"

I raise my eyes up in the air, "I thought you hated him after what happened yesterday."

She smiles coyly at me, "We made up – he apologized to me."

"Really? He doesn't seem the type to apologize."

"Well, he did, and he told me a few things about this place. He thinks this place is haunted and it's after us."

"Why?"

"That's what the deceased do when we living enter their world. They hunt us down the same way they were hunted down in their prior lives. They want revenge for the cruelty done to them."

"And you believe in all this crazy stuff?" I ask as I stand up.

"Of course," Yolanda cuts me off. "After last night, I believe everything. It was so real. You must believe me," she says. "At first I was just like you – not believing his crazy stories, and I also thought he was trying to scare us, but after last night…" she stops and looks out the window with her clothes in hand, shaking like a leaf.

"And you truly believe him?" I ask her in a softer tone of voice. I don't want to upset her even more. She nods. "Well, I don't," I lie to her. I know very well that there is something among us. I felt it and saw it a few times but what Yolanda saw or experienced is nothing compared to what lies beneath our feet. It is still dormant and I hope it will stay that way, but I have a strong feeling that our time is running short.

"I just want you to keep your eyes, and most of all your mind, open to other possibilities," she says and I nod.

Pleased she saunters into the bathroom with her change of clothes in her hands.

William

"How do you feel?" Alice asks.

My head is better. I reply and swallow an aspirin.

"I told you not to go overboard with your research," she scolds. I swear, Alice's caring can get on my nerves from time to time. I never had anyone care for me before. I was pretty much left to myself. My adoptive parents weren't too happy with me, and soon after my father's death, my mother sent me to live with Carmen and her family. Carmen's mother is the older sister of my adoptive mother.

For years I tried to search for my real parents, for my past. Nothing. At least not until the night Alice came to me. She told me our mother's name. Kate Williams. I also found out that she was only seventeen years old when she gave birth to Alice. My mother's family cast her away on this island. They were super religious and as soon as my mother told them that she was pregnant, her father made a few calls to some of his associates. The next day my mother became a permanent guest of St. Clara.

"Ready to go down?"

Not, yet. I smile at her and she crosses her arms. *I want to make a quick stop at Tony's room.*

"Why?" she asks and starts to tap her foot on the floor.

I want to see his files. I couldn't find anything about our mother except that she was here – in the asylum. Do you know if our dad was here too?

Alice's body stiffens, as always. I don't know what's with her. She simply shuts down at the mention of our father.

Please.

"You don't need him. He is of no use to us and he is not my father. He's yours."

Why won't you tell me anything?

"He is the reason for all of this. He's the one who caused my mother's death and mine."

"Tell me what had happened and who my father is?" I raise my voice and Alice disappears right before my eyes.

"WAS!!!!" Her voice echoes through the room. Frustrated, I slam my fist on the wall repeatedly and stop only when the bathroom door opens.

"Are you all right?" Phillip asks, staring at the dent my fist has made in the wall. I nod and without a word I leave.

Before I join the others I make a quick stop in Tony's room. Cautiously, I open his room and peek inside. The room is empty. I enter and start to search for his files.

"Bingo!" I tell myself. The files are stacked underneath his bed. I begin to go through each folder. I'm looking for my mother's name when something catches my attention. Some of the files are red and carry the names of some the contestants in this house. I stare at the three folders with the names:

Yolanda Perez
Seth and Selene Holloway
Phillip Stewart

I toss them aside. Not interested. I keep looking through the rest of the files. There it is, Kate Williams. I pick it up and beneath my mother's folder I spy another familiar name:

Lilly Holloway

I stand motionless for several seconds, pondering if I should peek inside the folder or not, when something else catches my attention. There is a notepad beside the files. I pick it up and read:

Yolanda Perez – Retrocognition
She has the ability to see past life and events.

"Yolanda – a retrocognition? Who knew," I whisper and ponder how far the Roma brothers went with their research. How convenient that she is here to help them or – not.

I keep searching and come across a family tree folded into three parts. It is the Seapeak family tree and at the top there is a familiar name circled in red:

Phillip Stewart

I sit in the room going over the family's trees unable to believe how deep the brother probed into their research. I'm wondering if they know about me and if I too play a role in their book, or should I say – plot. Something doesn't feel right.

I grab the Holloway folder and find copies of old news paper articles and written notes. According to the notes and articles, the Holloways come from a long line of criminals and they were all females. I start to read one of the notes:

Lilly Holloway, also known as Cut Throat Lilly, was one of the rare women who dressed as a man and became a fearless criminal. She and her crew crossed the Wild West stealing and killing. Lilly was considered a violent and unbalanced criminal, and was a mortal danger to anyone who had the misfortune to come across her.

Rumors are that she became pregnant and decided that the criminal life wasn't a lifestyle she wanted to give to her child. She bought a large piece of land in Louisiana and with a group of faithful followers.

Lilly spent the next ten years raising her daughter and working her land but her peaceful life didn't last very long.

Five male bodies were found on her land. Lilly Holloway and her daughter weren't among the corpses. Some say that Lilly got tired of her lovers and killed them all, took her treasures, and left with her daughter for another adventure.

I continue to flip through his notes and something else catches my eyes. It is about Selene.

Selene Holloway – psychometric.
She has the ability to obtain knowledge about a person or object through personal contact.

"This is why she acts so odd and dresses strange," I think aloud.

Confused and concerned about the Roma brother's research, I decide to leave and to do some of my own investigation about Tony and his brother. They know too much and I don't like it. I grab my mother's file and leave.

Down in the dining room everyone including my departed little sister is sitting around the table.

"Did you find her?" Phillip asks.

"Who?" I ask in confusion as Carmen approaches me.

"No. I've looked everywhere."

"Who is missing?"

"Jennifer," Carmen replies and sits in the first empty chair.

"So," Phillip begins, "we are now down to thirteen."

"And soon more of us will be their victims." Tony appears out of nowhere.

"Oh, please!" Carmen jumps in. "Give it a rest." She jumps up from her chair and stands before us. "I can't take it anymore. Since we entered this damn house you keep telling us that the house is haunted and it will come after us.

"You may think that I'm dumb but I'm not. I know your game."

"What game?" Tony yells. "I'm not playing any game."

"You're trying to mess with our heads."

"No. I'm not," Tony raises his voice at her and I have to smile. He reminds me of a child just scolded by his mother. "Who do you think is behind the disappearance of the others?"

"Definitely not the house," Carmen states.

"It's the show," Phillip declares and winks at Carmen. Poor fool. He has no idea who Carmen really is.

"The show – right," Tony protests. I hear Carmen clicking her tongue. She always does that when someone inferior to her doesn't give her the proper respect.

"Do any of you know the real reason this place closed?" Tony continues to push his point.

"A few years ago a vile massacre happened in here," I say.

"Everyone died, causing the asylum to be shut down indefinitely."
Tony nods his head with a weird smile that doesn't make me feel
comfortable.

"Yes, yes, but do you really know the truth behind the
massacre?"

"No. No one knows."

He smirks, "I thought so."

"Tell them," Yolanda whispers. "Tell them what you told
me."

"Tell what?" Maria asks.

"Some of us are connected to this place," Tony starts. "For
example Phillip is a direct descendent of Sir David Seapeak. The
Holloways are the grandchildren of Cut Throat Lilly."

"Who's that?" Ivy asks.

"She was a feared outlaw in the early nineteen-hundreds.
The people of the West were terrified of her. Cut Throat Lilly left
no one alive. She cut the throats of anyone who had the misfortune
of crossing her path."

"You are the grandchildren of a criminal?" Priscilla asks,
looking at the Holloways. I notice the indifference on the faces of
the two siblings. I guess they know about their grandmother, or
should I say, grandmothers.

"Actually," Tony steps in with a satisfied smile, "The
Holloways come from a very long line of criminals and they were
all women."

"Cool," Wayne says loudly. "There is nothing hotter than
kick ass chicks carrying a gun or two."

"I don't see anything cool about coming from an ancestry of
criminals," Carmen states and gives the two of them a disgusted
glare.

Seth cuts her off. "I personally don't care what you think."
Carmen starts. She seems frightened by him. I never saw her react
that way, not even with her parents. This is a new side of her.
Selene places her hand on her brother's shoulder. He says nothing

74

more.

Selene looks over to Tony and in a calm tone asks, "What does my family's past have to do with this place?"

"You don't know?" Tony smiles. "Cut Throat Lilly, AKA your grandmother, was the prior owner of this place. She and her new clique bought the place. They lived on this island for a few years until…"

"Yes, this is great," I interrupt him. "I already know the rest of that tale. All I want to know is what I don't know. For example, how does all this connect to the massacre or to what is happening to us?"

Tony taps his fingers on the table. "What I'm trying to explain is that…" and he stops. He is searching for the right words and the best way to explain it to us. "Isn't it a bit of a coincidence that all the direct descendents connected to this place are here on this island with us?"

"Not all of us," Carmen raises her voice.

"Look, even William is connected to this place," he says and everyone's attention is now directed on me.

I gesture toward him. "Let me help you," I say. "My mother was a patient in this place." I start to explain all I know about my mother and about my intense search to find more about my real family.

I finish my story and can feel their eyes burning with curiosity and anticipation. I immediately know what they are thinking by the way they look at me:

"William Hawthorn, the child of a crazy person and one day he too will be locked in a place like this, just like his mother."
"He'll meet his mother's fate. He deserves it."

I really don't care what they think because I know she wasn't insane. She was forced to be here and if she turned out to be crazy it's because this place made her that way.

"You haven't answered our questions," Selene says, drawing the attention away from me. She gives me a shy smile and quickly looks away, "What does all this have to do with us?"

"Oh!" Tony says. "I'm sorry. I do get carried away from time to time." He smiles. "The castle is cursed and it brought the curse here from England.

"You see, Sir David Seapeak had a trusted servant, George. George was a warlock and he introduced Sir David Seapeak into black magic soon after the death of his wife.

"Rumors are that Sir Seapeak made a deal with the devil to have his wife visit him every night in return for young fresh souls.

"Sir David Seapeak agreed to the deal but never pursued the agreement. That's when things between he and George became violent. They fought for days. George even brought young peasant girls to his Master's room for him to sacrifice, but he refused. That's when George lost his temper and stabbed Sir David.

"Years passed and mysterious deaths occurred in and around the Seapeak family. Accounts say that Elisabeth, granddaughter of Sir David Seapeak, was the re-embodiment of the devil and was responsible for the death of all those young missing girls. She was caught and severely punished for her crimes, but the deaths never stopped. More and more people were found dead and the Seapeak's were forced to abandon the castle.

"Many, many years later John Kane bought the castle and re-erected it on this island only to find out that the legends were true. The castle is cursed and it needs to feed on human souls…..."

"Oh! Please," Carmen shouts furiously. "Doesn't anyone see what he is trying to do? He is trying to put bugs in our minds. He is trying to make us forget our purpose by scaring the shit out…."

"I am NOT!" Tony looks offended. He reminds me of a little boy accused of stealing goodies from the cookie jar. "I can prove it."

"You can't even answer a simple question."

"Like what?"

"What your pathetic theory has to do with the disappearance of your brother, Joanna and Jennifer?"

"Didn't you hear me? I said the castle feeds on human souls."

"Oh! Please. I'm out of here," cries Carmen. "If any of you have any sanity at all, you should follow my lead," she leaves with most of the group right behind her. I smirk. Carmen always had a touch for drama and is a born leader.

I too decide to leave and before I walk out I say to Tony, "I'll talk to you later." He nods.

Tony

"I'll talk to you later," William tells me. I nod. I know what he wants and I'm more than happy to tell him all I know about his mother, grandparents and father.

Yolanda places her hand on mine. "Don't let them bother you," she smiles. Together we observe the Holloways and William leaving the room. I have to admit to myself that the Holloways are quite puzzling.

"I won't," I tell her and she smiles at me. "What do you say we explore the basement?"

"The basement?" she answers with uncertainty in her voice.

"Yes. Scared?"

Yolanda places her hands on my face and says, "Just for today, no spooky stories about the castle. Please, just for me."

I stare into her frightened hazel eyes and nod. "Fine. I won't. I promise."

She gives me a firm hug followed by a kiss on my cheek. "Thanks."

"For what?"

"For the kiss," I tell her with a smile and notice her cheeks turning red. She looks down, grabs my hand and pulls me forward to the crypt.

The basement isn't exactly how I pictured it. It is dark, cold, wet and it has a horrible stench, a mix between mold, chlorine and human waste. Yolanda sinks her nails into my flesh. She is terrified. I hope there are no rats or mice or anything that could cause her to sink her nails even deeper into my skin.

"What was the basement used for?"

"Do you really want to know?" I ask her, and she stays silent for a moment or two. Then she nods her head. "It was used as a chamber of horrors. They conducted compulsory sterilization, also known as forced sterilization."

"They forced sterilizations?"

I nod, "To prevent the reproduction of defective genetic traits."

"That's cruel."

"Don't worry, they stopped forced sterilization a long time ago. It has been acknowledged as a crime against humanity," We enter a bare room except for a chair in the middle of the floor. Electric cables run beneath the chair. "I guess Electroconvulsive therapy was practiced in here."

"Electro what?"

"Electroconvulsive therapy. Also known as electroshock or ECT."

"Oh! Electroshock. I heard of that."

"Insulin shock therapy was also practiced in here," I continue. When I see Yolanda's confused face I continue to explain. "It was a treatment where the patients were continuously injected with large doses of insulin in order to put them in comas for several weeks."

"That's nasty. I wouldn't like to spend weeks of my life in a coma."

"They stopped practicing Insulin shock therapy in the 70s," I explain. We keep moving, searching until our flashlights reveal a bathtub. I move the light from side to side and discover five more bathtubs.

"Hydrotherapy," Yolanda gasps.

"You know about hydrotherapy?" She glares at me. I guess

I must have offended her.

"Of course I know what it is," she snaps at me and moves across the room. "I saw it in a movie."

"Ah! Movies," I smirk. "What would we do without Hollywood?"

"Don't make fun of me, Anthony Roma," she scolds. I smile. She reminds me of my mom. "Did they practice lobotomies too?" she quickly adds in a softer tone.

"You know about lobotomies too? Let me guess, another movie?"

"Don't look down on Hollywood. It can teach a thing or two," she smiles. "For example lobotomy is a neurosurgical procedure. It consists of cutting the connections to and from the interior part of the frontal lobes of the brain."

"Wow. I'm impressed," I tell her and she gives me a theatrical bow.

Then she continues on to the next room and yells, "I found something."

"Found what?"

"A box," she replies as I walk toward her. I find her behind a large, half corroded metal box. It must have been the heater. She is scuffling, puffing, and cursing in Spanish. I stay behind and observe.

Suddenly I hear water pouring into the bathtubs. Yolanda stops and moves closer to me. Together we enter the Hydrotherapy room and direct our lights to the bathtubs but, there is no sign of water – just the sound. My skin starts to crawl, and when I see Yolanda running for her life down the hall I follow her example.

We don't stop running until we reach the kitchen. Before one of us says anything we chug down a glass of water.

"What was that?" I ask.

"One of your ghost friends," she snaps, and starts to curse in Spanish.

"What happened?" Ivy asks as she enters the kitchen.

"We were down in the basement and…" Yolanda stops in the middle of her sentence when she sees Ivy's enthusiastic face.

"You mean the basement is open?"

Yolanda nods and asks, "Why?"

Ivy quickly shuts the fridge, "It was locked before. Priscilla, Wayne, Warren and I tried to go down there last night," and with that she runs out. Probably looking for Priscilla and the Jones.

"What if they find the money?" I ask Yolanda.

"At the moment I really don't care. If they find the money we'll take it away from them."

"I'm impressed," I tell her. She gives me another sweet smile.

"Who knows," she adds, "maybe one of your friends will make sure Ivy and Priscilla won't find the money," and winks at me.

Ivy

"Priscilla," I call and motion her over. She glares at me and I keep waving her over. Finally she stands up.

"What?" She growls at me. I grab her hand and pull her toward the basement. "Where are you dragging me?" she asks as we pause in front of the open basement door.

I point to the door. "It's open."

"So?"

"What do you mean, So? I thought we wanted to win."

"We don't need the money. We swim in money. We're rich, remember?" I glare at her with annoyance. "Do not forget the real reason why we are here."

"Yes, but we need the money to stay in the game longer."

Priscilla is silent. She thinks it over and then says, "Fine. But as soon I see a rat or a spider or anything revolting – I leave."

"The entire place is revolting and old and dirty and creepy," I state. She agrees with me.

I toss a flashlight to Priscilla and she raises her nose up. "What? No lights in the basement?"

I shake my head and start to descend the stairs with Priscilla right behind me, holding my shirt firmly in her hand. With her other hand she flicks the flashlight right, left, up and down.

"I hate this place," she complains. "It's smelly, dirty and… wet," she lifts her foot to show me her shoe soaked in water.

"Come on. Let's keep moving." I press on with Priscilla moaning and swearing behind me.

"Do you believe Tony's little ghoul stories?" she asks and I burst into laughter. She looks away and says nothing.

I stop laughing and ask, "Why? Do you?"

With a shrug of her shoulders, she replies, "Maybe – I don't know – I just hear things at night."

"Like what?"

She halts in her tracks and places her hands on my arm. "At night when everyone is asleep, I hear people talking, screaming, crying, scratching and knocking on our bedroom door." I say nothing. "You must believe me. I'm not lying or make it up. It is true."

"Didn't you tell me that it's someone pulling a prank or two?"

She looks down at the ground then raises her head to me. "You know what? Oh, never mind." She starts moving forward without waiting for me.

I run to catch up and watch as she points the flashlight around the dark narrow corridor. She looks agitated.

"Carmen is right not to trust Tony. He is trying to put dirty, little suspicions in our minds. He wants to have us occupied with false facts so he can win the show, not to mention the money," I tell her, trying to comfort her.

"Maybe," she murmurs, "but do not forget he doesn't need the money."

"Neither do we and yet I still want to win."

"So – he – is just playing a game?"

"Yep, he is just playing a game. Trust me – this is all part of the show, and so are the noises you hear at night," I add. "Carmen said so."

"Speaking of Carmen," Priscilla interrupts. "Have you seen her?"

"No. Why?"

Priscilla starts laughing, "Someone took her beauty products, push-up bras, and Maria's diary. Carmen looks awful without make-up and her 38B breast size is now 32A." She continues laughing. "Maria, on the other hand, is devastated and is going from room to room looking for her diary. It must have some juicy stuff in it the way she's franticly looking for it."

"Who do you believe took it?"

"I don't know, but Carmen thinks Selene and Yolanda are behind it."

"Why?"

"She thinks Selene is trying to sabotage her – you know – William."

"Aaah," I say. "I don't think she is capable of something like that. She seems nice."

"So do I, but I kept my opinion to myself. She was out of control and wanted to go after Selene but William stopped her at the last moment."

"He really does like...." I stop in mid-sentence as my flashlight shone on something in one of the cells. I open the door wider and enter. There, in the farthest corner, I notice a gold charm bracelet wrapped around a chess piece. I move in closer. "It's Jennifer," I say.

"She must be the latest victim," Priscilla states and moves her flashlight around the room.

I turn the pawn upside down and notice Jennifer's name painted on its pedestal.

Suddenly we hear footsteps on the wet surface of the concrete floor.

"Hello!" I call. "Who's there?" Nothing. The footsteps come closer. "Who's there?" I demand.

"Come on," Priscilla commands and pulls me back. "Let's go." She yanks me away from the cell. Out in the hall we notice the cell doors swing slowly open and then shut tight.

When the doors open once again we start to run. I look over to my right and in one of the cells I can see a man sitting on a chair with cables strapped to his head. He is shaking and screaming. I quicken my pace and pass Priscilla. I don't stop until I reach my bedroom. I run to the toilet where I vomit up my lunch.

Feeling better, I join Priscilla, who is sitting half in shock on her bed playing with the chess piece.

Something at the base of the chess piece grabs my attention. "May I?" I reach for the piece.

I scratch the base and a piece of paper comes off.

"What is it?" Priscilla asks.

"Look," I tell her with a proud smile. "We found one of the clues." I show her the base of the object.

"S." She reads the letter carved into the bottom of the chess piece and looks confused. "What does it mean?"

"It could be a code or a clue to the whereabouts of the money," I reply.

"We should go and take the other chess pieces," Priscilla suggests.

I nod. "When?"

"Tonight when everyone is asleep."

"Right."

Wayne

"What are you doing?" Warren snaps at me as he sees me pouring some laxative into Tony's water.

"What do you think I'm doing?" I reply, and he steps closer.

"It's wrong," he tells me as he watches me pour more of the laxative into four other glasses.

"You really don't think that I'm going to stay in the kitchen all day long cooking for them and I don't get some fun out of it, do you?"

"It's wrong."

"Don't worry. Trust me." With a clap on Warren's back I return to the kitchen.

After dinner we walk to the entertainment room and I hang around, waiting for the show to begin. I take the best seat in the room and wait for the five others to drink my concoction.

I watch Tony place the glass to his lips and gulp the fluid. I smile. It is so hard for me to keep from laughing, especially when I see the others drink my mixture. I bite my lip, and Warren kicks me in the shin to keep me quiet. I'm snickering, smirking, and tears of joy form in my eyes.

"Are you OK?" I hear Yolanda. I turn my attention to her and watch Tony giving her a ridiculous smile as he holds his stomach. He crosses his legs and bends forward. "Are you all right?" Yolanda places her hand on his back. They have everyone's attention.

"Yes, I'm great," he says with a ridiculous smile, half embarrassed and half in pain. Then he lets out a grunt. "I'll be right back," he mumbles, and runs off.

I smile.

"Happy?" Warren whispers as I see Seth, Phillip, Maria, and Carmen run out of the room with their hands on their stomachs.

"Very," I reply with a content smile. Warren grunts and shakes his head.

I stay put and gleefully watch the five of them enter and leave the room repeatedly. It is hilarious.

The clock chimes ten times, and after that, the five of them stop coming back down. I decide to go to bed. The entertainment is over.

I'm walking down the hall and hear moaning and the sound of flushing toilets. I see Carmen and Phillip running down the hall with toilet paper rolls in their hands. Seth and Maria must have confiscated the toilets from their roommates. Carmen and Phillip will be fighting over the only gust bathroom in this house, I chuckle to myself. Yolanda and Selene will fight over their bathroom, just like William and Raul. They will be up all night. Ha! I'm wonderfully devious. And with this wonderful thought I enter my room and hear painful cries coming from the bathroom. Tony. I forgot we share the same bathroom. Damn it! I'll be up all night too. Damn it! Damn it! Damn it!

13 contenders remaining

Day Four

Monday, August 16, 2010

Raul

Phillip and I have been walking throughout the house for hours. It might sound crazy but it seems as if the house is changing its floor plan. The hallways appear to be stretching out, and I can hear and feel the walls moving around us. It's very creepy. I hear screaming, crying and foot steps coming closer. It is rather disturbing.

Phillip is calm and tells me to keep moving. I could smack him if he weren't so cute and I do have to admit – it kind turns me on.

"Look," Phillip says and points to a small flap concealed behind a mirror. "An exit."

We walk closer to the flap and I can smell moldy air coming from the tunnel hidden behind the mirror. "I don't know. It wasn't here a few hours ago and it feels wrong to me."

"It's an exit – the only exit we have found in hours. We have no other choice."

"It could be dangerous."

"So what? Do you want to stay here?"

"No – but…."

"Come on. Let's go," he says. "I'm going. I'm not staying in here." He walks down the narrow, dirty corridor.

I look around, and when I hear whispers swiftly coming closer, I jump into the tunnel and yell, "Hey! Wait for me." I start to chase after Phillip.

We've been walking up, down, left, and right in what seems like a giant maze built between the castle walls. It is cold, wet and dark. Centuries of dirt begin collecting on my clothes. I can't stand dirt. It makes me tense and I'm about to scream. I have cobwebs and dust on my hands and in my hair. If Phillip weren't here I would probably smack something around. What was I thinking wandering around the castle? I should have let him explore this haunted place by himself. But when he came to me with his sweet smile asking if I was interested in exploring the fourth floor I couldn't resist. I had to go.

Part of me wants to win. I need the money. And the other part wants to spend some time alone with Phillip. He is very cute. But what he didn't tell me was that he is also on the hunt for the extra guests living among us. He has this crazy idea that the TV station has hired some actors to drive us nuts. He told me this an hour after we began wandering around the fourth floor. I have another suggestion. I believe one of us is an infiltrator working for YTV. I told this to Yolanda and as always she dismissed my hunches. She believes Tony's theory. How idiotic is that? She always had bad taste in men.

"Say," I start, "why did you decide to take me on this crazy adventure?"

Phillip keeps walking. "Out of the people living in the castle, I trust you the most."

"What about Maria?"

"At the moment, I trust her the least," he says. I simply nod. I don't know what to say. I wonder if he knows about his fiancé and Seth. I stay silent.

"Look, a light." He points straight ahead and starts to quicken his pace. I'm right behind him.

"What the hell is this?" I ask as we enter the room. It looks like the room of a small girl. The walls are pink, the bedspreads are pink, and in a corner are dozens of porcelain dolls. I shiver.

"I really don't know," he mutters, looking around.

"You were right," I tell him, "Someone is living among us….."

"Yeah, but I didn't imagine it would be an old guest of the asylum."

"What do you mean?" I ask, knowing very well where he is going, but too afraid to admit it. At the moment I'm too preoccupied about those dolls in the corner with their big, bright blue eyes fixed on us. I gulp.

"I thought our extra guest was an actor or someone they hired to scare the shit out of us, but it seems our guest might be one of the original inmates of St. Clara...."

"That's impossible. How?" I ignore him and move quickly around the room, searching for clues to dismantle both his hypothesis and my gut feeling.

"Do you remember what Tony said about the massacre a few years ago?" He asks. I give him a quick head bob. "Everyone was found dead except one guest. A little girl around the age of ten was never found..."

"You cannot be suggesting that a girl of ten could go around this place slicing everyone's throats?"

"It's a possibility – a very strong possibility."

I snort, unable to believe that someone like Phillip could possibly believe such a pile of bull crap. "Of all the people in this house, I would have thought you'd be the last person falling for Tony's garbage," I sneer.

Phillip laughs, "Why?"

"You seem like a very intelligent person, not to mention strong," I explain. His face becomes serious and deeply concerned.

"Trust me – I'm not what you think I am. I'm just thinking that Tony's stories might hold some truth," he explains while I open the trunk at the base of the bed.

"What is this?" I ask him as I lift a white shirt.

"Hospital garment," Phillip replies as he walks closer to the trunk. He bends down and takes out another garment and examines it.

"You shouldn't have come here," says a small female voice. Phillip and I drop the garments on the floor and look around the room. We search frantically for the owner of the voice.

In the corner, where the dolls are cramped together, I swear, their heads turn towards us and their freaky ice-cold eyes are fixated on us. Then, someone cries "Mommy. I want my mommy!"

Phillip and I jump. Goose-bumps spring up all over my body.

"We've got to get out of here," I yell at Phillip. I'm freaking out. I'm having breathing problems and my heart is about to burst out of my chest.

The voices continue, "Mommy. I want my mommy!" If that isn't terrifying enough, lullaby music begins to play.

Phillip and I move closer to each other and stand back to back. I sense Phillip's body quivering.

"You shouldn't have come here," says the same small female voice. "You shouldn't have come HERE!!!!"

Suddenly the floor parts beneath our feet and we fall through the opening.

We scream and scream until we hit the ground and find ourselves in a dark, humid and horrendously putrid place. A mix of mold and human waste smothers my nostrils. I start to gag.

"Are you all right?" Phillips asks. I try to stand up but my left ankle is throbbing.

"No, I think my ankle is broken. What about you?"

"I'm ok. I was lucky to land on a mattress." Phillip walks over to me and takes a quick glance at my ankle. "It's swollen." He turns away and starts moving objects around.

"What are you doing?"

"I'm looking for something to put around your ankle until we find our way out."

After a minute or so Phillip says, "Do you see that?"

"What?"

"The fog."

I look down and notice a white mist arising from the concrete floor like water evaporating from the pavement on a hot summer day.

"Twelve little trespassers are exploring. One little trespasser is not." says the chilling voice of a little girl next to my ear.

Then, something grabs my ankles and pulls me. I plunge to the floor and scream. Phillip turns around and promptly grabs my wrist.

"DON'T LET GO!!!!" I yell. "DON'T LET GO!!!!"

"I WON'T!" he yells, and fights very hard to pull me back. From behind me I hear little children laughing and singing. I turn my head slightly to the right and see a small figure emerging from the mist.

"And now there are twelve little trespassers left," the shape says. I'm deathly frightened.

The small figure rises from the vapor and reveals that it is not a child at all but one of the dolls that we had seen a few minutes ago. Behind that doll, more dolls were emerging and rapidly coming closer.

"PLEASE DON'T LET GO OF ME!" I beg Phillip with tears streaming down my face. My body is slowly drifting into the mist toward those dolls.

Phillip falls down and his hands slip away from mine. I scream as I'm being pulled inside the mist.

"RAUL!!!!!" he screams after me and his petrified face is the last thing I see before I'm dragged into darkness.

Yolanda

It is one in the afternoon and some of the groups haven't returned from their search. Everyone is determined to make it to the final. They've been searching every space, but it is easy to tell from their discouraged faces that they haven't found the money yet.

The Holloway's, Phillip, and my cousin Raul are not back yet and I'm starting to worry. We agreed to meet by lunchtime, and the four of them still haven't shown up. Tony, William and I are anxiously waiting for their return while the rest of the contenders happily entertain themselves in the game room. Carmen is exhilarated at the news that Selene is not back. She is hoping for Selene's departure from the show. I could have knocked that smile off her face but I was too saddened by Raul's absence, and Tony was there to keep me calm.

Strangely, Maria doesn't look too upset that her fiancé is missing as well. She was indifferent to the news and went straight to her bedroom.

"Here," Tony says and places a cup of warm coffee in front me. "Milk?" I nod and he pours some into my cup.

"Thanks," I tell him with a timid smile. I turn my attention to William who is reading a book. Since I met him, I've never seen him pay attention to anything other than books and Selene. She is the one thing that can make him put books aside. His eyes look empty and lost. He feels the same way I do at the moment. Raul – where are you? And a giant knot is building up in my throat. I hope he hasn't left the show – I need him.

I do hope Tony is wrong and Phillip or Raul are right, but I start to see things – strange things. I wake up in the middle of the night and find myself in undiscovered part of the castle half naked. I've been having strange visions since I arrived at this place. For example, this morning as I woke up, I found myself back in the library, a place that I swore never to enter again. Yet I was there in a white gown that didn't belong to me. An older man with dark blond hair and dark eyes dressed in a Victorian gray suit walked toward me and kissed me on the lips. I swear it felt so surreal and yet it seemed true. His kiss felt so genuine, but when I opened my eyes the man's image vanished along with my hallucination. Oh, God! Please help us all if this place is after us.

"Everything will be fine," Tony whispers in my ear. He places his hand on mine and gives it a gentle squeeze.

Unexpectedly, the windows begin rattling. William looks up from his book and peers outside. "A storm is approaching," he says, and he turns to stare at the open living room door. Tony and I do the same.

In matter of seconds, the hall is filled with the sound of running feet. My heartbeat grows more and more furious. A strange feeling is awakening inside me.

We stand up and Phillip appears, followed by the Holloways. Their faces are pale and their breathing is labored and unsteady.

"Raul…" Phillip starts.

I interrupt him by saying, "Gone," and the three of them nod their heads in unison. I look back at them not knowing what else to say, so I sit back on the couch. I knew he was the next to go. I could feel it.

Outside I hear the booming of thunder and the sound of rain hitting the windows.

"What happened?" William asks.

"I don't know," Phillip snaps. "He was right behind me and the next moment a fog or mist started to build up in the basement……"

"In the basement?" Tony asks. Phillip nods his head.

"Raul and I were on the fourth floor and…." Phillip stops. He is unsure of what to say.

"And what?" Tony pushes him to keep talking.

"And the corridors of the fourth floor kept changing. It seemed as if they were stretching on and on, and when we found an escape door we used it, only to find ourselves in another maze," Phillip eyes us and sees the looks of incredulity on our faces. "You have to believe me – it's true."

"What happened to my cousin?" I cry as tears trickle down my face. Selene comes up beside me, and holds me tight, trying to keep me calm. For some strange reason I begin to feel better, more secure. It bothers me that my cousin is missing and I'm no longer upset. I'm ashamed.

"As I said before, a white mist rose up from the floor of the basement and covered our feet. Suddenly I heard that same childish voice from three nights ago, and Raul started to scream for help. I grabbed his hand and tried everything I could to pull him away from the mist but I wasn't strong enough. I tried to reach him, but that white mist was solid – like a wall. I punched and kicked at it, but it was like I was pounding a concrete wall. Then

Seth and Selene came and…."

"We tried our best," Selene says with a quavering voice. "We tried everything." She shows me her red and bruised hands. "We kicked, punched, and threw things…."

"Nothing worked," Seth continues, "Then – the screams stopped and the mist was on the move once again. It was after us – we panicked and ran away." The three of them looked down at the floor. All three shared an expression of shame but Phillip is still holding something back.

"What aren't you telling us?" I ask in a sharp tone. Phillip focuses on me.

"I don't know how to tell you, but I was right. We are not alone in this place," Phillip starts. "What I'm trying to say is that there is someone else in this asylum other than us."

"Who?" Tony demands.

"A girl. At least I think it's a girl."

"Are you sure?" Tony asks.

"Of course I'm sure. I know what I saw and I think it is that girl you've been researching. What's her name again?"

"You mean Alice? Alice Williams?"

"Yes! That's her!" Phillips snaps his fingers with a smile. "I know it was her. I'm sure of it."

"How?" William asks, slowly approaching our circle.

"Because she was the only survivor of the massacre and they never found her, not to mention that she was found responsible for the massacre. I believe that the girl I saw today was her …."

Tony smirks, "You truly believe that a ten year old girl could be responsible for a crime that would be impossible for a child to commit?"

"And what's your theory?" Phillip snaps back at him.

"I don't know, but I'm definitely sure that Alice Williams isn't responsible for the massacre. She was blamed because she was the only patient not found among the other cadavers, and at the time they had no idea that Alice Williams was only ten years old."

94

"And who do you think lives in between the walls of this forsaken place?" I ask.

Tony shrugs, "I don't know. It could be Alice or someone else," he states, and withdraws into his own thoughts.

Warren

As I come down the stairs seeking a glass of water, I notice light emanating from the living room door. Curious, I walk into the room and find Selene sitting on the couch comforting Yolanda, who looks like her dog just got run over by a truck. Seth is pacing up and down with his eyes fixed on the floor. William is, as usual, sitting in a corner with his nose stuck in a book while Phillip is by the window watching the storm outside. Rain is hitting the glass like a machine gun and Raul…. I look around and ask, "Where's Raul?"

Everyone turns their eyes to me. Yolanda starts to cry and I understand that he is the latest candidate to leave the show.

I sit in a chair and ask, "What happened?"

Phillip takes a deep breath and starts to go over his story, including his strange meeting with our mystery guest or should I say host? Anyway, it doesn't matter because their story seems very questionable to me and I don't know if they also switched to Tony's side and are trying to confuse us. I inhale and sit back. We are all deep in our own thoughts. The rain is still pouring down and an eerie feeling creeps over my body.

"The others won't believe you," I finally tell them. "It is hard for me too, to believe your story."

"Like I care," Phillip replies in an offended tone.

I smirk.

"Tell me a bit more about this – massacre," I request. I'm curious about the tragic event. Tony doesn't look too happy. I guess he thinks that it is one of my usual traps designed to make fun of him at the end. "Really. I want to know. I'm very curious."

95

"Eighteen years ago, on October fifth, a small group of policemen came to this island after receiving many complaints from family, friends and business partners," William begins. I'm a bit in shock. I didn't know that he too is obsessed with this place. "The police weren't prepared for what awaited them." He stops, takes a quick look at the weather outside and then continues, "When they walked through the gates of St. Clara, they saw the fields covered with human bodies placed side by side underneath the sun with their throats cut." Shivers ran down my spine. I'm trying to picture the scene. "According to newspaper articles, the grass was red, the bodies were mostly decomposed, and the air was putrid. Some of the policemen ran down the hill and started vomiting and crying. Never in their careers had they seen a crime that horrific. The scene left a deep scar on them for years to come."

I swallow and with a faint smile I ask, "How do you know so much about this place?"

William stands up and in an ice cold tone of voice replies, "I told you before, my mother was one of the patients and one of the victims."

My heart fills with sorrow. I want to say something nice but I don't do nice unless I get something in return.

"Right. I forgot." I say and observe William leaving the room. I head off to look for Wayne.

Half an hour later, I finally find him in Priscilla and Ivy's room looking through their things too.

"I thought we wouldn't touch their stuff," I whisper angrily as I enter the room. Wayne starts at the sudden interruption.

"Don't do that," he snaps at me.

"What? Catch you?"

Wayne turns around with a pair of black underwear in his hand. He takes a deep breath, "We have to or they'll find out that we are behind the disappearance of their belongings and much more."

"I don't know. I kind of like them."

"I know but we are here to win, and we made a pact not to go off course, not even for girls." With a disappointed leer he states, "Not much stimulation among their lingerie," and tosses me a bra and some underwear, "they're pretty plain," he whines.

"What do you expect?" I ask, and study their panties. Wayne is right. They are not much of a turn on. They are very simple.

"I hoped they were a bit more like Yolanda, Maria, or Carmen. Now – those were sexy." A mischievous smile appears on his face and I can detect some saliva forming at the corner of his mouth.

"But they are a lot better than Selene's lingerie."

"Yeah, well I didn't expect anything more from her than white sport bras and simple white panties. She's from Montana and spends most of her time around horses."

"What's this?" I ask, raising an eyebrow. "Do I sense compassion from you?"

Wayne smirks, "I just state the facts."

I smile and we continue to go through the room, tossing stuff out the window. I begin to tell my brother about Raul's disappearance and William and Phillip's story.

"So, Raul is gone and everyone is slowly losing their brain cells," Wayne grins.

"Pretty much." I dump a bag filled with make-up out the window. I hear Wayne sigh. "What's on your mind?"

"I was just thinking that I have no idea who the infiltrator could be. I was so sure that it was Raul..."

"Raul? Infiltrator? Why?"

"Ivy said something interesting."

"Yes – and?"

"She and some of the other contenders believe that there is a mole working for the show to drive us mad, to push our buttons..."

"Isn't that what we're doing?" I ask and motion toward the room.

Wayne smiles. "True, but there must be someone working for the show. There are too many special effects involved."

"I guess – but Raul …"

"He was the perfect candidate. He was pretty much liked by everyone and was no threat."

"Yeah – well – I don't think it was him. He's flabby. He has no muscles and he is not strong enough. He wouldn't be able to drag the other contenders out of the show!"

"He didn't need to force them out of the show. They probably went willingly. They had no other choice."

"From what we saw or heard, none of the candidates left the show willing or peacefully," I clarify. Wayne thinks about this and agrees with me.

"One thing is for sure, he or she better be strong. I won't leave so easily." We laugh and keep going through the room. "And what's with the chess pieces?"

"That, my dear brother, I can answer," Wayne proudly announces. "The chess pieces hold some kind of a clue or code."

"What?"

"I discovered it last night when I threw the piece at the bathroom door. I wanted Tony to shut up. I wanted to sleep…"

"Yeah, yeah, yeah, and?"

"The figure broke and when I picked up the pieces, I notice a letter A written on the base."

"No way."

"Way," my brother mocks. "I think, once we are finished in here we should look for the other chess pieces."

I agree.

Phillip

Maria enters the room and doesn't seem too happy to see me. "Upset that I'm still here?" I ask.

With a forced smile she says, "Of course not. Why would

you say something horrible like that?" She walks over to me and gives me her usual arctic hug and kiss. She always does that when she is mad at me for some reason and doesn't want anyone to know. She needs to keep up the appearance of our bogus blissful life together, even though deep inside we are not happy. I'm so tired of all these charades.

I push her aside and walk out of the room. I need to be alone and digest what has happened. I have no time or patience to deal with her at the moment.

I lay on my bed and take the latest chess piece out of my pocket.

As we were kicking the wall I discovered a pawn piece lying on the ground. And as the Holloways began to run away from the basement, I took the pawn and placed it in my pocket.

I haven't told anyone that I have found another piece or about my discovery.

I was outside their door last night when Ivy discovered the clues. Stupid of her not to close the door or at least make sure that no one could hear of their discovery.

Suddenly my bedroom door opens. I quickly place the chess piece under my pillow and look up. It's Maria. She looks sad and agitated but I really don't care.

"What's up?" I ask. She says nothing. "What?" I shout in frustration.

"Have you seen my diary?"

"Not again. I've told you. I don't have it. Are you sure you didn't leave it at home?"

"I'm sure," she says, looking doubtful.

"Come here," I tell her, and open my arms wide. She smiles and jumps into my arms. She feels so good and smells magnificent. As I said before, I DO love her but not enough to settle down and have a family with her. I'm too young and I think I will never be the type of man she wishes me to be. But for the moment, I'll try to be the best I can be, which doesn't mean much.

"What are you thinking?" she asks. I stay silent, just enjoying her in my arms. "Tell me. What are you thinking?"

"Nothing. I just like your company," I tell her. I feel her pulling me even closer.

After a while Maria says, "Seth told me what happened."

"And?"

"Who do you think that person was?"

"I really don't know."

"Do you believe the house is haunted?"

I pause, trying to make sense of things. "No. I still believe its part of the show. I don't believe in ghosts or anything paranormal."

"Are you sure?"

"Look at me," I tell her, and she lifts her head from my chest. She is so beautiful. "There's nothing to be afraid of. It's all part of the show. They want to entertain the audience."

"But," she interrupts, "the way Raul was pulled away from the show – it is not normal. It is barbaric. He was hurt after all. Aren't they afraid that we might take legal action?"

I shake my head at her. "Don't forget that we signed fifty pages of legal papers. We gave away our rights."

Maria sighs and places her head back on my chest. "I'll tell you one thing," she mumbles. "If something like that happens to me, I'll sue. I'll get a good lawyer who can find a loophole in the contract and break their savings account. Next time they'll think twice before they mess with me."

I smile, "I know you will."

She lifts her head up, "I know you know," and smiles back at me. Then she stands up, grabs my hands and pulls me up. "Come."

"Where?"

"Join the others."

"Do we really have to?" I mope like a little kid. "I want to be alone."

"No. I'm not leaving you here alone," she complains.

"Something could happen to you. I want to make sure we are safe and for that we should stay in large groups."

"Fine." She's right. Staying in groups would protect us from whoever is in this house. At least I hope so.

Carmen

I enter William's room and find him on his bed. I smile at him and he just glances quickly at me and goes back to his catnap. Frustrated, I sit on the bed beside him. Normally, I would lie on him, but in the last few months he's become very distant from me. In the last few hours he's become unfamiliar. I wish I could say it's that little cow girl's fault, but it isn't. William and I started to come apart a few days after his car crash. I, of course, didn't want to believe that he might leave me one day because I can offer him fame, success, and wealth. That's something he's always desired, and I knew that as long I could offer him those things he would be mine.

"Why didn't you tell me that you've been looking for your past – for your true family?" I finally ask him. He takes a deep breath and blinks his beautiful clear blue eyes. How I've always loved his eyes, and could lose myself in them.

"Is it that important to you?" he replies and I nod. "Why?"

"What do you mean why?"

"Why now? Why all of a sudden am I so important to you – so worthy of your time?"

His words are icy and sharp. My heart feels heavy and my head light and woozy.

"Why are you so cruel to me? What have I done to deserve such cold treatment from you?"

William sits upright and stares at me. I can see my reflection in his eyes. Old emotions awaken in me. I remember the first time I met him. It was ten years ago. He was sad, angry, and malnourished. His hair was uncombed and his clothes were too big for him.

My aunt couldn't have children and I guess she wasn't too upset about it either, because she wasn't too fond of kids. But my uncle always wanted to have children, at least one. He needed an heir for his family fortune so he adopted William. My aunt was infuriated with his decision and mistreated William as much as she could. She never showed him love or affection, and when her husband died she sent William to live with us.

It took years before William opened up to my parents, and especially to me, but once he did, we became inseparable. It didn't take long for us to become a couple. I protected him and comforted him while he supported and guided me through my career. I guess, I took his love and affection for granted.

"You never gave a damn about me and now, all of a sudden, I'm interested in someone else, you're all over me."

"That's not true."

"You always do that, and as for me not telling you about my fixation to find my true family, that's my business…."

I glare at him in anger. Tears of rage are building in my eyes, "It is my business. We promised each other to never have secrets or lie or grow apart."

"We were children when we made that promise," he snaps. "I've changed and you've changed." He takes another deep breath. "Look – my priorities changed after Julia's death." The mention of that name causes me to shiver.

"And that farmer girl is one of your new life priorities?"

"No. She is nice, refreshing and honest. I enjoy her company and I would be lying to you if I told you I wasn't attracted to her. I am, but at the moment I'm the number one in my life. I want to find out who I really am and where I want to be in life…."

"Mighty words for someone like you who only cared to party through life."

William smiles, "I told you – I've changed."

"You may believe that you have changed but you HAVEN'T!" I yell at him. I have the sudden urge to whack that big, fat smile off his face. "I know you better than anyone else – even better than you and I'll never give up on you. You belong to me."

"I'm sorry but you can't force me to be with you or to love you…."

"Yes, I can and I will. Don't forget you owe me your loyalty. I saved your life," His face darkens and the little William I met for the first time returns. Misery is back in his eyes.

The bedroom door opens and Ivy walks in.

"Yes?" I bark at her. She jumps and looks at William, as if seeking help.

"I came to inform you that dinner is ready and – well – I better go." She quickly leaves.

"I think we should go," William says and starts to walk away.

"We're not finished!" I yell after him.

"I am," he replies, and leaves me behind – alone in his room. Tears start to run down my cheeks. Never in my life have I felt so much pain and loneliness. I'll make her pay for my pain, and I will do what ever it takes to keep them apart.

Priscilla

There she is walking hand in hand with her fiancé and flirting with Seth. I'm wondering if Phillip knows about his fiancé sneaking out in the middle of the night to meet Seth, down in the small reading room to have wild sex. Warren and I caught them last night.

I look over to the Jones brothers and see them chuckling as the newest love triangle emerges. I just hope I'm not around when this gets out. To be honest I don't like love affairs. It's too much drama, violence and tension. Ivy on the other hand lives for stuff like this. She feeds on gossip.

"I have them," Ivy says in a soft voice as she sits next to me.

"Where were they?" I ask her, thinking of the endless hours we spent looking for the chess pieces.

"In the garbage, but we're still missing two pieces."

"Which ones? And you stuck your hands in the garbage?" I grasp my nose, and my mouth frowns in disgust.

"I had to do what I had to do," she says with a smile. "Don't worry. I washed my hands." She holds them up, and I look away. "The two missing pieces are Joanna's and Raul's."

"Where do you think are they?"

"The better question is who has them?" she said and I start to look around the table. It could be any of them and the upsetting thing is that Ivy and I are not the only ones who know of the clues.

"This is exciting," Ivy whispers in my ear. "Look at her! The way she's flirting with Seth, and Phillip doesn't even know." She starts to giggle. Suddenly she snaps, "Oops." She stares down at her plate.

"What?" I ask.

"She noticed us talking about her. She's glaring at us."

"So?" I glance over at Maria, who is trying to stare me down. I'm not backing down – not for someone like her, and as I imagined, she drops her gaze. I smile and, satisfied with myself, start to eat.

Maria

I know what they think of me and honestly I don't give a damn. I know how everyone feels sorry for poor Phillip having his fiancé going around his back. He is so nice, so intelligent. He could do much better, blah, blah, blah. I heard it all and I really don't care because no one knows him as well as I do.

So many nights I've gotten phone calls from strangers informing me that Phillip is at some bar, drunk and beaten. He always picks fights with strangers about random stuff and always gets injured. And as always I'm the stupid one who puts up with his mood swings, saves him and drives him to my house to take care of him.

Yes, I'm the dumb one who let him emotionally dance, step, and kick me around.

I turn my attention back to Phillip. The staring contest is a bit too childish for me and I decide to give Priscilla the satisfaction of having won her low IQ confrontation.

Phillip is holding my hand and gently caressing it. I take a deep breath and think how much I love him and how important he is to me, but I don't feel sorry for what I did with Seth. I actually enjoy his company and attention. I know I should feel guilt or shame but I don't. When I think of the many times I found Phillip in the arms of another woman or the endless messages from other women on his phone, or the many times he stood me up for other women, I can't feel shame for what I'm doing. And at the thought of those horrible times, I pull my hand away from Phillip and start to eat. Anger is slowly building up in my stomach but when I hear Seth's laugh my bad mood lifts away. I smile and think to myself that I do deserve some enjoyment and pleasure. Seth is so caring and gentle and for the time being I'll enjoy every moment with him. If Phillip should find out, I do hope it will hurt him as much as he's hurt me.

12 contenders remaining

Day Five

Tuesday, August 17, 2010

Selene

Another beautiful morning with a bright blue sky. The storm of the day before has passed on, unlike our worries.

"Selene, I'm afraid," Yolanda says, interrupting my daydream. "Something in this house is after me, and I think there're multiple forces."

"I...."

"Please," she beseeches me, "Don't come up with some tedious excuses – not from you. I know you know what is after me and why." She glances at the cameras positioned in all four corners of our purple room. I know what she wants to say.

"I'm a retrocognition and I know what you are," she whispers in my ear. I'm frightened. She is the first person outside my family to know my deep, dark secret. Without giving it any further consideration I just nod.

"How?" I ask her.

"Tony."

"What?"

"He has bunch of research papers about all of us."

"And you're fine with that?" I snap at her. It is wrong and sick.

"At first I wasn't but he explained that it is all part of his new book," she says. I'm still not happy. Actually, I'm uneasy. He knows too much about my family – about me. "Now, to my little problem," she quickly changes the subject. "I believe that…"

"Old residents are trying to tell you something," I interrupt.

"Yes – and how did you…"

"Know?" once again I interrupt her and she nods. "They have been trying to tell me something too."

"The Kanes?"

"No. The patients."

"The patients?" she repeats in a confused tone. I nod. "What are they telling you?"

"125."

"125? What does that mean?"

"It's the library," I explain. "I went there with Seth but I found nothing."

"No, you're wrong," she tells me. "125 is a room down in the basement. Tony wanted to take me there but after what happened two days ago…" I nod in understanding. "The library room number is 1125. The first number 1 fell off," she continues. "I'm reliving their lives over and over. Old memories are slowly reawakening within me and they all feel so real it scares me." She moves closer to me. "Last night, I dreamt I was standing at the bottom of this island staring up, admiring the re-erection of this castle. Hundreds of people were rebuilding this horrific place stone by stone. And all the time I was observing the fortress becoming bigger and stronger, I felt a dark pressure calling me. "You'll be my aide and I'll make you my queen," the house whispered to me.

"I looked over to my side and an older but very attractive man was standing next to me. He seemed so happy and excited watching the work. 'Here we will be happy and free to pursue our love without anyone judging or persecuting us,' he told me. I gently caressed his cheek and he pulled me closer to him. We kissed. It was so perfect – so passionate and so real."

"Watch out," I tell her, "not to fall in love with someone who doesn't belong in our world. You don't belong in his…"

"Yet," she interrupts me.

"You don't mean…..."

"I don't know but in the same dream I saw people dying while they were rebuilding this place. It needs to feed on living things and I think it wasn't John's brother killing him and his bride, but the evil resident in the house."

"Are you sure?"

Yolanda stays silent and after a long pause she says, "I think they are trying to warn us. There're trying to show us something important. But what? It drives me insane."

"What should we do?" I ask her. At that moment the bathroom door opens. Carmen walks into our room. She looks aggravated and as beautiful as always, even without her make-up.

"I need to talk to you," she demands, peering at Yolanda. "In private."

Yolanda looks to me for an answer. "It's ok. You can leave. I'll be fine." Yolanda nods, then grabs her clothes. "Call me if you need me." She glares at Carmen, "If you put a finger on her I'll rearrange your face."

"Is that a threat?" Carmen snaps. She places her arms over her chest and begins tapping her foot furiously.

"No, just some friendly advice." Their eyes lock.

"Don't worry. I won't touch your precious little Selene," says Carmen. "I'm just here to give her a warmhearted warning."

Yolanda storms from the room.

"Honestly, I don't know what the buzz is about you. To me you are annoying, weak and deadly boring," she smirks. "For some strange reason William is attracted to a dimwitted girl like you but not for the reason you think." She steps closer to me. "He always had a taste for innocent little girls," This begins to anger me. She is only two years older then me. "He likes to be the first – if you know what I mean," and gives me a mocking smile. I shake my head because I really have no idea what she is trying to say. "He likes to pop the cherry."

"Oh!" I blush and feel suddenly vulnerable.

"He enjoys it."

"And why are you telling me this? I thought you didn't like me and you would be more than happy if he takes advantage of me."

She grins. "Actually, I can't stand you and I really don't care what happens to you as long it doesn't affect us." Carmen takes a piece of newspaper from her pants pocket and tosses it to me. "Two year ago William went out with a young actress. Her name was Julia Smith. He was as charming and funny as always and as always he got what he wanted. This time it was her prominence." She walks to the window and stares out toward the horizon. "Since I can remember, William has always been very selfish and aggressive. It never bothered me because I always knew he would come back to me. He dated girls for their innocence, popularity or to gain their business contacts. As soon he got what he wanted, he broke their hearts and returned back to me.

"He always took sadistic pleasure in hurting and destroying people. I guess it has something to do with his childhood." Carmen turns back to me. "We've been together for almost five years and all this time he never told me why he did what he did. He won't fully open to me." Her eyes turn watery and she gives me a sad, forced smile. For the first time I see kindness and vulnerability in her thick dense shell. "To make the story short, this girl – Julia Smith – killed herself after William broke her heart. She took dozens of sleeping pills, and while she was slowly dying, wrote a very emotional letter to William." She smirks. "Actually the letter was more for the world and her fans to remember her one more time and to make sure William would pay for what he had done to her. And he did."

"Her father is a big Hollywood producer and he destroyed both of our careers. We tried everything to resurrect our names and reputations. Nothing worked until a few months ago. We were lucky to be chosen to play the two main roles in 'Blue Vein'." I get the impression that she is acting for the camera – for the spectators back home. She is playing her role pretty well, and I remember that she was a horrible actress who was miscast as the heroine in my favorite book series "Blue Vein".

"And?"

"And, what?" she snaps at me. "I don't need another Julia Smith in my life," she screeches. "We are just recovering from the scandal and, no offense, but William is into outgoing blonds and red-headed girls like me and William belongs to me – he always has, so back off."

"And if I don't?" Her face turns dark, and thick, blue veins begin to emerge at the surface of her neck and forehead.

"Are you stupid or what?" Carmen says. "I forgot. You people are a bit slow."

"What do you mean, you people?" I quickly stand up and walk towards her.

She looks down at me. Carmen is a head taller than me. "You country people," she smirks, "are – a – bit – slow – DUH!!!"

I want to pull her pretty red hair from her head and knock her perfect white teeth out of her mouth. Instead I hold my anger in and stupidly glare at her. Thankfully, Yolanda returns from the bathroom. Carmen takes a step back.

"I love him and I'll do anything to have him back," she tells me as she walks through the door. She stops, turns around and with a stern glare says, "And I do mean anything." She leaves.

Yolanda

I come out from the bathroom and see Selene staring at a piece of paper. Her eyes are watery and angry. She looks like she is about to kick that red-headed snake's ass. I do have to admit – I wouldn't mind kicking her ass myself. She, William, Phillip and Maria think they are better then everybody else. They are so arrogant with their noses up high in the air as if we were piles of shit.

Honestly – I do not understand what she sees in that third class actor. He and Carmen can't act. They destroyed a perfect movie with a perfect storyline from one of my favorite book series, "Blue Vein". Their acting was so amateurish, and at the end when they asked Carmen if she read the book, she said in her weird high-pitched voice, "No – I'm not into romance books and I'm not into drama," she told the reporters. Yet, here she is in this Reality TV Show creating all the drama. OK – fine, I do understand her getting all angry and jealous over William giving all his attention

111

to Selene, but she and William aren't a couple anymore and in my book that means he is back on the market even though he is not my type. I'm into nerdy looking guys just like my Tony. He is so smart, and the way he talks makes me tingle.

"So long, Carmen," I call after her sarcastically. William and Carmen, two very unknown actors (and may I add awful actors) are now so famous. Everybody wants a piece of them, especially William. Eww. I do not understand what they see in him. His features are hard and disproportioned, not to mention his unattractive body. A fifth grade boy has more muscle on him then William Hawthorn. He really does look like a troll.

I stop glaring after Carmen and concentrate on Selene. She is so naïve and innocent. I'm worried about her moving to New York City. People are not friendly – not in New York, anyway. They will take advantage of her. She'll be a little fawn in the middle of the Coliseum surrounded by big, hungry aggressive wolves.

I do hope she has better taste in friends than in men. At least she has me for a friend, so that means maybe her taste is not so terrible after all.

Selene is reading a piece of paper. It looks like an article from a magazine. "What was that about?"

"Did you know about this?" she shows me the article with a picture of a pretty young girl in an evening gown. Standing beside her is William in a tuxedo with his arms around her waist. The headline blares:

```
William Hawthorn Responsible for the
    Death of Young Actress Julia Smith
```

"Yes," I reply and see her disappointed stare. "I thought you knew."

She shakes her head, "It's not like I can get every gossip magazine where I live."

"It was on the news for weeks and all over the papers for

months," I reply. Selene looks like she is about to cry. "What happened?" I ask her again. She tells me the whole story.

"Carmen is right," I respond. "William got caught drunk and in possession of drugs a few times. He is a loose cannon and you should drop him before he breaks your heart." I can tell this doesn't sit too well with her. She is confused and I need to push her to come to the right decision and drop William Hawthorn. "William and Carmen have always been a couple – a strange one, but a couple nonetheless. They have been on and off constantly.

"Don't you think William flirting with you and Carmen's outrage temper could be just an act?"

I can sense quickly Selene's mind pondering that, "An act?"

I nod, "Think about what she said and how she was acting in front of the camera." I point my index finger at the four cameras in the room. "They're trying to capture the audience once more by using you, or, as matter of fact, all of us."

Slowly she walks over to her bed and sits down with the piece of paper still in her hands. Selene looks lost, beaten and most of all confused. I feel bad for what I said but I had to do it. She is so clueless when it comes to real life experience. Her family must have raised her beneath a glass top. She has no idea what people are willing to do for money or fame or both.

"Get dressed. I'll wait for you," I tell her, but she shakes her head.

"I'm not hungry."

"Then – I'll see you later," and with that I leave the room. I can't wait to see my little genius again. Today will be the day that Tony and I will kiss, and with that thought I run down the stairs. Ten pairs of eyes turn toward me as I wish everyone a good morning. Seth looks behind me searching for his little sister. He notices that someone else is also seeking Selene. William.

"Selene doesn't feel too well," I say. Seth nods. Carmen triumphantly grins, and William shoots her a nasty glare. Perhaps I was wrong. Perhaps, he truly likes her.

Nah!!! William Hawthorn only cares for himself and nobody else.

I saunter over to my Tony who, as usual, has his nose plastered to the monitor of his laptop. He is writing and reading some files at the same time.

"Good morning," I smile. He raises his eyes at me briefly, and turns back to the monitor.

"Morning," he says and keeps typing. He ignores the beautiful and very short dress that I have chosen specially for him. It exposes all my rounded curves and my fully ripe breasts. I take a deep breath and sit next to him.

"How did you sleep?" I ask.

"Not well. I was writing all night." He yawns. "It was quite exciting yesterday. I can't wait to continue," he says. For the first time today he is actually giving me his attention. "We will go up to the third floor."

"When?" I ask.

"I thought later," he tells me. A chill runs through my body. I have had more than enough of ghost stories for today.

"Not today," I say, and Tony stops typing. "What about tomorrow?"

"Tomorrow sounds fine," he kindly replies. "I could use a day off from the supernatural hunt."

I smile at him and think to myself how crazy I am for nerdy guys and Italians. Sooner or later I will have that kiss.

Wayne

It's late in the afternoon and we sit around the table waiting for one of us to stand up and admit what we all feel is going on but none of us has the guts to say.

"Four of us are now gone and some of us are on edge," the cowboy starts. "Some of us think there is some kind of a conspiracy." He looks over to Tony.

"You don't?" Priscilla's voice sounds stressed.

"Strange things are happening here….." Ivy quickly adds.

"Everyone knows the channel is famous for its extreme shows," Seth says, trying to control the situation and taking the lead. I'm fine with that. My brother and I do not want to be leaders but disruptors.

"I agree with you on that, but we weren't informed that day by day some of us would leave the house in the most cruel and horrific way," Ivy cries out. She is a mess. The way her body is constantly shaking reminds of Crème-Brule.

"Ivy, please. Not you too," Warren jumps in. "I think we should stay on the realistic side of the matter and not on the imaginary."

Tony snorts. He really believes in ghosts and the supernatural. I couldn't believe my brother when he told me what happened yesterday afternoon, but now – the way Tony acts, I have to laugh.

"My grandfather was here – twenty years before the massacre," Tony states. His face is red and his fingers are compressed together on the table. "You should hear some of the stories he told us about this penitentiary. Not to mention about this castle. It's haunted – the castle is a living organ." A loud chuckle from the other side of the table startles Tony. "WHAT'S SO FUNNY?"

"You should hear all of you," that red-head snob mocks. "The place is haunted – the castle is alive – Matt, Raul, and the Johnson sisters are dead – we will all soon meet their fate. Blah, blah, blah." She continues to ridicule him. "They are probably back on land in a luxurious penthouse eating a five star meal, watching us and laughing their butts off about how stupid we are acting after spending only four days in this place."

"Do you really believe that?" Priscilla and Ivy ask her in unison.

"She is a third class actress and not a fortune cookie," I utter through clenched teeth. I have very little patience when it comes

115

to Carmen. I can't stand her. "She hasn't a clue unless it's written on a manuscript."

"EXCUSE ME!!!" she yells. Her eyes bulge out, and her face is as rigid as a chopping board.

"You heard me," I retort.

"Take it back!!!" she grunts, and grabs one of the plates.

"No." Suddenly she curses at me and begins throwing plates, cups and food.

I dodge a cup that misses my forehead by inches. Her boyfriend, or ex-boyfriend what ever they are, is sitting in a corner reading a book. He doesn't look or react to what is going on.

"ENOUGH!!!!" I hear cowboy's voice.

"Let me GO!!!!" I hear psycho Raggedy Suzanne screaming and stomping. "I said – LET GO OF ME!!!!"

I lift my head carefully making sure no further crockery is coming my way. Cowboy has that lunatic in his arms. He is trying to contain her while she is doing her best to free herself. Meanwhile the other third class actor is still reading and shows no reaction. He really is strange.

"Quiet!!!" Phillip hushes us. "Do any of you hear that?"

Everyone is silent even Raggedy Suzanne. The faint sound of a violin can be heard echoing through the empty hallways.

"What is that?" Carmen asks.

"A violin," I snort sarcastically.

"OH! GOD," Priscilla panics, "Is the house. It's calling us."

"No it is not the house," Cowboy exhaustedly replies. "It's Selene." Then he turns to Yolanda. "Did something happen?"

For the first time William shows some reaction – concern. He lifts his head away from his book to listen for Yolanda's answer.

"No, nothing. She doesn't feel well," Yolanda replies and quickly looks down, away from Seth's inquisitive eyes.

"Are you sure?"

"Of course I'm sure," she snaps. There is a defensive tone to her voice. "Why?"

116

"She only plays her violin when she is upset."

"Can you blame her if she is upset? We have no idea what is happening. I just lost my cousin and I don't know if he is safe or not." Cowboy releases his grip on Raggedy Suzanne.

Carmen breaks away, and her face twists once again into an ugly mask. "Where is William?" she demands. Everyone turns to the chair where William was sitting and reading a book a few seconds ago.

"I saw him leaving through that door," Maria says and points to a side door connecting to the living room. "I guess it must have been too loud for him."

Carmen, without another word, leaves the room through the side door. She is right behind him. I'm laughing inside, because I can see her boyfriend climbing up the stairs. I know where he is going. Everyone in this house knows how badly he wants to have a piece of that weird country girl. She is cute but strange – too strange – and so is her overly protective brother. I wouldn't mess with him.

Out of the blue Priscilla asks, "Is it true? We are not alone in this forsaken place?"

Seth looks at Phillip, Waiting for him to answer. After all, he was the one who was with Raul when he vanished.

Before he can speak, Warren butts in. "As I said before, it's all part of the show. They could have hired actors to dog us, or it could be one of us working for the channel to take each of us out of the show." They all seem to be considering this.

"Who?" Maria inquires.

"I don't know," Warren says. "It could be anyone, even one of the four missing people."

"What? How?" Phillip gasps.

"It could be Matt." I observe Tony gloating. "He was one of the first to vanish, and that could give him a great advantage. No one would suspect him or his brother of working for YTV…."

"I've had enough of your false facts and accusations!!!!"

Tony slams his fist on the table. "My brother and I are innocent. We only came here to investigate St. Clara....."

"Blah, blah, blah." Warren mocks him, and Tony's face is getting redder by the second. "We've already heard your crazy theories and, trust me, no one is buying it. You're nuts!"

I smile and give my brother a head bob. It was our plan all along to set them against each other and it seems to be working superbly. Warren is on a roll today.

"You..." and I see Tony jumping across the table to my brother. His hands clutch Warren's neck. Food, plates, and utensils fly across the table.

We rush over and split them apart. Seth and Phillip hold Tony to one side while I leave the room with a firm grip on Warren.

In the hallway, I release my brother and say, "Good job, man." Warren smiles at me and gives me a high five. "Are you all right?" I ask, after noticing red marks around his neck.

He nods, "Yeah, I'm fine but who knew that little spaghetti bender had a Mafioso side to him?" He rubs his neck and shoulders.

I smile, "We should stay out of his way for a day or two," and Warren agrees with me.

Ivy

"I want to leave this place as soon as possible," I cry out to Priscilla.

She shakes her head and says, "We're stuck on this island. All we can do is wait until they come back to pick us up...."

"If we survive," I quickly answer.

Priscilla turns around and whispers, "Or if they come back," and walks away, leaving me with that thought. I hate when she does that to me. She always puts more doubt and worry into my mind when I need reassurance and consolation.

I walk back to my room. I need to be alone, even though right now it is not such a good idea to do that. But I want to assess our

118

chances of survival, and on the possibility that something is after us. Maybe some of the others don't believe in the supernatural or the afterlife, but I do.

I remember one occasion when I was ten years old that there was a strong odor of Jasmine in our house for a whole week. It reminded me of Wai Po's perfume. During that week I also saw, for a brief moment, the dark ghostly shadow of an elderly woman.

I told my parents but they didn't believe me until a letter arrived from my uncle. The letter informed us of the sudden demise of Wai Po. I then realized that instant I knew that the dark shadow I occasionally saw and the perfume I smelled was hers. She stayed with us a whole week, watching us and making sure we were fine and then she left.

Once in a while I still smell her perfume and know she is with me, protecting me. I smile at her and thank her. I wish she could be here with me now to guide me through this nightmare. I have a feeling that it will be me next. I don't know how or why. I just know.

I barely sleep at night. I start to hear crying, whispers, and sometimes shouting too. My rational theories are slowly fading from my mind, gradually being replaced by Tony's improbable reasoning. Funny, I swore not to fall into his trap and it seems that's exactly what I'm doing. I guess it's the lack of sleep.

I don't know what to do and talking with Priscilla doesn't help. She is too preoccupied with her career. I'm wondering if she'll start to think about something else besides being famous once I'm gone from here. There isn't a day that goes by without her shouting at me for not playing the dimwit role she wants me to portray. She really wants to be famous. She schemes constantly to become a famous actress one day. I'm even included in her plans, although I don't want to be. I dream only of a simple life. I would like to have a loving husband, a few children, and a bakery shop where people come from all around the world travel just for my delicious low calorie cookies, cakes, donuts and so much more.

I've already come up with some recipes and my dad wants to invest in my business. If I wasn't such a coward, I wouldn't even be on this island. I would be in San Francisco planning the grand opening of my bakery shop. Instead I'm here, only because I'm afraid to tell my best friend about my future plans.

"No!!!" A shout interrupts my reverie. "Don't touch me!" I start to run down the hall thinking someone is in trouble.

One of the bedroom doors is open. I look inside and see William standing between Carmen and Selene. Carmen looks infuriated. Her face reminds me of a rabid dog. Selene is standing behind William. She is frightened.

"Stay away from me!!!" Selene hysterically cries out. "Don't touch me."

"What's the matter," Carmen snarls at her, "are you afraid of me?"

"Enough!" William shouts at her, "Get out."

Carmen glares at him, and then shoves him out the way. Selene takes a few steps backward to escape her, but grabs her upper arm. Selene lets out a scream of pain. I place my hands over my ears. Her heart-rending screech makes my body tremble. Selene collapses and convulses on the floor. William runs to her and calls her name several times.

"What's going on?" I hadn't noticed Seth come up behind me. The color drains from his face as he sees his sister lying on the floor. His eyes open wide in terror. "Selene," he calls and pushes me aside. He kneels next to her. He wants to hold his little sister but for some reason he doesn't. It seems as if something is holding him back. William's hand moves toward her face.

"Don't touch her!" Seth shouts, and pushes him away. "This is your fault!" he yells. "If you had left her alone she……"

"He loves me," Selene says, but the voice is not her own. She rises to her feet looking dazed. I'm freaked out, and so are the others.

"He doesn't love you." Selene speaks again, only this time

120

in Carmen's voice. "He loves whoever can give him an easy life."

"He loves me. He wants to marry me." Selene is now using the first voice again. She stretches her hand forward, toward Carmen. "As you can see William wants to be with me and not with you. I can give him everything his heart desires. My family is very wealthy and powerful, unlike yours."

"Shut up you little witch!!!!!" Carmen snaps at Selene, and slaps her across her face. William immediately slaps Carmen. "William," she gasps, placing her hand on her cheek. "How could you?" Hot tears run down her face.

Selene flashes a wicked grin. "If he loves you that much why do you think he spends all his nights in my bed and not in yours?"

"SHUT UP. SHUT – UP – YOU WITCH!" Carmen spits at her and then glances at William. "Don't believe her. It's not true. They are all lies."

"No, they're not," Selene says in the mysterious female voice. "Why are you doing this to me? I thought we were friends."

"Friends do not steal from friends," Selene replies in Carmen's voice.

"I've never stolen William from you," Selene counterattacks in the other female's voice. "He told me that you two were just friends and nothing more – just friends."

"We're more then just friends," and Selene extends her arm as if she is holding something. "Read." She shakes her hand.

Selene now shifts her body forward to grab the object – think it might be a magazine. She reads it. Selene lifts her head and tears begin running down her face. "It can't be. It isn't true." she says in the mysterious voice.

"It is all true. By tomorrow the news will be all over the world."

"GET OUT!!!!" Selene shouts in the strange female's voice. "And take your garbage with you!" Her right arm moves forward like she is throwing something. Then she collapses in hysterics.

Seth walks to his sister's bed and snatches a blanket. He

wraps it around her and draws her tightly to his chest. He whispers something in her ear while he gently rocks her back and forth.

"All this time I wondered what I'd done to Julia. I asked myself what I did wrong to cause her death and now I know," William states to Carmen.

"No, William, please," Carmen pleads, "Listen to me. She is lying. You must believe me." Her eyes glisten. "She pulled this charade to get even with me after our little talk."

"What talk?" Seth and William both ask at once. William turns to meet Seth's enraged glare. I swear – if Seth wasn't so preoccupied with Selene, he would probably assault William.

Carmen says triumphantly, "I told her about Julia's suicide and the car crash... and the alcohol and drugs...."

"You had no right to do such a thing!!!!" he snaps at her.

Carmen smirks, "I do. You belong to me."

"I do not!"

"I want everyone out of here," shout Seth. When no one moves, he bellows, "NOW!!!!!" I quickly go out the door. Seth looks dangerous. I don't wait for him to tell me twice.

Behind me I hear Carmen confront William. She is crying and stamping her feet on the floor. She reminds me of a little child begging her mother for a toy.

"William, please," she begs. "You must believe me. I love you."

William stops, turns around, and shouts back at her, "STAY AWAY FROM ME!" Then, with a deep sigh, he adds, "I'm so angry. I need you to stay away from me before I lose my temper."

William looks into the hall at me. I start, and quickly enter my room before Carmen notices me. "Too much drama – even for my own taste," I say to myself, and take a deep breath.

"What was that?" I ask myself, rehashing Selene's outlandish behavior.

I lie down on the bed. A strange scratching noise from behind the bathroom door startles me.

"Hello!" I say and stand up. "Priscilla? Is that you?" I move closer to the door. "If it is you – it's not funny….."

I stop in mid-sentence as white smoke billows from underneath the door.

Instantaneously, I panic. I'm next! I try to run for the door, but my legs feel paralyzed. In the distance I hear, "Eleven little trespassers are arguing. One little trespasser is not."

My heart is racing wildly, and I feel faint. My vision is darkening by the second. Before I pass out the mysterious, childish voice whispers next to my ear, "And now there are eleven little trespassers left."

I start to scream for help and……

Phillip

Back in my room, I find Seth holding a dagger.

"What are you doing with that?" I ask.

"I found it on your bed," he replies.

"On my bed?" I'm confused.

"I was wondering if you changed your mind and decided to cut my throat," says Seth.

"Why should I?"

"Me and Maria," he answers. He places the knife down on my side table. "You might have changed your plans and……"

"Trust me," I quickly respond, "I didn't and won't. I would be lying if I said that I don't love her, but I know that we're not meant for each other. I do hope being with you she'll realize that…."

"And what if she falls in love with me?"

"That's what I'm hoping," I state. "When you came to me and told me about Maria wanting to start an affair with you, I thanked the Heavens. Someone up there must be pulling some strings for me."

"I don't understand you. She's very nice and sweet and…."

"Conniving," I interject. "I don't know how she is with you, but with me she wasn't always sweet, nice, adorable and all the pleasant things you think about her. She was very manipulative from the beginning.

"The one thing I still can't forgive her for is what she did to me a few weeks ago. Matter of fact, it was this specific incident that opened my eyes about her.

"A few weeks ago I went to a jewelry store and bought her an engagement ring. It wasn't expensive or fabulous. I'm just a student and my budget is kind of tight. You know what I'm talking about?" Seth nods. "Anyway, I bought her a ring and wrapped it nicely and put it away until her birthday. It's a dream of hers to be proposed to on her birthday. Girls," I say and shake my head at the same time. "In any case, two days before her birthday I received my credit card bill and guess what? Someone charged $ 10,000 on my account. I looked closer and found the jewelry store where I bought Maria's engagement ring had charged me for that amount. I immediately called the store and demanded to know what the deal was. They told me that a pretty girl with long dark hair had returned my ring and swapped it for a 2 ct. diamond.

"I was so infuriated and I still am. No one messes around with my money." I'm worked up now. "Anyhow, I drove to her house and confronted her and do you know what she told me?" Seth shakes his head, "She said, 'Less then a 2 ct. won't do for me,' in an arrogant tone of voice. I asked her why she was so obsessed about how much money I spent on her ring." I take a deep breath to calm myself down. "She told me the more I spend on her, the more I prove how much I love her. And that she was too embarrassed to show my puny ring to her friends.

"I was fuming and before I stormed out, I called the wedding off. Since then she's been trying to convince me to propose to her again.

"Of course she told everyone that the wedding was still on. That's what she told the producers of the show, too. I can't trust her. I don't even know if she is pregnant or not and if she is – is the baby mine? I asked her a few days ago about why she wasn't showing any signs of pregnancy and she gave me some lame excuse. 'All the women in my family don't look pregnant until very late.'" I mimicked Maria's voice.

Seth smiles. "Like I have any clue what that means. We men are so clueless and women know that very well, it's so easy for them to take advantage of us.

"Think about it. If the bill hadn't shown up, I wouldn't even have known what she did. And I'm supposed to marry someone like her who goes behind my back? She wants me to trust her about being pregnant and believing that the child is mine? I don't think so," I ended.

"What did you do with the ring?"

"I brought it back of course. I'm not spending $ 10,000 on some stupid ring. For God's sake it's a ring not a car!"

Seth drops onto his bed, "And you're still ok with me and Maria?"

"I'm more than ok," I explain. Seth nods in understanding.

I lie down on my bed and start to doze off.

Carmen

"Will," I call. He shows neither reaction nor emotion. He is standing in an empty dark corridor facing a window. "Will, I…."

"You gave me your word that you wouldn't touch her. You promised me that," he calmly says. His new tone of voice scares me to death. He is so indifferent and cold toward me. "You saw how I threw myself into drugs and alcohol in order to forget Julia. You knew how much I loved her," William says. "How could you. I trusted…"

"NO!!!" I yell, and grab him in my arms. He pushes me aside and moves a few feet away, "It's not true. I love you."

"Love," he laughs mirthlessly, "You don't know what love

125

is. You only know how to love yourself."

"Don't forget that I gave you life. I saved you."

"Yes, I know," he grunts. "You remind me of that every day."

"I wouldn't have to if you'd remember where your place is. Right next to me. You belong to me. I own you."

"YOU do not OWN ME. No one owns me. I told you. I'm done with you. I want you out of my life." He steps closer to me. His mouth is just an inch or two away from mine. I can smell his breath. My heart beats rapidly. "I'm warning you," he growls. "Stay away from Selene."

His last words leave me feeling deflated.

"Why is she so important to you?" I murmur. "She's a little liar. She lied about Julia. She made up the story. She wants to get even with me after our little conversation." I try to win him over but he won't listen to me. He keeps shaking his head. William seems spellbound by that little cowgirl. Why is she so important to him?

"What did you show Julia?"

"I don't know what you mean."

"What did you show Julia that caused her to commit suicide?"

"Let me tell you something about your beloved Julia," I snap. Now my patience is wearing thin. "She was weak, insecure and withdrawn just like....."

"YOU WERE THE ONE WHO FORCED ME TO BE WITH HER!!!" he shouts, startling me. "Now, what did you show her?"

"I showed her evidence that you were just playing with her. Sure you were in love with her, but sooner or later you would have become bored and left her." I smile. "She really thought that her fantasy would come true. Julia had everyone believing that you two were getting married – as if," and I start laughing in his face. "I know you, William. You and I belong together." I caress his face. He grabs my hand and pushes it away like it was a dirty rag. "Between me and Julia, she was the selfish one. She knew she couldn't keep you for very long, so she decided to destroy herself, and that's what she did." I start to laugh out loud. Soon my laughter turns into sobbing. I walk to the window and look up at the full moon, thinking about my next steps to win William back.

I can help you, a voice whispers in my head. I turn around and see only an empty and dark hallway.

Near the end of the hall, written in red paint on the wall, I read:

Vengeance is engaging and I can help.
Give yourself to me and I'll give myself to you

Tiny electric sparks begins to run through my body. When all the windows in the corridor suddenly open, I run down the stairs. Cold air hits my face, and I can hear the agonized wail of a woman. I don't stop running until I reach the living room. But before I enter, I try to collect myself. I don't want to give Tony the satisfaction that he was able to scare the crap out of me for a few minutes.

Finally calm and collected, I enter the room with a big smile. I try not to appear disappointed when I see William has his full attention on that girl. For some reason, for the first time in my life, I feel threatened. It just pisses me off that it had to be someone like her. A country girl.

I sit in my usual place and glance around at the others. Everyone is conversing. They seem happy, but I sense some tension. Their eyes look empty, and several appear nervous.

William's laugh breaks my train of though as I glare at the two love birds, and the words "Vengeance is engaging and I can help. Give yourself to me and I'll give myself to you," come to mind.

11 contenders remaining

Day Six

Wednesday, August 18, 2010

William

Down in the third floor corridor I found Selene shifting furniture around. I smile at the sight of her hair covered with dust and cobwebs. She is sneezing and coughing.

"Bless you," I call out. She jumps as if stuck with a hot poker. "I'm sorry, I didn't mean to scare you," I quickly add. She shakes her head and turns to whatever she is looking for. I follow her as she walks around. She appears distant. "What are you looking for?" I ask. Her delicate features bear a look of concern. She hesitates to answer, seeming annoyed or bothered by my presence.

"You shouldn't be here. If Seth finds you…."

"Your brother doesn't scare me a bit," I retort.

"He should," Selene quickly advises me. "He is twice your size and he was about to break you into pieces…"

"But he didn't," I interrupter her.

"Because he knows how much I'm…….."

"In love with me," I finish her sentence.

She smiles. "Attracted to you." Her gloomy expression returns. "He – forbade me to see you or talk to you ever again," she says. I can see that this upsets her.

"Do you always obey your brother?"

She stops and stares at me, "No."

"Then why now?"

"Because," she says in a loud voice, "he is very important to me and…"

"And I'm not?" she turns red again.

"He says that you are playing with me. He says that Carmen is trying to get even with him by hurting me, through you."

"Why would I do such a horrible thing to you?" I ask and step closer to her. I'm wondering what's going on between Seth and Carmen. Knowing Carmen it must not be too good.

"William – don't!" Alice says, moving between us.

Why not? You wanted me to gain her trust.

129

"Not like this," she snaps at me. She is angry and sad at the same time. "I don't want you to hurt her."

What's with you? Why are you so protective?

"I love you William, but what you are doing to her is wrong," she states, "Let me show you something." Images start to form around me. I'm confused and feel a bit lightheaded.

I'm standing in a room with light pink walls, white furniture, mint green curtains and bedspread. I notice that one of the walls is covered in posters of – me. I smile.

Outside I hear a commotion. I walk closer to the window and look down. Two people are arguing and by the look of things, this isn't the first time.

A figure appears beside me. It's Selene crying as she watches the two figures argue. I notice some resemblances between Selene and the two people. They must be her parents.

Selene wipes her tears away and takes out her violin. She starts to play in an effort to drown out the voices as well as to express her anger and misery.

Now I understand how important her violin and music is. It is an escape from her discontented life.

"I don't know," Selene says as I come back to reality. Alice is gone and I'm disappointed. I want to wring her neck for what she just did to me.

I shake my head trying to wake up. I feel strange and I've forgotten what we were talking about.

"Are you ok?" she asks.

"Yeah, yeah." I smile at her and sit down on one of the empty beds. "Say – what are you looking for?"

"Money or clues," she smiles. "Between Seth and me, I'm the one who has the eyes and the good fortune to find things," she explains. Then, she stops her search and looks at me. "Is Seth right about you and Carmen?"

"Don't lie to her," Alice warns me.

Get – out, I grunt at Alice and with a smile I reply, "Of course not. Your brother is lying. Why should I or Carmen get even with your brother? We've never even met him before."

Selene nods her head, and I begin looking for my irritating little sister.

"My brother and I used to be very close, but since my parents sent him to a private boarding school we've drifted apart," she explains and sits next to me. "I hoped this little adventure would reunite us, you know, like before, but…" and she stops. She glances out the window. The sun is high up in the pale blue sky. Selene looks so sad deep in thought.

I move my hand forward, wanting to touch her's.

"Don't you dare?" Alice shouts at me and grabs my hand.

What's wrong with you??? I yell at her. Once again I'm standing in Selene's room, only this time its nightfall and the windows are covered in fresh, soft, white snow. It has been quite a while since I've seen snow. I never thought I would miss it.

In the background I hear shouting and yelling.

"It is your fault," I hear a woman shouting. "If you had told me…."

"What? That my family is cursed?" a man shouts back at her.

"YES!!!" the woman cries. "I would never have married you. I would have had a normal daughter."

"She IS normal," the man shouts back. "She's beautiful, smart, and…."

"She won't have a normal life. She'll spend her life locked away from society…"

"And?"

"AND?" the woman raises her voice. "What man do you think will want to be with someone like that?"

"Plenty!!!" the man snaps at her.

"Oh Please," the woman pouts. "We had a normal life before Selene was born. You were a veterinarian. You had your own clinic and I was a teacher…"

"I'm still a veterinarian. I still have my own clinic and you are finally living your childhood dream. You are a published author."

"We're poor. We struggle day in and day out."

"That's not true. We have a roof over our heads and food on the table. We're fine."

"What about Seth?"

"What about him?"

"He deserves to have a life."

"He has a life…"

"What? Taking care of his sister for the rest of his life? Nice life."

Behind me, I hear sobs from beneath the blankets. Selene is crying.

"William! William!" I hear Selene calling my name.

I snap back to reality.

"Are you all right?" she asks.

"Yes, why?"

"You look so sad and in pain."

"I'm great." I force a smile and grab her hand, all the while as I'm searching for Alice. I pull her arms up, revealing her hands encased in gloves. "Why are you always covered from head to toe? Why do you fear contact? What are you hiding?"

"Aren't we full of questions." She pulls her hand away from mine and stands up. I quickly wrap my arms around her upper body, not letting her walk away from me. She doesn't push me away. "Do you believe in magic?" she whispers, and entwines her fingers into mine.

"It depends on what kind of magic."

"Curses," she specifies.

"Sure," I lie to her.

"What about witches?"

132

"You mean – real witches?" I ask. Her head bobs up and down. "Do you mean fairytale witches – you know, transforming humans into frogs, flying on broomsticks and so on? Or modern age witches, performing rituals, dancing naked underneath the full moon, reading cards…"

Selene rolls her eye and turns around. "I mean …. I'm trying to tell you that…..How can I make you understand?"

"Just spill it out," I tell her. She takes a deep breath.

"Sit." She presses on my chest forcing me to sit back on the bed. Selene stands in front of me looking nervous. She cracks her knuckles while staring at the floor.

I place my hand upon hers. "I won't judge you."

"You say that now, but you'll change your mind in a few minutes."

"No, I won't. I like you too much," I notice her cheeks becoming redder by the second.

"I'm a psychometric," Selene blurts out, studying my face. I pretend to be confused, but I'm not. I knew all along what Selene was. I just want her to open up to me. I want her to trust me.

"I have the ability to obtain knowledge about a person or object just through contact. But in my case, my power is much stronger then other psychometrics. It is – painful – as you have witnessed."

"That explains quite a lot," I smile at her.

"Explains what?"

"Yesterday."

"Yeah," she whispers and turns around. We are silent. None of us want to speak about yesterday's event. We're both embarrassed.

Then she calls my name.

I lift my head up to her. "You know," I start. "Only my family calls me William. Friends call me Will."

"Oh! Ok," she whispers. "Our welcoming is about to expire." I look around the room not grasping what she is talking about. "We need to leave, now," and she tries to pull me up.

On the threshold, I find Alice glaring at me with her arms crossed over her chest.

"I warned you," she says. "Be careful not to hurt her. I might be your sister but my alliance lies with someone else's bloodline, and that is NOT the Hawthorns."

What? I ask. Alice disappears.

As I descend the stairs, I watch Selene carefully and wonder what the relationship between she and my sister is.

"What?" Selene smiles at me.

I shake my head, "Hmm, Nothing." I continue to descend the stairs, still deep in my own thoughts.

Tony

"This was the children's dormitory," I tell Yolanda and point my camera at the rows of beds. There must be at least one hundred of them.

"I can't imagine how horrible it must have been to spend a childhood in here," Yolanda says. She walks to a bed with a small chest box at the end.

"Most of the children were born in here. They didn't know a life outside of these walls."

Yolanda stays silent and opens the chest. Inside is a teddy bear, a diary and some old clothes. Yolanda turns to the first page and read aloud, "Alice Williams. The diary belongs to a girl named Alice."

Williams, I think. *Alice Williams*. "May I see it?" I ask. She seems more than happy to give it to me. I flip through the pages and read:

June 22, 1992

Today, I saw my mommy after a very long time. She has a big belly. Nurse Katherine told me that my mommy is

134

carrying a baby and that I'll be a big sister.

"You'll have to take good care of your little brother once he is born," she said and gave me a big kiss. I love Nurse Katherine. She is like a mommy to us. She loves us all the same. That's what she keeps telling us when we fight over to who she likes the most.

The children in St. Clara are not allowed to have contact with their mommies. It is forbidden and I tried to warn Julian but he wouldn't listen to me. Julian and his mother were brought here together and separated soon after their arrival. Julian cried for days. My friends and I tried to help him but he pushed us away.

"They will take you away from here and you'll never see your mother ever again." Jennet told him soon after she kicked dirt in his face.

Julian stood up and pushed Jennet to the ground. Then Jennet cried and ran to Mr. Dubs. He is mean. He likes to pull us by the ears and slap our hands with sticks. It hurts a lot. I was once punished by Mr. Dubs too. I took an apple from Johnny. I know it was wrong but I was so hungry. They feed us very little here.

Anyway, Mr. Dubs yelled at Julian and pulled him by the ear while he was dragging him away from the play ground.

"That will show him not to mess with me," Jennet smirked after them. I felt so bad and sorry for Julian.

Two nights ago Julian snuck into his mother's bedroom but he was caught and sent away from the island the next day.

You had to hear his mother scream. It was horrible. My friends and I had to keep our ears closed.

She is better now. I saw her today. She was sitting on a bench watching the ocean. I tried to talk to her but she won't reply. Nurse Katherine told me that they gave her *happy medicine but she doesn't look happy. She looks like the walking dead.*

I take a deep breath and close the diary. I try not to imagine the horrible life these children had in here.

"Are you all right?" Yolanda asks, and I slowly nod my head. In reality I'm not. I'm deeply saddened but I don't want to show it. Yolanda has her own problems and I don't want to pile mine on her. She came up here for me, but I also know that she came here to find some clues about the mysterious person living among us. She wants to make sure that her cousin is safe and sound and not locked in a dark cell somewhere in this castle to be the pet of a deranged woman.

I take the bear and place it in my rucksack together with the diary.

"Don't," Yolanda tells me. "It belongs to the dead."

"It belongs to the brother of this little girl."

"Who?"

"William," I reply and observe her eyes widen.

"You mean Alice is his sister?" she asks, and I nod. "Does he know?"

"I think he does."

"And if he doesn't?"

"Please, don't tell anyone about this – not even Selene."

"I won't." She smiles at me and then wraps her arms around mine. "Do you think Raul is fine?"

"I don't know. I really don't know," I whisper. "I wish I did know."

Yolanda nods and we remain silent during our excursion. She walks ahead and searches each chest. Some are empty, while some contain clothes and toys.

Then we enter a large room with small chairs and tables. To one side of the room is a large round green carpet. Behind it are small book cases running the length of the wall. Some contain books and others toys.

Yolanda and I start searching the room and discover a bundle of children's watercolor paintings.

"What's this?" she asks. "This can't be possibly be painted by children." She sounds dismayed.

I say nothing and continue to examine the horrifying pictures. The colors used on them are dark. There are no bright yellows or vibrant greens. There is a lot of red paint, which seems to represent blood spouting from the bodies of screaming patients.

Another picture shows a graveyard with bleeding red crosses. The blood runs down the bottom of the paper, taking the form of a river. A river of blood.

I take my camera out and start to snap a few pictures of the paintings.

Out of the corner of my eye I observe Yolanda taking Alice's diary out of my backpack and looking through its pages.

After a while I hear her talking to herself in Spanish. She sounds sad and angry.

"What's wrong?" I ask her.

"July 04, 1992," Yolanda starts to read. "Today is Independence Day, and we decorated the hall for the big evening party. All the children, doctors, nurses and some of the patients attended the party. I was looking for my mommy but she didn't come. I cried so much because I was worried she was sick. Dr. Hawthorn saw me crying and came to me.

"What's wrong little Alice?" he asked, and I told him that my mommy didn't come and I was worried. He took me by the hand and brought me to see my mommy. She doesn't look good. Her skin was as white as her lips and her body kept shaking. Dr. Hawthorn told me that my little brother was giving my mommy some trouble.

"Mommy," I called. But she was sleeping. So I placed my hand on her belly. I felt my brother kicking. I laughed, as did Dr. Hawthorn. Then I placed my ear on my mommy's belly and whispered to my little brother to be nice to our mommy – she is all I have – she is all we have, and went back to my room so I could write this in your pages. It was the best day I ever had since I was born." Yolanda closes the diary and in a soft tone she said, "Can we leave? I've had enough for today."

"Sure." I put my camera away.

We descend the stairs, and before we join the others, I walk into William's room. I place his sister's diary and teddy bear on his bed. I turn around to leave when I hear something hit the floor. I spin around and notice Alice's diary sitting open on the floor. I pick it up and see Alice's last log. I start to read:

September 09, 1992

Today, I'm a big sister. My little brother is born. His name is William and he is so cute. Nurse Katherine took me to see him and I can't wait for the moment they bring him to me. I'll teach him how to sneak out from these walls and . . .

I flip through the pages looking for more, or for an explanation to her unexpected conclusion, but the rest of the diary is blank. I always wanted to know what had happened to her. Alice's body was never found and she still remains one of St. Clara's unsolved mysteries.

I close the diary, replace it on the bed next to Alice's stuffed bear and walk out of the room.

Seth

"We should leave this island," Priscilla declares in one of her usual panic attacks.

"And how do you think we should do that," Phillip snaps at her. "We are miles away from the coast. It took us an hour on the boat to come here."

"Maybe this damn place has a small boat," Priscilla retorts in a non-too-convincing tone.

I walk across the living room and sit on the first empty seat. To my satisfaction, Selene is ignoring William. My talk with her last night must have convinced her to drop him. He is a scum bag. He and Carmen both.

William is sitting in a dark corner reading a book, as usual.

"I don't care," Priscilla screams. "I want to leave!!!!"

Tired, annoyed and curious I ask, "What's going on?"

"You don't know?" Maria asks.

"Know what?" They look away.

"It's Ivy," Selene replies. "She's missing."

"Since when?"

"We think since last night," Phillip explains. "Priscilla and Ivy had an argument and….."

"I thought she was just mad at me and wandered off," Priscilla says. "Ivy always likes to be alone when she is angry."

"Well, maybe she is still angry. She might still need some time alone," I state.

Priscilla shakes her head. She is silent for a moment, then says, "I found this today lying on her bed." She holds up a chess piece. A pawn. "You know what it means?" She asks, and I nod in understanding.

She starts to cry and once again Maria runs to comfort her. I never liked girls who constantly cry. Thank God Selene is tough. I wouldn't be able to deal with that.

"What now? What shall we do?" Phillip asks and slams his fist on the armrest of his chair. "We are caged in like birds."

"More like rats," Wayne utters, "Birds can fly."

"All we can do is to wait until the YTV comes back to pick us up," Warren says.

"You want to wait," Priscilla snaps. "Until they come and pick us up! Are you insane? What if they don't come? What if we are going to die? What if….." and she continues to cry.

"What's the big deal," I snap at her. "I don't understand why you are so upset. We were informed that one of us would leave the show everyday."

"Yeah, but no one told us about a lunatic living among us," Priscilla shouts. She points up at the ceiling. "This nut could be the one who killed everybody years ago in this forsaken place. After all, the culprit was never found. What if this woman is now after us, and what if Ivy, Raul, Jennifer, Joanna and Matt are the latest victims of this woman and not of the show?"

"You have a lot of ifs and not enough facts," I tell her. "I'm leaving. I can't stand it anymore." I turn to Selene and ask, "Do you want to come?"

She shakes her head.

"Let me make you something warm," Maria tells Priscilla. "It will calm you down."

Priscilla thanks Maria and before I leave, Priscilla takes center stage one more time. I don't know if her tears and emotions are real – after all, we all know why she joined the show, and she could just be pretending. "You are allowed to believe in whatever you want to believe but do not ridicule my...."

I start to laugh out loud. Priscilla and the others stare at me. "Thank you for allowing me to express my opinions," I tell her. She squints and purses her lips. No one says anything. I guess I frightened them too much. In their minds I'm the crazy, hot-headed cowboy, but I didn't encourage them to think of me any other way. I came to this game to win, and my strategy is to act like a crazy, hot-headed cowboy so they'll be scared of me and leave me alone.

I turn my attention to Maria, who is walking towards me. I open the door, "After you," I smile at her. She smiles back at me and walks into the kitchen. I follow her.

Maria putts some water in a pot and places it on the stove. She looks up. "What?" she smiles.

"I'm admiring you."

She shakes her head at me. "I told you what we did was a

mistake," she says. "I should have never done it."

"What? Get even with your cheating fiancé?"

"You knew?"

"Of course. Just because I live in a rural part of the country, it doesn't make me stupid."

"Then why….."

"Why did I do it? Why not? I love women, especially when they are attached to someone else.

"Listen, I'm not looking for a relationship – at least not now. I just want to have fun, and if someone as gorgeous as you wants to use me to get even with her cheating boyfriend – I'm in. It doesn't bother me a bit. You get what you want and I get what I need."

"You men are all the same," she snaps at me. "You don't care about our feelings. You only care about your five minutes of satisfaction."

"Hey! Hey! I do more than five minutes," I correct her. She frowns. "So, what about you and I in the pantry?"

"You are such a pig," she utters in outrage. She turns away to pour the hot water into a mug. I embrace her from behind.

"Come on," I whisper and she moves her head aside. "I know you want it."

"Why don't you go and bother someone else?"

"I thought about it, but there isn't much of a choice left," I respond. She pushes me away.

She turns around and glares at me. I grin. Her face is too funny, and the more I smile, the madder she gets. She wants to say something but instead storms out of the kitchen.

"You forgot your tea," I shout after her, smiling. She returns, grabs the tea and glares at me before running off again. I laugh.

Then my second least favorite person in the house walks in. Carmen Skylark.

"What did you do to Maria?" she asks. I shrug, not willing to talk to her. The less I talk to them, the happier I am. "It was quite a show last night between the two of you."

"I know what you are up to," I tell her. "I know you too well, and I also know you two are just playing a role to suck us all into your fake soap opera. What I don't like is that you made my sister a target. Watch your back."

She smirks, "Or what? Are you going to spank me?"

"Tell me – does your dimwitted boyfriend know about our deal?" I ask and watch her body stiffen. I smile. "I guess not."

"Beware, Seth Holloway…"

"Or what?" I interrupt her.

"You'll have to do more than just mend your sister's broken body."

That's it. I'm angry and can feel my blood boiling. I rush over to Carmen and shove her against the wall.

She laughs. She always had a macabre sense of humor. "It brings back old memories."

"You do NOT mess with me," I tell her and release her.

"And you DO?" she shouts. "What will your precious little sister do or say when she finds out what you've done?"

"And what will your boyfriend do or say when he finds out what *you've* done?"

Carmen smirks and as she walks over to the window she says, "Did you like my little present?"

"What present?"

"The knife," she explains and turns around with a frightening smile. "You didn't think I would forget the promise you made. You know," and stops in mid-sentence waiting for me to finish it, but I won't. Instead I turn around and take my leave.

"You owe me," she shouts as I leave. "Remember."

I keep walking. I'm trying to ignore her and at the same time I'm trying to find a way to tell Selene about my shameful sin.

Priscilla

I can't stand being in here any longer. This house is evil –

142

haunted. I want to go home and once again I start to sob.

"It's OK," Warren whispers in my ear. I'm glad he is still here with me. "I'll go see where the tea is," he says.

I quickly shake my head holding onto his hand tightly. "No, don't. I don't want to be alone. I'm scared."

"I'll leave the door open. I'll be right back. I need to use the bathroom."

I let him go even though I don't want to be left alone. "Please, hurry," I tell him, still holding his hand in mine.

"I will," and he leaves me all alone in the living room.

Wayne went to his room. Tony and Yolanda went wandering around in the third floor while Carmen quickly ran out of the room soon after Seth and Maria left. Selene left, too, for her daily violin practice. Phillip went with William to search the basement. They were either looking for the money or clues. I should probably tell Warren since Ivy is out.

Oh, God! I just pray she is all right. I start shaking and crying. I'm losing my mind.

I look across the room and see a small bust of Mozart on top of one of the many shelves in the room. For some reason the bust reminds of a statue that I unintentionally broke. It was back in middle school. I was in eighth grade, and at that time I was so horrible and bossy. Ivy was so weak and easy to command. Anyhow, my boyfriend had broken up with me, exactly a day before the spring dance. I was so mad, I took my anger out on a statue sitting in the school court yard. The statue was donated by a previous principal. It was a hideous thing. It made no sense to me how something that ugly was permitted on our school's grounds or, for that matter, on any school's grounds.

Well, to make the story short – I broke the statue. I hit it so hard that it fell to the ground. I was so mad that I didn't really care if someone caught me or not. Ivy, on the other hand, looked as if I had just stabbed her in the heart. She panicked and placed some parts of the statue in her bag.

"What are you doing?" I asked her.

"I'm trying to hide the statue," she said and ran away from the scene.

Days passed by, and everyone in the entire school was wondering who the culprit was. Ivy and I kept quiet, and in the end the principal punished the entire school by canceling the spring dance. We were devastated until Ivy did the gutsiest and noblest thing I ever saw anybody do. She marched straight into the principal's office and confessed to a crime she hadn't committed.

We had our spring dance while she was suspended for a whole week, but from that day on, Ivy had my respect and friendship. We became best friends.

Tears begin building up in my eyes and I turn my attention to the TV. A black and white movie is playing. I have no idea what the movie is about, nor do I care. Suddenly the living room door slams shut and the TV turns off. I scream and grab the blanket to wrap around me. I look around and in the quiet, empty room I hear, "Ten little trespassers are curious. One little trespasser is not."

Then the lights flick off and the TV turns back on. I see myself on the screen sitting on the corner of the couch. I move in closer to the TV and notice big yellows eyes reflecting off the screen.

"And now there are ten little trespassers left," says a little girl's voice from behind me. The room goes dark. Two strong hands wrap around my wrists. Someone or something starts pulling me. I scream, but no one comes to my rescue. I'm all alone.

Maria

A shrill, high pitched cry reaches my ears as I walk down the hall.

"Priscilla," I gasp. Out of the blue Warren appears next to me. I try to open the door, but I can't. Warren starts kicking it violently.

"What happened?" I turn and see Carmen with Seth right behind her. Warren doesn't answer. He continues to kick the door and finally is able to break it open. The lights and TV are on. The coffee table is upside down, the pillows from the couch are scattered around. In the middle of the floor I see it. Another pawn.

Warren grabs the chess piece and declares, "Priscilla is gone."

The four of us say nothing. We no longer have the words.

"And then there were ten," says Phillip as he enters the room. He's so calm, so cool.

"Where's William?" Carmen asks, after noticing that William isn't with Phillip. Selene is missing too.

"He joined Tony and the others," Phillip replies, looking around. "He didn't look too good," he adds. "He had this long face and he didn't say much. Something seemed to be bothering him. When he saw Tony, he left me."

"Oh!" Carmen says. She starts to bite her fingernails.

"I've been thinking," says Phillip. We turn our attention to him. "We should hunt down our host."

"What? Why?" I blurt out. "It's too dangerous. We don't know who this person is."

"Exactly," Phillip replies with his usual superior smile. He always does that when he wants to impress the public. I notice that he is looking at Carmen. I clench my hand into a fist and start to grind my teeth. "We don't know if this person is working for the show or if she is one of the patients," Phillip continues, staring at Carmen's body. I can see the desire in his eyes growing stronger by the second. "We're becoming paranoid. As more of us mysteriously disappear, we begin to believe some of Tony's crazy stories..."

"Not me," Carmen interrupts, clicking her tongue.

"I didn't believe that crap either, but strange things are happening around here. Some of us see dark shadows, others hear

whispers. Let's be fair, we don't know if this is part of the show."
Phillip smiles at her.

"Oh! Please," scoffs Carmen.

"So, what do you have in mind?" Warren finally says.

"I think the three of us should search the house," Phillip explains. "We should start now."

"But – it's almost nightfall," I protest.

"Phillip is right," Warren jumps in. "We're going to search the house."

"And we should start from here," Seth says. He throws open a small door concealed behind a large oil painting. "Whoever took Priscilla must have come from here."

We peer into the opening and see a long, narrow tunnel extending behind the wall.

"It must have taken Priscilla through here," Warren claims triumphantly. He steps into the corridor.

"Wait!" Seth snaps at him. "We need some equipment."

"Ok. Fine. Make it quick," Warren pauses while Seth, and Phillip, go off to search for what they need.

"So," Carmen says, "you believe the crazy stories of loony Tony too?" Warren says nothing. I guess he is confused. He, too, does not know what to believe. Just like me. "You are so pathetic," she states and turns her back on us.

"What a …..." I stop, not wanting to swear.

Warren exhales loudly and sticks his head back into the tunnel. Seth and Phillip re-enter the room with two backpacks and flashlights in hand.

"Ready?" Warren asks them.

"Ready," Seth and Phillip say in unison. I hug Phillip and wish him good luck.

"I'll be back soon." He follows Warren into the dark corridor.

"Will you tell the others what's happened?"

"Of course," I assure Seth. "Good luck, and be careful."

"Thanks. We will."

"Seth," I call. He stops and turns around. "Will you keep an eye on Phillip – for me – please?"

Seth nods and with a smile says, "Sure." He disappears into the tunnel. I close the door behind them and quickly run up to my room, where Carmen is lying on her bed. She doesn't look too happy about seeing me, and the feeling is mutual, but it's better than being alone.

Warren

We start to climb up, down, left, and right following steps carved deep into the dusty floor. It's an endless maze filled with the dust and debris of several few decades. Candies, chocolate wrappers and soda bottles are scattered across the floor in all corners of the labyrinth. Curiously, Seth moves into one of the small nooks searching through the garbage for some clues.

He calls us over. "Look," he says, and points to two small holes in the wall. "It's Selene and Yolanda's room." Phillip and I take a look while Seth moves to the other side of the nook. He whispers, "And this is Carmen and Maria's room."

I walk to the other side and peer through the holes. I can see Maria sitting on the bed, combing her long, curly hair.

"Hey!" Phillip whispers. I whirl and find Phillip lying on the floor with his face pressed to the floor. "I can see their bathroom. Guess who's taking a shower?"

Seth dives onto the floor, and at the same time he pushes Phillip aside. "Carmen. Carmen Skylark," Phillip says with a hint of lust. Seth is no better. He doesn't move or say a word. Matter of fact, I think he forgot to breathe.

"Come on," I snap at them. "Let's go."

Seth and Phillip stare at me. When they finally leave the nook, I quickly dive to the floor and spy on Carmen too.

Behind me I hear snickers. Quickly, I lift my head and I find Phillip and Seth standing in front of me with huge smiles on their faces.

"Enjoying the view?" Phillip laughs.

I stand up and shake the dust off my clothes. "What view?" I reply. "She is as flat as a chopping board."

"What are you talking about?" Phillip steps in, somewhat offended. "She's hot."

"She's flat," I reaffirm my point. "I like curvy women. I don't like to feel every point and bump. You know what I mean?" I walk past them with a big, satisfied smile.

"Are you telling me that you don't find Carmen attractive or sexy?" Phillip continues.

"Yep," I say, and keep walking.

"Priscilla isn't curvy either," he states.

I stop. "What are you, blind?" I snap, "She has a nice fruit basket and two wonderful ripe melons too."

"You ARE strange." Phillip glares at me. "Do you and your brother always have to talk like you're reading a menu?"

"We love food," I state and keep walking.

"Whatever, man," Phillip grunts from behind me.

It was actually Wayne who came up with the idea to talk in menu terms. He thought it would make us sound more authentic.

After some time, we begin to hear music coming from somewhere further down the hall. Seth motions us to move quietly ahead. He leads the way through the maze. Then he stops and grabs a piece of wood lying across our path.

Phillip and I follow his lead. Phillip finds a wrench and I come up with a small rock. I know, not much of a weapon.

Seth opens the door and the music stops. A warm, bright light welcomes us into an oval room. Antique-looking mirrors cover the walls.

"This must have been the ballroom," whispers Phillip. "Do either of you have any idea which floor we're on now?"

Seth and I shake our heads. None of us have any clue as to

where we are. According to my watch, its midnight. We have been wandering behind the castle walls for over two hours, and haven't discovered much beyond the peepholes.

"You are on the ground floor," says a little girl's voice.

"That's the voice!" Phillip shouts. "That's her!" He points towards the floor. "Look." Seth and I follow his finger and discover a thick, white mist emerging from the ground. Phillip grabs our shirts and starts pulling us towards the maze. "We have to get out of here," he shouts.

Seth and I don't argue, and start to run down the hallway. Phillip reaches the door first, with Seth right behind. As I get to the door, it slams shut. I start to punch and kick at it. From the other side I hear Phillip and Seth calling my name. They pound on the door as well, but are unable to open it.

"Nine little trespassers are together. One little trespasser is not," the little girl says.

"Stay the hell away from me!!!" I yell at the voice.

Then something cold grabs my ankles and yanks me to the floor. I feel drowsy and I'm slowly slipping away. I can hear the little girl finishing her rhyme, sounding far off. "And now there are nine little trespassers left," and hear nothing further.

9 contenders remaining

Day Seven

Thursday, August 19, 2010

Wayne

I open the refrigerator and notice that some more provisions have vanished.

"We're missing more food," I tell myself.

"What did you say?" says a voice from behind me. I jump and quickly turn around. William is standing in front of me. "What did you say?" he repeats.

"I said that we're missing more food." I start to shove food left and right, searching, just in case I missed the meat.

"What do you mean?" he asks. I frown. I don't have much patience at the moment. Warren is gone and he didn't even have the decency to wait for me or, for that matter, inform me about his stupid plan. He knew I would stop him.

"Over the last two, three days, Warren and I noticed that provisions were gradually vanishing from the fridge – mostly meat.

"Last night we hid the remaining steaks, and now they're gone," I grunt. "Who the heck comes in here in the middle of the night and eats steaks?"

"I'm just curious about who, in general, would eat raw meat." William states. I stop searching and turn around. I stare at him with a confused look. "What?"

"Eat – raw – meat," he repeats slowly.

"What are you talking about?"

"The pans are untouched. The dishwashing machine is empty, and there is no smell of cooked food."

I stay silent, trying to think of a plausible explanation. "He or she must have cleaned and put everything back in its place so we wouldn't notice. And as for the odor – he or she opened the window."

"It's possible but…"

"Are you going to tell me that you, too, believe the crazy stories of loony Tony? Come on, man."

William says nothing. He is considering my point. Then he says, "You can't deny that there are some pretty strange things going on in here."

"Like what?" I snap at him knowing very well what he's insinuating.

"Things are vanishing," he says and I have to hold back my laughter. "We hear strange sounds, especially at night," and once again, I have to stifle a chuckle. I bite down on my lower lip, on the verge of exploding with laughter. Man, Warren and I are good.

I take eggs and bacon out trying to calm myself down. William starts to make a batch of pancakes.

"I want American pancakes, not whatever you call them over there," I utter.

"We call them pancakes, too," he snaps back at me.

"Those are not pancakes," I tell him. I can see William starting to lose his cool. "They're deflated...I don't know what to call them. They're not very appetizing."

"Did you ever eat them?"

"Of course. Warren and I spent a whole year in England," I blurt out. From the expression on his face, I can see that I've misspoken, "Exchange students," I quickly add, trying to cover my blunder. He nods and goes back to his pancakes.

He probably won't mess them up. They are from a box, and he can read and follow instructions very well. He had plenty of training with Carmen, the tyrant.

"Wayne," he calls. "I think we should tell the others about the meat."

"Why?"

"Just to see their reaction? Maybe we can figure out who it is."

"Sure. Why not." I reply, and continue with breakfast.

"Are you – worried about Warren?"

"Nah," I lie. I recall how uneasy he became in the last few days. He barely had any sleep. He was constantly tossing in his bed, and when he finally fell asleep, he began to have horrible nightmares. The disappearance of Priscilla didn't make the situation any easier for him. Priscilla and Warren became pretty close, and for him to go after her and not tell me anything about his decision must mean that he really does care about her.

"Wayne! Wayne!" I hear William calling me. "Your bacon is burning."

"Shit!" I yell and quickly push the pan away from the flame.

"What were you thinking?" I don't answer. "Are you ok?"

"Yeah, yeah. I was just daydreaming, that's all," I puff. "Why don't you go to Selene?"

"What about?"

"Never mind," I reply. "I'll take care of it. I just need some time alone."

"Fine with me." He places the pancake batch aside. "If you need anything just give me a call."

I nod and wave him to go. He leaves and for some strange reason Nana Cecile and all the crazy things Warren and I did to gain her love come to mind. We were so competitive. Every year we used to bake two birthday cakes for nana and hope she would pick our cake as her favorite. But she never did. She loved us both equally, and of course, she loved to have Warren and I baking two cakes for her. Triple Chocolate and red velvet.

I smile and start to feel calmer than I did a few seconds ago. I continue preparing breakfast.

In a matter of minutes, the kitchen is filled with smoke and sizzling sounds. I run to the window and open it. I gaze in astonishment as the smoke won't leave the room. I run to the range and turn off the gas. I place the bacon in a large plate along with the pancakes. The coffee machine just finished brewing the coffee and I'm anxious to drink a nice, strong cup. I pour some into my mug and before I place the bacon and the pancakes on the dining room table, I put some water on the stove for tea. William and his tea.

"English people," I tell myself, and shake my head.

I walk back and forth and the smoke is still lingering in the kitchen. Grabbing some cardboard lying near the stove, I use it to move the air around.

From behind me I hear a grunting or moaning sound. I turn around and yelp at the sight of an old man crawling on the floor. He is wearing hospital garment, and keeps moving forward with his grey eyes fixed on me.

I start to panic. Blood pours from his mouth as he emits a chilling shriek. Then I hear a girl singing, "Eight little trespassers are assembled. One little trespasser is not."

I dash to the door, but it's locked. I try to call for help but the others are too far away to hear. There's no one else on this floor.

"And now there are eight little trespassers left," concludes the small voice.

I take a deep breath and prepare to fight my way to safety. I turn around and…

Selene

Something startles me. I open my eyes and find someone wrapping me in a blanket. Relieved, thinking Seth has finally arrived, I sit upright. But as my vision focuses, the figure starts to take form, and I see William standing over me.

"Not happy to see me?" he asks, with a semi-hurt tone of voice. I quickly shake my head not wanting to hurt his feelings. In truth, I'm not. I had hoped it was Seth.

"It's just that…"

"I know," he says and sits next to me. "You hoped that I would be your brother." I nod. "You shouldn't be here by yourself."

"I'm not. Wayne is…." I look around. "He was here a minute ago."

"He went into the kitchen. I guess cooking calms him down," William explains, and gently grasps my hand. I'm beginning to calm down. "You shouldn't be here alone. I'd rather you were in the bedroom with Yolanda."

"Well – she's not in her room – she's with Tony," I tell him. He has a confused look on his face.

"Oh!" he smiles. "So, they're finally together."

"I don't know if they are together together but at the moment they are together," I tell him. My cheeks feel hot. William starts to smile sweetly at me. I blush even more, and when he carefully wraps his arms around me and rests his head against mine, my heart begins to pound. He sniffs my hair. A bit creepy, but nice.

I start to trace his hand with my finger. I love his hands. Strong and delicate all at the same time. I look up into his beautiful blue eyes. The way he is staring at me makes me both uncomfortable and blissful. In this precious moment I'm the only thing on his mind and soul, and I like that a lot.

"What are you thinking?" he asks. I shake my head and don't answer. "Tell me."

"I was thinking that I'm – going – to miss this," I explain, looking away from him.

"Miss what?"

"You know – you and me. We can't stay together."

William jerks his head up, "Why not?"

I turn my attention back to him. "Look at me," I snap at him. I show him my hands that, as always, are enclosed in gloves. "I can't have a normal or healthy relationship with anyone. My own parents are afraid to be around me. My brother is scared of me and my grandmother felt sorry for me." I try to stand up but William won't let me.

"We can find a way," he whispers in my ear, still holding me by my shoulders.

I click my tongue and look away from him. I'm disappointed and most of all, I'm angry, but not at him. "I can't. I can't have you hating me or being afraid of me or – feeling sorry for me. I just can't."

"I wouldn't – I couldn't….."

"You say that now, but wait a few days or weeks," I interrupt, "when I start to act strange or tell you about your past or future."

He pulls me forward, closer to him. He places his head next to mine and whispers, "I know what I'm getting into," he whispers.

I can't believe what he is saying. Is he serious or is he just playing with my heart like Seth keeps telling me. But why? What did I do to him or to Carmen to deserve such wicked treatment?

I move away, but he draws me back into his arms. "It will be fine," he whispers, and gently kisses my hair.

I grab his hand and place my head on his shoulder. I'm so confused. What to believe? Who to believe?

"Something troubling you?" he asks. I ponder his question, but remain silent.

"May I ask you something?" William says. "Why haven't you ever asked about my past?"

"Meaning?"

"Everyone in this house is so interested in my wild nights on the Hollywood scene, including your annoying brother."

I smile and caress his bruised left lip and cheek. "He can be very – protective."

"Yeah, well, he is a bit too protective, but that shows that he does care for you, very much in fact."

"I don't know if it's for me or for him," I declare and in that moment I regret my quick answer. The look on his face makes me want to elaborate on my answer. I take a deep breath. "It was three years ago, actually. Seth came home for winter break. He brought one of his best friends with him. His name was Mark Martin and he was – cute. Anyway, we both liked each other until we kissed…"

"You kissed?" he asked, shocked.

"Yeah, well it wasn't the first kiss I dreamt about. We were in the barnyard…."

"The barnyard?" he says with a hint of sarcasm and a big smile on his face.

"Yes, the barnyard." I repeat. His smile grows by the second. "Anyway, as I was saying, we were in the barnyard and we – kissed.

156

It was horrible. I had visions and when I woke up he was standing over me, glaring. He was furious and called me names. My parents were disappointed in me and didn't speak to me for days.

"Seth left the ranch the next day with Mark. From that day on, Seth became distant and his visits became more and more infrequent.

"Another disappointment I gave to my parents. This is why I need to win. I gave them so much agony. I want to make it right, and by winning the money – it would ease the pain I gave them." Tears fill my eyes. William gently places his face in his hands on my face. "I also hope to improve the relationship between my brother and me, but he is too busy chasing skirts."

"Don't say that," he whispers in a scolding manner.

"But it's true."

"Enough. I don't want to hear you speak like that again."

"I saw his future and I told him. His face got dark and the veins of his neck were throbbing in."

"What did you see?"

"On September 11th, 2010, he'll be charged with the murder of his girlfriend. I saw it happen. I saw him cutting and burning her. I saw everything."

"And will you try to stop him?"

"You can't stop death," I tell him, and see disappointment in his eyes. He doesn't push the subject any further. "As to your question," I quickly change the topic, "I never asked because all my question were answered when Carmen touched me."

"And what did you see?"

"Someone lost, unhappy, and disappointed with life and himself." I look into his eyes. "You know where you want to be and who you want to be but you're not there yet. You have to find the courage to let go of your fears."

"You're good."

I smile. "Carmen. I saw everything through her eyes." After a small pause, I add. "You know, I shouldn't tell you but she truly loves you."

William releases me. "She doesn't love me. She thinks she does." The tender William I care for disappears within seconds.

"But – I saw it. I felt it, just like I felt Julia's love for you."

"Please, don't. Don't go there," he snaps. "That's the past." His face softens, pulls me onto the couch. We stay in each other's arms, waiting for Seth and the others to return.

Yolanda

"Hey!" I say aloud as soon I find William.

He raises his index finger and points to Selene who is sleeping in his arms.

"Sorry," I reply softly. "Tony wants to talk to you."

William nods and gently shifts Selene to the couch armrest. William stands up and before he walks over to me, he takes a blanket and tucks her in. He gives her a gentle kiss on her head. The kind that makes you want to say, "Aww, how sweet." I don't say it, but I'm thinking it.

"Keep an eye on her," he tells me. "Please."

"Sure." I sit next to her. I glance at Selene's face and notice her lips are curved upward into a content smile. She looks happy – very blissful. "You're a stubborn girl," I grin.

"What did you say?" Selene yawns and starts to stretch.

"I said that you are a very stubborn girl."

"What? Why?" she sits upright and looks around the room, "Where's Will."

"Where's Will? What does he call you now, Sal?" I don't know why I'm so irritated. I should be happy for her instead of bickering with her. "Since when are you two on a nickname basis?"

"Last night," she smiles. "And no, he does not call me Sal. I wouldn't have it. It's a horrible nickname. Can't you be happy for me?"

"I am," I say, not too convincingly.

She grabs my hands and pulls them closer to her. "I think – I'm in love."

I roll my eyes up and let go of her hands. "Please!"

"What?"

"He's William Hawthorn – the actor – the one who has girls dropping from clouds – the one who jumps from one flower to another, and, forgive the expression, but it's too early in the morning to use vulgar terms."

"I know all that…"

"Then why are you falling for him?" I ask. I notice her good mood is disappearing. She pulls the blanket up to her neck. "Seth is still missing. You didn't forget that?"

"Of course not," she snaps back at me.

"And?"

"And, what? What's your problem?"

I glare at her and feel horrible for the way I feel. I take a deep breath. "I'm sorry," I finally say. "I'm just mad, frustrated and angry, and I'm taking it out on you. Forgive me."

She nods. "Why so tense?"

"I think Raul was right about my horrible taste in men. But please don't tell him that I said so." Selene smiles at me and points to the cameras. "We kissed and….." I continue and in an instant I have her full attention. "Nothing."

"Nothing? What do you mean – nothing?"

"I felt nothing. It was like I kissed Raul or my aunt or my mother," I explain. I can feel my temper rising and voice getting louder. "Everything was perfect. The light, the food, the mood, and when we kissed, all my expectation went – poof."

"What about Tony?"

"I think he liked it," I smile and Selene grins back at me. "He was all over me," and we both start to laugh.

After awhile, "I don't know what to do?"

"About what?"

I lift my eyes. "With Tony," I exclaim. "I don't know how to tell him. He looks so happy."

"You can wait until after the show."

"I don't know. What about you and William? Is he a good kisser?"

Selene's face turns crimson. I have to laugh as Selene pulls the blanket over her face and giggles like a little girl.

"What?"

"I asked if he's a good kisser," I repeat.

"I don't know. We didn't kiss – yet."

"Why not?"

"It's complicated."

"Complicated?"

"It's me," she says and I nod in understanding. I have to admit that maybe, and I do mean maybe, that I was wrong about William. He seems to genuinely care for her.

"I'm worried about you."

"Why?"

"You, moving to New York City. They'll eat you alive."

She smiles. "Thank you for caring so much about me, but I'll be ok. William wants to move to New York, too. He wants to attend NYU."

"Really?" I'm in shock. "Is he that serious about you?"

She shakes her head and starts to blush once again. "He wants to study cinematography."

"And he always wanted to go to NYU?"

"At first he wanted to go back to England, but he decided to stay."

"And this decision came to him, when?"

"Last night," she timidly replies. "But he won't immediately attend college. First he has to fulfill his contract."

"What contract?"

"Blue Vein," she says.

I make a sour face.

"He really doesn't have to. The movie can survive without

160

him and Carmen. Who knows, maybe it will be even better."

"No way. William Hawthorn is the one who makes the movie a success."

"What? No way."

"Way," she yells back at me. We begin to argue back and forth about William's acting, and whether or not he makes the movie better.

The door opens and we stop quarreling. Tony smiles at me and I smile back. But mine is not as sweet or genuine as his. I take a deep breath and wonder if perhaps I should give him a second try.

"Hungry?" he says, and Selene and I nod.

We step outside, and I see William coming down the stairs. Carmen is a few steps behind, watching him closely. She looks so sad. Tony seizes my hand and I rush into his arms.

"Feeling better?" William asks Selene. He kisses her gently on the forehead. Carmen's face contorts in anger. "Don't pay attention to her," William whispers to Selene. Tony and I follow them to the dining room. Behind us, Carmen screeches in frustration and throws something. We don't turn around. We simply keep moving.

The dining room is, as always, filled with delicious food. The Jones's are magnificent chefs. I'm glad they took over the job. I can't cook. I've tried before but the only thing I can do is throw something into the microwave or oven.

I put some bacon and eggs on my plate and start to eat. To my disappointment, the food is cold. I take a sip of coffee, and it is cold as well.

"Everything is cold," I say and Tony agrees with me.

William stands up. "I'll check on Wayne. Maybe he needs some help." He walks out through the side door.

Five minutes pass before William returns with a concerned look on his face. "He's gone. I can't find him."

Tony stands up. "Come on. Let's look around for him." He

says. "You and Selene stay here just in case Wayne or the others come back." I nod as they disappear through the kitchen door.

Carmen

As I leave my room, I notice that the door to Tony's room down the hall is open. I hear William's voice. I stop to eavesdrop on the conversation.

"Did they come back yet?" Tony asks. I can't make out William's answers. "How is she?"

"How do you think she is?" William replies. "She's shaken but she'll be fine. Now back to my answers," he continues. I move closer to the door. My curiosity is increasing.

"Yes, yes," Tony keeps repeating. Well, no shock there. He sounds like the lunatic I think he is. He fits perfectly in this place. "I spent most of the night searching."

"Really? Not from what I heard." William states.

Tony giggles. "Nothing happened. Yolanda gave me a hand with my research."

"I asked you to be discrete and, no offense, but Yolanda is quite a gossip box …."

"She is not." Tony interrupts. "She can keep secrets. Trust me."

"If she goes around and tells anyone about my private affairs – I swear, I'll rearrange your face…"

"Don't come to me for help and then threaten me," Tony yells back at him. "I'm doing you a favor and you should be grateful."

William grunts and after a few seconds I hear him sigh.

"Why so tense?" Tony asks.

"Never mind," William snaps. "Did you find something?"

"No, I'm sorry. Without the net, I can't find what you need. But I found something that might come in handy."

"Yes?"

"Your father was a doctor in this institution." Tony pauses

162

dramatically.

"And?"

"Your adoptive father was your real father," he finally says. I can feel the tension building in the room. I'm on tip toes, and the hair on my body is standing on end.

"What?" William gasps.

"Your adoptive father was your real father. Here, look at your birth certificate. Mother, Kate Williams. Father, James Hawthorn, AKA Dr. James Hawthorn – your mother's physician," Tony explains. "I'm sorry, I wasn't able to find your sister's cause of death."

"William has a sister," I whisper to myself.

"So, it was you," William says. He sounds like an injured puppy. "You were the one who dropped my sister's diary on my bed. Thanks."

"You're welcome. I hope it helps in your search and I'm sorry….."

"Good morning, Carmen!" Maria shouts. I jump, and Tony's bedroom door promptly slams shut. "Is snooping on your to do list today," she mocks.

"And yours is how to……" I stop. The door opens, and William steps out with Tony behind him. "Hey!" I smile to William. He looks indifferent. We haven't spoken since that little witch acted eerie. How can he believe her and not me?

"We need to talk," William says to me, and my heart gives a small flutter. Those four words are a woman's nightmare. They never bring happiness.

"Sure," I reply not showing my fear. We move to a corner in the hall, and once Maria and Tony are out of our sight William begins.

"I'm done playing. I don't want to hurt her or any other girls."

I laugh, "Are you telling me that you are actually falling for her?"

William looks down. He is uncomfortable. "What I'm saying is that I'm done playing your bloody games. I'm done."

"You never complained before…"

"I DID!!!" he shouts at me. "Right after Julia's death, and I don't want Selene to meet her fate."

"Oh Will. Will, Will, Will. You always had a soft spot for naïve, innocent and dimwitted little girls."

"Why her? Why not Maria?"

"She is not naïve, innocent or dimwitted, and most of all, a little girl." I smile at him and try to kiss his lips, but he stops me at the last moment.

"No, no more. I'm done." He pushes me away.

"You owe me. I saved your life and gave you all you desired."

"I didn't know the price would be this high."

"What? To love me?"

William stops and turns around. He takes two steps toward me. "No. To be your puppet – your servant from hell. I'm done with you and with this thing living inside of me. I'll find a way to save myself and Selene," he whispers.

"Then you'll die," I whisper back to him.

"At last, for the first time in my life, I'll do something right, and I'll do it myself." He walks away.

"Wait!" I yell after him, and grab his hand. My heart starts to beat faster and butterflies are building up in my stomach. I haven't felt this way for a very long time. His hand feels so warm and strong. I look up. His eyes are cold, and I miss the love and excitement he gave me whenever he' peered into my eyes. His love and devotion for me ended when he met Julia. I feel empty and miss his company.

"What?" he grunts. "I'm busy."

"William, please, talk to me. I can't stand it anymore."

"I told you – I'm done – we're done." He shoves my hand aside, "and I would advise you to be a little more careful with your craving. The Jones brothers have noticed some of the food supplies are missing."

"I wouldn't have to sneak around in the middle of the night if you would give me what I want," I snap back at him.

"And you won't. Not as long I'm around," he retorts and walks away.

At the bottom of the stairs, I see Selene and Yolanda step out of the living room. Yolanda jumps into Tony's arms and – and William walks towards Selene and holds her hands in his. He gently kisses her on the head as if she is made of porcelain. Selene hugs him, and when she sees me glaring at them, she freezes. William looks up at me with the same hatred he showed a few minutes ago. He turns his attention back to Selene and whispers something in her ear. I stand there, all alone, watching him share his love with someone else.

It breaks me, and when I see him pull her into his arms, I start to scream and rip the paintings off the walls until my rage is finally gone.

More controlled now, I start to smooth my hair and straighten my clothes. I take a deep breath and decide that it is time for me to join the others.

I enter the dining room. The three girls sitting around the table have long faces, while the guys are nowhere to be found. I guess Seth, Phillip and Warren aren't back yet. Good, although I wish that little farmer girl was also gone.

I sit in the first empty chair and pour some coffee into a mug. I look around and see that the food is untouched. I sip the coffee. Cold.

"Where are the guys and why is everything so cold?" I ask. Yolanda glares at me.

"They went looking for Wayne," Selene replies. "He's missing."

"Missing how?"

"We don't know," Yolanda explains. "We walked in and

breakfast was waiting for us as always, but this time it was cold. William went looking for him, wondering if he needed any help and.....”

“He told us that Wayne is missing,” Maria continues. “The kitchen is a mess. I think Wayne put up quite a fight.”

I nod and, curious, walk over to the kitchen. Pots, utensils, food and shattered plates cover the floor. The fridge is open, and some of the doors have been ripped off the cabinets.

A breeze from the ocean is gusting into the room. It is pretty cold. I shut the window.

Then a loud commotion from the dining room startles me. I hear shouts, screams and furniture being smashed. I rush back toward the noise.

Phillip

“Come on!!!” I keep yelling at Seth. After many hours we have finally found an exit.

We emerge from the chamber and find ourselves in.....

“The basement,” Seth confirms. I nod. Seth tugs my shoulder and leads the way out. The bright sunlight blinds us. In the commotion trying to help Warren, we lost our flashlights and were forced to find our way back in the dark.

We hear familiar and welcome voices coming from the dining room. I hear Maria shouting and Yolanda’s irritating voice answering, but at this point they are music to my ears.

We start to quicken our pace and I want to run into Maria’s arms as soon I see her, but when we see all the good food on the table, Seth and I dive right into it.

We shove bacon, pancakes, coffee, and eggs into our mouths while everyone watches us in astonishment. Selene runs to Seth to hug him but she stops at the last second. “I’m so glad you are back,” She says, and squeezes his shoulder.

Seth takes her hand, “Me too,” he smiles at her and turns

back to the food.

"What happened?" Maria asks, and sits next to me.

"Warren is gone," I tell them and in between bites, I start to narrate our little adventure. Seth adds bits and pieces. He wants to incorporate his views into the story. I don't mind, it gives me more time to eat.

Carmen walks in and sits across from me. "Wayne is gone too," she states.

"What?" Seth and I ask simultaneously.

"We're not sure," Yolanda quickly clarifies, and glares at Carmen.

"We are," Tony enters the room with William.

"How?" I ask them.

"We've found blood," William explains.

"A lot of blood," Tony adds. "In the pantry."

We don't know what to say, except for Carmen of course. She raises her mug and exclaims "Congratulations to the final eight."

I look around, trying to gauge the emotions of the group. Some of them are happy about still being here, but others are frightened. They all seem to be wondering who the next victim will be, and if this is really part of the show.

I decide to go snoop around the Jones's room to see if they found the money. They were a tactical duo. They liked to goof around and prank people but they weren't stupid. I've been watching them carefully the last few days, and discovered what splendid illusionists they are. One stayed with the group and kept everyone's attention while the other snuck out of sight to do whatever they had planned.

I open their bedroom and an unpleasant smell assails my nose. I look around and see their clothes spread across the floor. Dirty plates and glasses with mold on them lie under their beds.

I unbolt the window. Fresh wind blows into the room, driving the odor out into the hall.

I don't know where to start. There is so much stuff all over the place. I turn to my left and begin in the closet. I find a suitcase inside containing an E-Touch and a bottle of laxative.

"You mother f….." I start to say out loud when something catches my sight. A black book. I open it and on the first page it reads:

Private Diary

Maria Sanchez

I feel conflicted about reading Maria's diary, but a small voice inside me keeps urging me to do so. I decide to take the diary to my room, and once there I jump on my bed and begin to read:

August 3, 2010 – Phoenix

Dear Diary:

Phillip is asking too many questions about the child. I want to confess that I've lost it, but I'm afraid I'll lose him forever. Even my parents and friends are asking too many questions. The pressure is getting to me. I have to tell him. I'm going to tell him as soon we win the show. He'll be so happy with a million dollars in his pocket that he'll forgive me. I know he will.

Angry and highly enraged I keep scanning the pages. I want to know what other lies she's told me.

May 13, 2010 – Phoenix

Dear Diary:

168

I find myself in a very difficult situation. I did something horrible and I do not know how to resolve it. I tried to spill my troubles to my friends...

I flip through more pages:

July 3, 2010 – Phoenix

Dear Diary:

Two days ago I lost the baby. I was sad but I'm starting to feel better now...

I realize now that our entire relationship was built on lies and deceptions, so I decide to confront her.

I storm into her room and find her on the bed reading. She looks up and with a smile she says, "You found my diary," and runs over to me. I grab her by her shoulders and push her against the wall. "Phil, you're scaring me. Phillip!" She pleads with me to let her go.

"Show me your stomach," I tell her. She recoils and tries to free herself, but it's too late. I've already lifted her shirt up and my hand touches her flat stomach. I feel neither a bump nor the movement of a child.

"How could you lie to me?" I shout at her. "How could you push someone else's child on me and then still lie to me after you lost it."

"I love you. I didn't want to lose you," she sobs.

"No, no, no. Stop crying!" I yell. "Your crocodile tears won't work on me anymore." Maria starts to cry even louder. "Once we are back in Phoenix, I want you to pack up all your stuff and move out of my apartment." I walk away unable to look at her. I've lost all the respect and love I ever had for her.

"Please, Phillip," she shouts, running after me. "You need to listen to me."

"I've had enough of you and your plans and lies," I slam the door in her face and lock it

"PHILLIP!!!!" she cries, and bangs on the door.

I ignore her and turn my stereo on. I raise the volume up as high as possible. I'm done with her. I don't want to see her anymore.

8 contenders remaining

Part Two

The Enlightening

Day Eight

Friday, August 20, 2010

Maria

After many hours of pleading, crying and yelling for Phillip's forgiveness without any result, I decided to spend the rest of my remaining time on this island locked away in the Johnson room.

I'm so ashamed, and with good reason. I know what I've done is morally wrong but Phillip was, and still is, the one person I can't live without, and I would do anything to have him.

And you practically did, says a small voice within my own conscience.

I agree. I pretty much used all the tricks in the book to force Phillip to stay with me. There is nothing I can do or say to keep him. I've lost him for good. A giant knot builds in my throat and tears fill my eyes.

"Seven little trespassers are dreaming." I hear the voice of a little girl singing. "One little trespasser is not."

I jump. It has come for me and I'm not ready to leave the house – not yet. I need to mend my relationship with Phillip.

"NO!!!" I yell and run out of the room.

I rush down the hall, knocking on each door and begging for help, but the house is dark and empty.

I begin to cry as I feel my body shake uncontrollably.

"Please. Please," I beg, "let me in." I keep knocking on doors in the hope that someone will hear me and come to my rescue, but all my efforts are in vain.

I turn my attention to the floor and watch helplessly as the white mist slowly rises, reaching for me.

In the background I can hear the little girl coming closer and closer. I start to run again, only to crash heavily into a wall. I slump to the floor.

"And now there are seven little trespassers left," continues the little girl.

Then, something snatches my wrist and…

Carmen

Where is everyone? I think to myself as I walk from room to room. The house is empty and it freaks me out.

I enter the living room and hear William's soft gentle laugh.

He seems to be in a very good mood. I'm happy to see him content after such a long time.

I start to say something to him, but the soft sound of a guitar stops me.

I move the curtains gently aside and peek into the room. There, on the small couch, I see William admiring that cowgirl while she plays a country song. I don't know which one. I'm not a big fan of country music, and at this point in my life, I loathe it. I hate everything that reminds me of Selene Holloway. And if my ego isn't hurting enough, Selene has a beautiful voice too. I can see from William's eyes that he thinks so as well. He has become too close to her. I need to do something to separate them. I need William to dislike her, but how?

I close the curtains and sit on the couch, pondering how this could have happened to me. I had always seen a future with William, happy, in love and married but now…

William's laughter interrupts my thoughts. I remember with horror the first time he met Selene. He was full of adoration for her and I dismissed it as another one of his escapades. I was so stupid and naïve; too proud and too self-absorbed to accept his lust for her. He always had been attracted to innocent, pure, sweet and naïve girls. It never bothered me before. As long as I had fame and money he would come back to me, but now – I'm not so sure. And I was the one who pushed him toward her. I thought she was no threat to me, but look at her now. I'm jealous. I don't know if I hate her because William likes her, or because I'm jealous of someone like her.

In the midst of my own thoughts I hear more giggling and laughter. Growing angrier by the moment and feeling betrayed, I

174

stand up and rudely enter the room.

William and Selene are just a few inches apart, gazing lovingly into each other's eyes. Selene looks shocked when she sees me, and drops her cat-like eyes to the floor. "Uhm, I – have to – go," she whispers, and when she takes a step William grabs her hand and pulls her back to him.

"No, you don't," he smiles at her. He turns his ice-cold eyes to me. "We're a bit busy," he tells me, with a look of annoyance. It seems that it is definitely over between the two of us. I don't want it to be over. I saved his life. I gave him everything he wanted, and this is how he thanks me? I don't think so.

"So," I start biting my lip, "is this what you want? Is this the path you choose?" He nods and my skin begins to crawl. "Do you know how hard your life will be and how weak your future will be?" William shrugs his shoulders, and I start to get angrier and angrier by the second. I turn to Selene who is looking down at the floor, "And you…"

"Don't talk to her," William barks. His face turns cold, and the dark William I first met is back. The William who has no respect or love for anyone but himself. His selfish attitude isn't his fault. It's mine. I was the one who made him that way.

He turns his attention to Selene and the oddest thing happens. He pulls his sleeves over his hands and presses them against her cheeks.

I can't comprehend his strange action. Is there something wrong with her? Of course there is, something wrong, but what?

William stands up, and pulls Selene with him. "I would appreciate it if you would stay away from us from now on," he tells me.

My jaw drops. No one has ever spoken to me that way before. If that's not bad enough, I notice something else. The shy, weak and, most of all, insecure Selene is no more. Now she stands strong and confident by his side. She knows William is now totally committed to her.

I have to destroy her.

I become aware of Tony standing in the background. Something in my mind clicks. Tony holds the knowledge I need and the secret to the vengeance I crave.

I run to him. He doesn't look too happy to see me. I can see the color drain from his face. He's scared of me. How sweet.

"I need to talk to you," I tell him, and pull him over to a dark corner of the hall.

Out of the corner of my eye, I can see the lovebirds, William and Selene walking to the dining room. The sight sickens me. I look around the hall, making sure no one can eavesdrop on our conversation.

The hallway is empty, so I ask Tony, "What's wrong with Selene?"

"What do you mean?" he replies. I shove him against the wall. I know he knows what's wrong with her and I don't like it when people assume I'm stupid, because I'm not. It ticks me off.

Angry and frustrated, I sink my nails into his upper arm and move my face closer to his face. "Don't play stupid with me," I snarl. "You seem to know everything about us, especially about the Holloways." I press my nails even deeper into his flesh.

He smiles and for the first time I see Tony under a different light. He is not the dorky guy he lets everyone believe he is. He is mischievous and conniving just like me.

"What's so funny?" I ask him.

"All right then," he chuckles as he pushes me away. "Selene is a psychometric."

"A what?"

"A psychometric," he repeats. "Selene has the ability to obtain knowledge about a person or object through contact."

I feel as if lightning has just struck me. That's how she knew about Julia and me. That's how she knows so much.

Shocked and confused I ask, "Does William know?"

He shrugs his shoulders. "I don't know," he replies. Nothing else matters to me at this moment than to show William and the rest of the world what a wicked and dangerous person she is.

"I need your help," I tell him. Tony moves two steps back. "I need to destroy her." He smiles at me. I realize that I am about to get my vengeance.

Tony

"What now?" I whisper as I study my notes. Yolanda won't help me anymore. She is too scared and won't use her sixth sense, which is the main reason she is on this show, in the first place.

"Damn it!" I shout, and slam my fist on the table. I had hoped with Yolanda and Selene on this island, it would help me solve the mystery that occurred a few years ago. After all, Yolanda is a retrocognition and Selene is the great, great granddaughter of Cut Throat Lilly, not to mention a magnificent psychometric. They should have picked up something by now.

Disappointed, I start to play with the ring that I believe belonged to William's mother. I found it on Abe. It cost us a small fortune but if this is really her ring, it could help us find out how the massacre occurred. Assuming Selene helps, of course. But with William constantly by her side and Seth maintaining steady watch on his sister, I don't know how to slip Kate's ring into Selene's hands.

I had hoped that being nice to William or Seth would bring me closer to Selene, but I was wrong. For some reason, the two of them don't trust me, especially William. He looks at me strangely and only talks to me if he absolutely has to. I expected that William would open up to me after I told him some very important facts about his real parents, and again, I was wrong.

I look over to my clock and it's almost time for lunch. Time for me to make my way to the others, even though I wish I could stay here and organize my notes.

On the first floor I see the two lovebirds, William and Selene, leaving the love room. That's what everyone in the house calls the study. It seems its old world charm attracts a lot of couples, including Yolanda and me.

I notice Carmen standing almost incoherent, watching the two of them walk away hand in hand. She looks up at me for a second or two, and it gives me the creeps. Her expression makes me very uncomfortable. When she begins walking toward me, I feel my pulse quicken, and not in a pleasant way.

"I need to talk to you," she says, and pulls me over to a dark corner of the hall.

Carmen glances back at William and Selene slowly disappearing from our sight. "What's wrong with Selene?" she asks.

"What do you mean?" I reply, and she pushes me against the wall. Her long finger nails sink into my upper arms. Her face is just inches from mine, too close for my own comfort.

"Don't play stupid with me," she snarls beneath my nose. "You seem to know everything about us, especially the Holloways," and sinks her nails deeper in my skin.

I smile.

"What so funny?" Carmen asks, now very annoyed.

"All right then," I smile as I push her hands away. "Selene is a psychometric."

"A what?"

"A psychometric," I puff at her ignorance, but then again, I shouldn't be too surprised with her lack of knowledge. She doesn't seem to be the type of person who would give up an evening in a club for the library.

I begin to explain as Carmen contemplates the meaning of my words.

"Does William know?" she whispers.

"I don't know." I tell her, even though I have a strong feel he does.

I watch Carmen move slowly and almost incoherently to the other side of the hall with her hands over her mouth.

"I need your help," she walks over to me. And once again, she intrudes upon my private space. "I need to destroy her."

I smile at my new opportunity. "I have an idea," I tell her and pull Kate's ring from my pants pocket. "This is William's mother's ring."

"And?"

I raise my gaze up in protest at her ignorance. "If you find a way for Selene to touch the ring, it will show William and the others what a freak she is," I specify, knowing right where to push her. She will come to my side and do whatever I want.

"I don't know – how?" she says.

I take her hand and place the ring in her palm, "If you want William back you'll find a way to place this ring into Selene's bare hand." I smile at her. "I know you will." With that I walk slowly away feeling very pleased and content. I can't imagine what she'll come up with, but whatever it is, it will be very positive for me.

Phillip

"She's gone," I announce as I enter the room with another chess piece in my hand. I place it in the middle of the table for everyone to see. "I found it in front of my bedroom door."

"Another chess piece and this time it's a knight," Seth says. He reads Maria's name carved into the base of the figurine. "What does it mean?"

"I think…" Tony starts to talk, then stops. He is insecure. He doesn't know if he should continue or not.

"Go on," Yolanda encourages him. She shakes his hand lightly and smiles.

"I don't want to sound crazy or….."

"You're already there," Carmen smirks. Tony glares at her.

"No offense, but she has a point," says Seth, taking Carmen's side. I should have known. Now with Maria out of the way, Carmen is the next best thing left in this house. I don't like it a bit. I need to talk to him. Carmen is out of the question. She's mine.

"What do these chess pieces mean?" Yolanda asks. I flash a devilish grin. It appears that I'm the only one remaining who knows the truth about these pieces. None of them have a clue. Poor, simple minded group.

"I haven't the slightest idea," I lie to them.

"So, Maria is gone now," Carmen whispers. I notice how tense she is, deep in her own thoughts.

"Yep, she's gone," Tony repeats. He stares intently at Carmen, who returns his gaze. They seem to be in agreement about something. They've stopped loathing each other and appear to be on the same page about – what?

Seth stands up and draws my attention away from the two of them. He leaves the room and it doesn't take long for Carmen to follow him.

I start to get nervous. Something is going on, and I need to know what it is.

I decide to go after Carmen. I need to confront her. I want to know what she wants from Seth.

I find them in the living room arguing about something. I'm not quite sure what. They keep their voices low. Seth turns around and is about to walk away from the argument, but he stops when he sees me.

"I know what she is!!!" Carmen yells after him. "She is an atrocity! Your family is wicked! I knew it all along," she adds.

"At least my family doesn't have to deal with someone as poisonous as you." Seth grins, and Carmen is now boiling over. Her face is red and one of her eyes is twitching.

From behind I hear foot steps approaching. I turn and see William and Selene join our little gathering.

"Ah! There you are," Seth smiles at William. William is shocked by Seth's calm tone of voice.

"Don't you dare…" Carmen snaps at Seth as she advances toward him. "Do not!"

"Have a seat and let me tell you a little story about your girlfriend…"

"Ex," William affirms.

Seth's eyes turn to Carmen and with a bright smile he asks, "Troubles?"

Carmen says nothing. She just glares at him and walks over to William. She grabs his hand, encouraging him to leave.

"You might want stay and find out what my connection is to your girlfriend," chides Seth. "Correction – ex-girlfriend," Seth adds with an amused smile. He looks so proud of himself.

"Come," Carmen says and pulls William's hand. "Don't listen to him. He and his sister are delusional people."

Seth laughs out loud, "Am I now? What about you, Carmen?"

"I'm staying," William tells her and let's go of her hand, "I want to hear."

"There you go." Seth grins playfully and drops onto the couch. "Have a seat."

William nods and sits on the first empty chair facing Seth. I too, sit. I'm curious.

"William. Don't!" Carmen pleads. "He's a liar."

"All I ask is for you to hear my story, and then it's up to you to decide if you believe me or not," Seth says. "Julia and I were friends – very good friends."

"Really?" William utters with doubt in his mind.

"Yes, we were friends. But the point of my story is not about my friendship with Julia, but my encounter with Carmen and the role I played kill Julia."

Everyone stops breathing.

"What the hell?" I say out loud and watch William glance repeatedly between the two of them.

Carmen smiles and looks over to William. "He was the one who told me all about her dirty little secret," and turns back to

Seth. "And she had many. You see, our Seth and Julia were not only very good friends. They were more then that. And when you entered her life, Julia broke off their relationship in order to be with you.

"Poor Seth. He was so full of pain, hatred, and bitterness when I met him. All he wanted was for me to destroy you both, and so I did," Carmen sadistically smiles at him. I start to shiver. Never in my life have I seen such a cold and morbid smile.

"No," Seth grunts. "You used me to destroy her."

"And you didn't care," Carmen steps in. Ashamed and hurt, Seth drops his gaze to the ground. "On the contrary – you loved it. You wanted her to pay for the pain she caused you."

Selene seems shocked and broken. She looks to Seth for an answer, but nothing comes. She takes a step back and walks out of the room, hearing no more.

I wait for Seth to follow her, to say something to her, but he doesn't.

"Yes, I wanted her to be hurt and I wanted you" Seth calmly proclaims as he turns his eyes back to William, "out of my way – to pay for all that you'd caused me but your guardian devil," and he points towards Carmen, "wouldn't have it." Carmen smiles proudly as she gently caresses William's cheek. William shifts his head as he pushes her hand away. "If I were you," Seth continues, "I would check those brakes of yours. She might have had something to do with your car crash. She's dangerous. She can't be trusted."

Seth stands up and walks away, leaving William and I alone to ponder his tale.

Yolanda

I watch Seth leave the room. He looks happy – happier than normal.

With a smile, I enter the living room seeking the joy and happiness that has touched Seth, but I find the opposite. Phillip is

182

sitting on the couch. He looks confused and shocked. Carmen is on her knees next to William, crying and begging.

"What happened?" I ask in a softer tone. The scene makes me uncomfortable.

"Leave me," William says icily to Carmen. "I don't want to see your face ever again." He pushes her to the ground.

Phillip jumps up, ready to hit William for hurting Carmen.

"William, please," Carmen sobs. "I love you. I had nothing to do with her death. You must believe me."

"Believe you!!!" William spits at her. "I should trust you? Why? When all this time you've schemed behind my back, lied to my face, and stepped all over me?"

"I didn't touch her," Carmen repeats again and again.

William moves closer to her and whispers something in her ear. "No!!!" Carmen cries out. "Please, William." But William just ignores her.

"What's happening?" Tony asks as he enters the room. I grab his hand and drag him into the next room. I don't want to talk in front of Carmen. She's a mess.

"Why?" Tony asks when I'm done explaining what I witnessed.

"I don't know. I found them in that state."

"We should investigate."

"I think this is a bad idea," I tell him as he drags me out of the room.

Down the hall we encounter Phillip and William throwing punches at each other. It's awful. Their faces are covered with blood, and the sound of fists striking flesh is ghastly.

"Do something!" I shout hysterically at Tony.

"What do you want me to do?"

"Stop them – of course."

"Let them fight," he says.

"What?"

"They'll stop soon," he states. He looks almost gleeful watching the two pound each other. He's enjoying it.

I'm disgusted, shocked and disappointed by his lack of concern. There's nothing I can say or do to make them stop.

Seth

Back in my room I find Selene sitting by the window. She turns around. "Is it true?" she asks. I nod. "Talk."

I walk over to my bed and lay there. "What do you want me to tell you that I was a fool and learned my lesson?" I utter in a groggy tone of voice. "Because I didn't. To tell you the truth I would do it again. I loved her so much and for her to throw me aside for him, like the months we spent together meant nothing," I stop and look over at my little sister. She is silent while she listens and observes my face.

She sits next to me, "Is that why you became so distant from me? You are ashamed."

"Not for the reason you think," I clarify.

"Then for what!!!" Selene raises her voice. I shake my head. "Please Seth, talk to me. I love you."

"And I love you, but what I've done is my own fault and my own problem..."

"I can help."

"NO!!!" I snap.

Selene automatically moves across the room, "Please Seth, let me help you. I can..."

"I said NO," I yell and see Selene lock eyes with the ground. A tear runs down her cheek. I can't stand it to see her like this. And it hurts me so much that I am the one causing her this much pain, my little sister. "I'm tired," I tell her, "Do you mind leaving?" Selene nods but before she leaves the room I yell out, "And stay away from Carmen and William." She nods once more and closes the door.

I try to close my eyes, but I can't sleep. So many thoughts are swimming through my mind, not to mention the guilt I feel for being so harsh to Selene.

I stand up and decide to make me something to eat. It might help me calm down.

I head down to the kitchen, and scrabble around looking for something to make a sandwich. I come up with bread, mayo, mustard, tomatoes, lettuce, onions, and a few slices of turkey. As I begin to put it all together, I hear a rattle coming from the pantry.

I look around for something sharp to use as a weapon. On the counter is a large fork. I grab it and walk warily toward the pantry.

I open the door and find a body lying on the floor.

Cautiously, I step closer, holding the fork.

Suddenly the body rolls over, and a very familiar face appears from beneath a cascade of thick black hair.

"Maria!" I cry and kneel next to her. I drop the fork on the floor and lift her head up in my arms. "What happened?"

She says nothing. She seems lifeless.

"Six little trespassers are alone. One little trespasser is not." I hear a little girl singing in the background.

"What?" I whisper. Maria opens her eyes and starts to kiss me.

"And now there are six little trespassers left," the voice concludes and then…

William

We are sitting in the living room. Some of us are tense and others quiet.

I look around and notice Seth is not among us. I'm glad and can't wait for the moment he leaves the house – if he leaves. I just hope he'll leave before me.

185

"Ahhaaahaaaaha!" Tony's laugh draws my attention. For some strange reason he and Carmen have become quite close. It's weird. I can see that everyone in the room thinks the same thing.

Phillip is sitting on the armrest of a chair with a soda in hand glaring at the two of them. His face is bruised and swollen after our fight. Yolanda is watching Tony and she is in disgust – or mistrust.

I honestly don't understand them. I don't know what they see in each other. Carmen and Tony are violent. I know how evil Carmen is. I always knew it, but it never really bothered me until Julia's death. I had a gut feeling that Carmen was behind that, but I never wanted to find out. I was afraid. And now – I know.

"William, William," I hear my sister calling. I look around and find her at the door. I turn away and ignore her.

"They have Mom's ring," she says, pointing to Carmen who is twirling a ring in her hand. Tony is moving toward Yolanda and Selene. He smiles at the two of them. I notice a cup of coffee in his hand. "You must stop them," Alice says out loud. She sounds hysterical. "They want to place Mom's ring in Selene's hands. Stop them!!!"

I say nothing. I do nothing. Morally I know I should run to her and protect her but my legs won't move. Something is holding me back. Something is telling me to stay and watch.

"Will!!!" Alice shouts. "What are you waiting for? Help her!!!"

I don't move an inch. I just watch Tony pour the hot coffee onto Selene's hand.

She yelps.

"I'm so sorry," he apologizes. I can see that he doesn't mean it.

Selene shakes her head. "It's OK. It's fine." She rapidly pulls her glove off.

"William – why?" Alice asks and I can hear disappointment in her voice. And to tell the truth – I don't care. After all, she, too, stabbed me in the back.

186

Supposedly she's my sister, and yet she is more preoccupied with Selene's well-being than my own. I won't forget her words: I might be your sister, but my allegiance lies with someone else's bloodline, and that isn't the Hawthorne's.

What does that mean?

From the corner of my eye I catch sight of Carmen walking toward Selene. She has my mother's ring in her hand and is ready to place it in Selene's grasp.

Selene looks up. She smiles at me and I smile back at her. She's unaware of what is about to happen.

I jump to my feet as Carmen grabs Selene's hand and forcefully slip my mother's ring onto one of her fingers.

Selene screams and tries to take the ring off.

"Get it off!!! Get it off!!!" she yells and Yolanda tries to help, but it is too late.

Selene faints and before she hits the floor I pull her into my arms.

"What did you do?" Yolanda shouts at the two of them and slaps Tony's shoulders.

Tony seems ashamed and Carmen looks proud. They make me sick, and I'm disgusted with myself. I could have helped her. I could have stopped them. Why didn't I?

Alice looks down at me with such disappointment in her eyes. "What did you do?" she says, "You fool! Do you want me dead?"

I glare at her, wanting to argue the fact that I'm no fool and I don't want her dead, even though she already is, but I can't bring myself to do it.

"Where is my son?" Selene asks. I look down at her. "Where is William?" she asks and I notice it doesn't sound like her. Could it be my mother's voice?

"He's dead," Selene says in my father's voice. It's creepy hearing my father's voice coming out of Selene's mouth.

"What? No. It can't be. I saw him moving and I heard him

cry."

"No. He was born dead."

"No!!! He was alive. I know he was alive. You're lying to me!"

"Calm down," Selene says in my father's voice and moves her hands as if taking something from her pockets. A syringe.

"NO!!! Stay away from me. NO!!!"

"It will calm you down."

"I'll be good. I'll be good. Please don't."

"Shhh. You know that I love you."

Selene sits on the couch and slinks into a corner like a defeated animal waiting for its death. She nods her head.

"That's my girl," Selene grins. I recognize my father's evil, cold smile.

Selene falls asleep. I move closer to her and gently lift her into my arms.

"She's a witch," Carmen smirks. If I didn't have Selene in my arms, I would have slapped her across the face.

Without a word I keep moving toward the stairs. Selene whispers in my ear, "I know you're not dead. I know you're alive. I'm your mother. I love you."

I stop and a warm sensation fills my heart as I hear my mother's voice telling me that she loves me. A tear crawls down my cheek. I wipe it off and continue to climb the stairs with Selene in my arms.

When we reach her room, I place her on her bed. My mother's ring is still on her finger. I pull it off and study it. There is an engraving. It reads:

Forever one

I sneer. My father loving someone else other than himself? Never. I know him too well. He was always too involved in his work. His heart had no room for love.

Angry, I throw down the ring and watch it bounce across the floor.

The door opens. It's Yolanda. I stand up and without a word, walk out.

Selene

I open my eyes. A shadow flits across my face.

"Good. You're awake." I hear Yolanda's voice. "How do you feel?"

"Not good," I confess. "Now everyone knows what a freak I am."

"It was Carmen, with the help of Tony." Yolanda snaps. "I punched him in the stomach before I came to you."

"Why did he do this to me?"

"Tony and his research. And Carmen wanted to get even with Seth through you. She knows you are Seth's weakness," Yolanda explains and sits next to me.

We are silent. I look out of the window and tonight the moon is as bright and beautiful as I have ever seen it.

"I found something interesting," Yolanda says. "It's Dr. Hawthorn's journal." she tosses it on my lap. "I found some disturbing things."

"Like what?" I ask, lifting the journal.

Yolanda takes it from my hands and starts to flip through pages. "'December 14, 1980'," she reads. "'Another child is missing. This is the seventh one to disappear into thin air in the last three months. We have no leads. We don't know who, where, how, or why.

"We had a meeting and we all agree not to involve the police. We don't want them to come here and snoop around, or worse, shut us down. They are unwanted children and no one will miss them." Yolanda looks up. "Nice isn't?" I agree.

"That's not all. 'April 28, 1989.'" Yolanda continues to read.

"Twenty children are missing now, and fifteen members of our staff have committed suicide. They walked up to the west wing with knives in hand, and before they leapt off the balcony, they cut their own throats. I don't know what's happening. None of us has any idea what's going on, and we are scared.'"

"You don't think – whatever was responsible for those events back then is now responsible for what is happening to us now?"

"I don't know," she says, looking up from the journal. "I'm not sure." She gives the journal back to me. "Read."

I look down and read:

September 22, 1989

I don't know if I too am starting to have hallucinations, but I hear things. And see things, the shadow of a black dog.

At night it comes to me. It whispers in my head. It wants me to give it a body of flesh. It wants to be reborn.

I refused his wishes and more people have died. I don't know how long I can last. I'm slowly slipping away.

December 06, 1990

I've done it. I gave the demon a human body – a baby girl. Tomorrow my brother in law will come and take her away from here as that thing wished.

Oh! Poor little baby. Hope God will forgive me for my sins.

"You don't think this baby girl is…" I stop and start to flip through the journal. I look for more logs, but Dr. Hawthorn had stopped writing.

190

"Carmen?" finally she finishes my sentence.

"Seth!" I gasp as a horribly sharp and raw pain emerges in the core of my stomach.

6 contenders remaining

Day Nine

Saturday, August 21, 2010

Selene

I open my eyes and role over onto my right side. I glance at the clock, and in bright red lights it announces that it is way past my usual wake up time. It is exactly nine o'clock. I had trouble falling asleep and once I did, I had horrible nightmares. Dr. Hawthorn's diary, Seth, and Carmen were haunting me in my dreams all night long.

I lift my head up and notice Yolanda has already left. Her bed is neatly made and her pajamas lie neatly folded on the covers.

I yawn, stretch, and make my way to the closet. I don't have much to choose from due to the limited amount of clean outfits. Eight days have passed, and our clean clothes and food supply are quickly becoming scarce. I just hope Tony is wrong. I don't want to be involved in anything other than a game.

I take a deep breath and with that thought I stroll to the bathroom. I open the door and find the room empty. Until now, Maria and Carmen have hogged the bathroom. Yolanda and I were forced to use the Johnson's bathroom most of the time, but now that Maria is gone, the bathroom is back in our control.

Unexpectedly the other bathroom door opens. It's Carmen. She doesn't look too enthusiastic to see me. I feel the same about her.

"Are you going to take long?" she asks in her usual annoyed and arrogant manner.

"Yes," I snap at her. She raises an eyebrow. "I just walked in." I know I promised Seth and Yolanda to keep my distance from the two of them and not to provoke them, but I can't.

She smirks "Don't get too comfortable..."

"Yeah, yeah," I reply and walk toward her. "Go and threaten somebody else for a change." I slam the door in her face and lock it.

Shaken because of what I just did to Carmen Skylark, I jump in the shower. "She'll kill..." I stop. "What the..." I start to say out loud as I discover my left arm wrapped in gauze. I unwind the bandage and find a long, narrow cut running along my arm.

A knock on the bathroom door startles me. "Who is it?" I yell, and hear the door opening.

A vivid black and white movie scene comes to mind, and my imagination runs wild. I expect to be attacked by a giant knife at any moment.

"It's me," Yolanda says.

I let out a deep breath. "Yes?"

"I just wanted to see how far you are. Breakfast is ready and Phillip wants to talk to us about – well – you know – the situation."

"What situation?" I play stupid for Yolanda's sake. She is pretty shaken. No wonder. She spends most of her time with loony Tony. I should stop calling him that. He's a good person, but his stories are starting to get on my nerves, and Yolanda is becoming more and more paranoid. She is splitting her time between me and Tony.

I just don't understand her. She told me she didn't have any true feelings for him and yet she wraps herself around Tony like a koala bear in a eucalyptus tree.

I begin laughing as that comical image forms in my mind.

"What's so funny?" Yolanda asks.

"Nothing. I'll be right there."

"Would you mind telling Seth for me?"

"Sure. No problem," I tell her.

"Thanks."

"Yolanda," I call after her, wanting to show her my arm. Maybe she has a clue as to what happened to me.

"Yes."

"Never mind." I decide not to ask her. She is already too uneasy. I can't put more stress on her. I'll talk to Seth.

"Ok then. I'll see you in a bit."

I quickly jump out of the shower, brush my teeth, comb my hair, and get dressed. Before going to call my brother, I rewrap my wound and cover it underneath a long sleeved shirt. At the last moment I decided to keep my injury to myself. I don't want to worry my brother even more. Hastily I make my bed and throw all my stuff into my closet.

I enter Seth's room, and to my surprise find that his bed is made. Correction, it's untouched. His dirty clothes are still lying on the floor and the medical book he was reading the day before is in the same exact spot on the bed where he left it.

I pick up the book and, to make sure that I'm not just panicking for nothing, I open it. My heart sinks. The bookmark rests at the end of chapter four. It's the same chapter Seth was reading the day before. I look across his bed and discover Seth's notebook sitting on the nightstand. I open it. His last log was yesterday morning.

Now I start to panic. My heart is pounding and my body is shaking. I can't lose Seth. What will I do without him? Who will keep me sane in case I lose myself in a vision? Who will be there to guide me back to reality? Who will protect me? And who will save Mom and Dad's ranch?

I begin to pace the room, trying to calm myself and find a reasonable solution.

Then an idea comes to me. Seth may have slept in someone else's room. After yesterday's confession he was pretty much tired of everyone and everything in this house. Seth is a great person and tends to get along with everyone, but I noticed that the more time he spends with these people, the more he wants to be alone. I think the show is getting to him too.

Truth be told, the show is getting to me too. I don't know what's real and what's not anymore. No wonder, between Tony's stories, Phillip's claims, Yolanda's visions and the many sleepless nights I've had – I'm lost too.

Tired of reflecting on my problems, I begin walking from room to room in search of Seth. I paused to look through everyone's belongings. Maybe someone has found the money or clues.

Finding nothing and unable to locate my brother, I decide to look for him downstairs.

At the bottom of the stairs, I hear the voices of Phillip, Yolanda, Tony and Carmen coming from the living room. I guess they just finished breakfast and, unexpectedly, my stomach starts to grumble. I pat my stomach, hoping it will calm down.

I stride into the dining room and find the table empty. They must have cleared it, I think. I enter the kitchen.

There on the countertop I find pancakes, muffins, bacon, eggs, and toast waiting for me. My mouth waters, and I grab a plate.

I begin to eat and glance at the four dirty plates sitting by the sink. Three people weren't present for breakfast today. One was me. What about the others?

Unexpectedly, I feel something beneath my foot. Looking down, I see a chess piece. My heart drops. I pick it up and slowly read my brother's name carved into the base of the piece. Distraught, I begin walking to the others, bringing with me the terrible news.

Phillip

Breakfast is quite strange today. Everyone is so civil and silent. Normally we can't wait to go off on each other.

"Where's the rest of the crew?" I ask looking around the table. William, Seth, and Selene are missing.

"Selene is getting ready," Yolanda replies. "She'll come down with Seth."

"They don't usually get up this late." I continue with small talk while watching each of their movements. So calm and secure, yet their eyes show fear.

"It's getting to them too," Yolanda states. "More bacon?"

I shake my head. "No, thanks." I turn my attention to Carmen, who is playing with her food. "Where's your other half?" I ask, and Carmen's face contorts at my joke.

196

"None of your business."

I smile. "I think at this point it is our business to know where everyone is."

Tony and Yolanda agree with me. With a sour face Carmen says, "He's sleeping – at least that's what he was doing half an hour ago when I walked into his room."

"Are you sure he was sleeping and not pretending to sleep in order to avoid you," I continue, teasing her. I can't help it. I just love making her mad. It really turns me on.

"Screw you," she grunts and I keep smiling.

"Coffee – tea?" Tony asks as he looks around the table.

"No, thanks," I tell him.

"Coffee, please," Yolanda smiles, and extends her cup towards him. He smiles at her and begins to pour the hot liquid into her cup. I notice a distant look in Yolanda's eyes. I glance over at Carmen and see the same thing in her eyes as well. I know what they're thinking, because I share the same thoughts:

"Who is this mysterious guest? Is she friendly? Is she an actor hired by the show?"

"Who is the mole?"

"Who is the next to go?"

"Is this still part of the show or are Tony's stories coming true?"

"I need to win. I want to win."

"Where the hell is the money?"

"Did one of us find the money and if so – who?"

"I'm going crazy. This place drives me insane. I need to get out of here as soon as possible."

"Could you pass the syrup," Carmen politely asks Yolanda, who complies without a nasty comment or frown. Happy to pass her the syrup. Yep, the four of us are acting completely normal, as if nothing gruesome is happening around us.

Carmen looks up and I wink at her with a dazzling smile.

She shakes her head and fixes me with her most evil glare. I smirk and glance out the window. The sky is gray today. The clouds are thick and dark. Heavy wind rattles the windows. The atmosphere seems to be gloomier than ever.

I clear my throat, "Now that we are done with breakfast, I think we should discuss who the mole could be."

"What?" Tony gasps. "Shouldn't we wait for the others? And I thought you didn't believe in an infiltrator after…"

"Raul's disappearance?" I conclude. Tony nods. "I've changed my mind." I continue to explain. "There is no way someone could have survived eighteen years without food or water."

"She might have survived on rats or ravens and rain water." once again Tony has come up with one of his ridiculous theories. I swear, if I wasn't so set on the Holloways, Tony would probably be my number one suspect. For the moment he is in second place. "It sure rains a lot here," Tony concludes. The two girls are still cringing at the thought of someone eating rats and ravens.

"You can believe in ghosts or hauntings or forgotten patients still roaming around or any other fairytale you can think of. I – on the other hand, believe in facts – real facts." I watch Tony's joyful face turn sour. "I believe the Holloways are working for the show."

"No way. It's preposterous," Yolanda snaps, and slams her hand on the table in protest.

"And why not?" Carmen smirks.

"What do you mean 'why not?'" Yolanda questions. Then she turns her eyes to me. "Carmen and William could be working for the channel. They're – mediocre actors but…"

"Hey!" Carmen objects.

"They would be more likely to work for the show," Yolanda continues. She turns back to Carmen, "William has pretty much screwed up his and your careers," she says. I watch Carmen's nostrils flaring. I'm expecting her to breathe fire at any moment. "You're pretty desperate to regain your status and would do anything…"

"You little…" Carmen stands up.

"Look!" I raise my voice and draw everyone's attention. "To me, every one of you is a suspect," I confess. "I don't trust any of you."

"Ouch! That hurts," complains Tony.

I glare at him. I've been trying to explain my point of view for the last ten minutes and keep getting interrupted. "As I've been trying to say," I grunt, "Seth and Selene were witnesses to the disappearances…"

"As were we all." Once again I've been interrupted by Yolanda.

"Not like them. On the night Matt disappeared, Seth and Selene were together, and another thing, they were never as scared as the rest of us.

"On the day Raul was taken, Seth and Selene magically appeared right after he vanished. And the voice of this mysterious girl, it sounds a lot like Selene."

"Oh, Please," Yolanda says and stands up. "I've had enough of these false accusations, but before I leave, I just want to state that Selene and Seth are not involved with the TV station or with what is happening around here. They're innocent."

"And are you sure?" I ask.

"Yes," she says with certainty. "And I, too, am very unsure about the rest of you." She looks around the room and settles her gaze on Tony. This shocks me. I thought they were pretty close, but yesterday's show might have pushed Yolanda away from him.

Yolanda walks out with Tony right behind her.

I turn my attention back to Carmen. "Here we are once again. Just you and me." I smile at her, forgetting about Yolanda, Tony, and the mole.

"Will you drop it!" she snaps at me. "I've told you over and over, you have no chance with me."

"What can I do to change your mind?"

"A complete make over."

"Ouch," I tell her. I don't know why I'm so attracted to her. I just know that I want her. "I'm way better looking than William." I continue. "You might just discover that I'm the one you've been looking for all along."

"Oh, Please!" She smiles, and I sense a crack forming in her icy shell. "Get down from your throne, your majesty."

I laugh. Then I stand up, walk towards her, grab her hand, and gently kiss it. She seems pleased, so I move closer and kiss her.

After a long minute she pushes me away. "You're not my type," and walks out.

"Keep telling that to yourself, my dear, but deep inside, your heart is burning for me and your hormones are out of control," I yell after her.

She doesn't stop and I don't want to give up. She will be mine and I decide to follow her into the living room. I guess she is looking for refuge with the others. She must be desperate.

She sits on the couch and I sit next to her. Then she moves to the other side of the room and I follow her. She doesn't know how much she turns me on. The more she rejects, the more I want her. I've always loved the cat and mouse game.

"Will you stop?" She looks past me. I turn and see Selene walk into the room with a chess piece in her hands. She looks up at us with a blank look and says, "It's Seth. He's gone."

"No!" Yolanda gasps and quickly runs over to her. She embraces her friend and whispers something in her ear. Selene nods.

"I…"

"We know," Tony says, "Take good care of her." And with that they leave.

"Damn it!" I shout. "There goes my theory. Or maybe not."

Yolanda

I'm with Selene in our room. She looks devastated and I understand how she feels. A few days ago I also lost someone very important to me, and I still don't know if he is ok.

"What are you thinking?" she asks.

"I don't know how to tell you without you attacking me," I confess. "There is something walking beside William."

"Like what?"

"He has a spirit guiding him."

"And?"

"This spirit is connected to you and him."

"How?"

"Don't know, but I have a strong feeling that it won't take long before we find out. Our time is running out. I feel it and so do the spirits in this house. They're preparing for something big," I explain, and sit next to her. "If something should happen to me…"

"Like what?" she stops me. Selene looks scared and beaten. I grab her hand.

"This morning I woke up down in the basement. Room 125," I explain, and can feel my heart beating faster and faster. "I stood in the middle of a circle drawn on the soil," and show her my wound, a deep cut at the base of my left hand.

She bolts upright and gasps. "What happened?"

"I think – I drew the circle with my own blood," I declare and watch Selene's eyes grow larger. I stand up. I'm unable to stay seated and calm. "The circle I drew wasn't any circle. It was The Key of Solomon, a portal used to summon gods, spirits, and demons."

"What did you summon?"

"I don't know. I don't know!" I cry out loud. I know the consequences. Whoever I freed will come back and hunt me down. It's the punishment for summoning them into our world.

"Yolanda," Selene whispers softly. I turn my eyes to her,

and she gently lifts her shirt up. A long, deep cut on her left arm appears.

"My God! What happened?" I cry. I take her arm and study the cut.

"I don't know. It was there when I woke up this morning."

"It was an athame…"

"A – what?"

"It's a witch's knife. It's used in rituals," I explain. "Your arm was cut by someone using an athame." I look up at her, "You were lucky…"

"Lucky!!!" she snaps and covers her wound. "How?"

"Whoever did this," and I point to her injury, "was very careful not to hurt you badly."

"Why?"

I shake my head. "I don't know," I whisper and stand up. "I have to go."

"Go where?"

"I need to think," I state. Selene says nothing, her eyes locked on me. She's frightened – so am I. "I have to be alone." Before I walk out I add, "I'll see you later. Everything will be fine." I close the bedroom door behind me.

In the hallway I watch in awe as previous lives pass by. They are continuously reliving their past existence life. I see nurses and doctors doing their daily rounds, and patients walking around me. By the stairs a woman with sheets wrapped around her neck is waiting for me to join her. She is trying to say something, but she can't. The sheets prevent any sound from coming out of her mouth.

"I'm sorry," I whisper. "I don't understand."

The woman raises her right arm and points with her finger.

I follow her gesture and see William entering the living room.

"What are you trying to tell me?" I ask, turning my eyes back to the woman. She vanishes.

"No, no! Wait!" I shout, but she's gone. "Damn it," I grunt, and kick the stairs in despair. I'm lost. I have no idea what they want from me, and time is running out.

Angry and stressed I decide to join the others and keep a very close eye on William. I open the door and find him standing in the middle of the room.

"How is she?" he asks.

"She's pretty upset." I walk next to him. "She wants to be left alone." I place Seth's chess piece in his hand. I look in his eyes, and for the first time something about him makes me feel uncomfortable.

He glares at me, and I think he senses my anxiety about him. There is more to William than I had originally thought. But what?

We stare at each other for a few seconds, then I drop my gaze and ask, "What now?" and sit in an empty chair away from the rest of them.

William

The house feels cold and empty, and as I walk into the living room a gloomy mood seems to linger. I look over to Tony and see fear and concern in his eyes. I notice that Yolanda, Selene, Seth, and Phillip are missing.

"Where is everyone?" I ask. Tony says nothing. Carmen remains seated by the bay window and hasn't moved an inch since I walked in. "Hello!!!" I yell trying to attract their attention, "Where is everyone?"

Carmen turns away from the window. "It's Seth," she says, and stops. I watch her, waiting for her to continue.

"He's gone," Tony concludes. I try to appear concerned and sorry, but I can't do it. I'm happy that he is gone. It was about time.

"Don't be so happy," Phillip says from behind me, and pats me on the back.

"I don't know what you're talking about," I grumble, and move away.

"You're the only one in this house who doesn't seem to miss him."

"Why should I? I never liked the guy."

"I didn't care for him either," Carmen confesses. Like that is a shock.

"Try to keep your opinions about him to yourself," Tony cuts in. "Selene is devastated." His last comment causes my mood to deteriorate. I haven't thought of Selene. How could I?

"How is she?" I ask them.

"She's pretty upset," Yolanda says. "She wants to be left alone." She places the next chess piece in my hand. A bishop. "What now?" she asks and sits in an empty chair away from the rest of us.

I sit as well. No one speaks for several minutes. I notice that Yolanda is watching me.

Seconds pass, then minutes and she is still watching me. Unable to tolerate her accusing eyes, I stand up. "I've got to go," I mutter.

"Will. Will," Carmen calls my name. "William."

"What?" I snarl in frustration.

"Don't go to her," she says. "Please."

"I can't deal with you right now," and I run up the stairs. My cheery mood is back. Seth is out of the way, leaving me alone with Selene. Maybe she can help me.

In the distance I hear Selene's violin playing.

I start to follow the melody and find her at the end of the third floor holding her legs tightly. Her head is on her lap. Her violin sits beside her like an old faithful companion. She is sobbing as she rocks back and forth. Seeing her like that breaks my heart. I don't know what to do.

I decide to stay and walk over to her. I sit beside her violin and hold her in my arms. I give her a gentle kiss on the top of her head, and she leans against me. I carefully caress her head. I'm not very good at comforting people. I'm not a people person, and tend to keep my distance when a relationship starts to become more complicated than just two people making out. I always take my leave when I start to care for someone other than myself. And if a girl says those three frightening words, "I love you," I'm gone. But with Selene it's different. I feel a strong bond with her.

Selene lifts her head. Her nose and eyes are red, and her face is sickly pale. I didn't think she would miss her brother that much.

"Feeling better?" I ask her

She nods and whispers, "A bit."

"He's fine. Don't worry."

"This show is starting to get to me," she whispers. "In fact, it's starting to get to most of us. Even Carmen, the winter queen."

"What?" I ask in amusement, knowing very well how cold Carmen can be.

"The winter queen. That's what Seth, Tony and Yolanda call her," she replies looking away from me.

"What did she do to deserve that name?"

"She is very beautiful," she explains, "and also very cold, hard and self-centered."

"She wasn't always like that," I explain. "Her real father killed himself."

"What?"

"She was three years old when she discovered her father's body hanging from the light fixture in his office. He killed himself.

"According to Carmen he lost millions in a movie production and couldn't stand to see everything slipping away from him.

"A few months later, Carmen's mom re-married her lover, who was Carmen's dad's best friend."

"No way," she gasps like a little girl. I smile. She is a breath of fresh air, filling me with joy and excitement.

"Way," I tease her. "Carmen caught her mom and Mr. Smith going wild in the garage. The car was bouncing up and down, her mom was screaming, 'Yes, yes,' and Mr. Smith was grunting like a hog."

"You're joking."

"No, I'm not," I tell her, raising my right hand as in an oath. "Carmen told me that, and it's one of the few things I believe coming from her mouth."

"Why did you call him Mr. Smith?"

"That was the first thing he told me, 'Boy, my name is Mr. Smith and you shall call me by that name. You are not my son nor are you related to me. You are here out of the goodness of my and Mrs. Smith's hearts. Do you understand?' I nodded and later that evening Carmen came to my room and told me that she, too, wasn't allowed to call him anything but Mr. Smith."

"What about her mom?"

"What about her?"

"Does she have to call her husband Mr. Smith as well?"

"No. She has permission to call him by his first name – Rupert," I explain. Selene's nose wrinkles up in dislike at the mention of Mr. Smith first name. "Except when they are having sex. 'Yes, yes, Mr. Smith, yes,' she screams his name out loud," I explain and watch as she blushes.

"Are they that loud?" she asks.

"No, not really." I flash an impish smile. "Carmen and I used to sit in front of their bedroom door."

"That's sick."

"Let me finish," I plead. "Mr. and Mrs. Smith had sex every Friday evening, and Carmen and I were not allowed to leave the house unless…"

"You snuck out."

"Exactly," I tell her and abruptly push her down to the floor with my upper body. I lay my head on her chest and can hear her heart galloping. Gently, she caresses my head and I start to kiss her shirt. An odor of lavender and vanilla enters my nose. The smell is cozy, and a warm sensation fills my body.

I lift my head and stare at her beautiful face. She smiles, and I move my lips closer to her ear. "I like you a lot."

She turns her head and whispers, "Me too."

Thrilled, I move closer to her lips until she stops me.

"Why not?" I ask her in frustration. I want her, and it drives me crazy being this close to her and unable to touch her to show how much I care for her.

She pushes me away and sits up on the floor.

"I need to know," she says in a soft tone, "are you pretending to like me?"

"What? No. Why do you ask that?"

"Seth," she says, and my blood starts to boil. "And Yolanda."

"What did she say?" I snap and take another deep breath.

"She told me that every girl you dated either committed suicide or vanished," she says, her bright eyes studying my face. "Why?"

I snort. "There's nothing…" Selene unexpectedly grabs my shirt and pulls me forward to kiss me. My heart starts racing and I'm unable to control myself. I push her back down on the floor and open her shirt. I begin to kiss her neck and move down to her breasts.

"William!" she cries, and attempts to push me away. But I persist. "William!!!" she shouts, and pulls my head up by my hair. "I have an idea," she says and my heart stops. It's not Selene's voice. It's Carmen's voice. "I want this one. I need her."

I sit upright, knowing all too well where this is going.

"No," she says with my voice. "I'm done. I told you I wouldn't do it anymore."

Selene moves towards me and runs her fingers along my neck, the same way Carmen used to. "Please, Will. Just for me," and kisses my lips. It's hard for me to resist her. I'm pretty turned on. "I need her."

"I can't. I won't," she says in my voice and my desire for her evaporates. It's a bit creepy hearing my voice coming from a mouth I just kissed.

"It will be simple and easy. It will be a piece of cake,"

Selene smiles, exactly like Carmen. "I'll play the jealous, hurt and betrayed girlfriend while you play the self-centered, arrogant boyfriend who is totally in love with this girl. Once she falls in love with you," Selene smiles, "You bring her to me and…"

"No. No more. I'm done. I can't."

"Oh, Will," she pleads. She kisses the base of my neck. "You owe me. I need you to do this for me – for us. You want to be happy, famous and rich, don't you?"

Suddenly Selene stands up. Her face is once again covered with tears.

I stand up as well and step beside her. "I…"

"You lied to me," she murmurs. "I trusted you!!!" she slaps me across my face.

Furious, I grab her by her shoulders and push her against the window. "Did your vision show you how I told Carmen I wouldn't play her stupid games anymore? I like you Selene. I mean it."

"It's too late for that," she says and tries to free herself, but I refuse to let her go. "Get away from me," She cries.

"Please, Selene. Let me explain," I beg. "Eight years ago I was diagnosed with leukemia. I had no chance of survival. I was too thin and weak. I've been that way since the day I was born." Selene's body starts to relax, and I loosen my grip on her shoulders. "Carmen came to me one day offering long life and happiness for my loyalty.

"At first I thought she was making fun of me and my situation until she showed her true self." I look down at her. "She was frightening and she showed me what she can do – who she really is.

"Initially I rejected her offer, but as death came closer, I pledged myself to her. Days, weeks, months and years went by. I became a monster, doing everything she asked me to do, except, hurting you, or even allowing her to hurt you."

"And you expect me to believe that?" Selene asks. She turns

around to face the window.

"I'm asking you to give me a chance, and yes, I'm asking you to believe me," I state. "Not long ago you asked me to believe your story and I did. Your brother. Seth…"

"What about him!!!"

"He and Carmen made a pact…"

"No. He didn't. It's not true."

"He did. She told me so and to get even with him for breaking their agreement…"

"She wanted you to hurt me," Selene interrupts and I nod. "No. He wouldn't. He couldn't."

"Listen to me," I tell her and pull her closer to me. Selene pushes me aside and walks away. "Selene!" I call her name, but she doesn't stop.

Frustrated, I start to throw things around.

My sister barges in. "I told you not to lie to her."

"Not now," I snap at her.

"She'll forgive you," she continues. "She will."

I look down at Alice. She smiles at me. "Here," she says and offers me a glass with something purple in it. "Drink it. I made it for you."

"I'm not in…"

"Please – for me," she begs. Just like the good little brother that I am, I can't deny my sister's request.

"All right," I tell her and take the glass from her hands. Alice smiles joyously.

I toss the juice down and all of a sudden my throat starts to burn. Then my stomach. I collapse on the floor.

"What's happening?" I gasp for air.

"There, there," I hear Alice's whisper next to my ear. Her cold hand is caressing my face. "Everything will be fine."

Carmen

Late in the evening, I find William sitting at the bottom of the stairs. He is watching Tony like a hunter. I know what that look means.

"What are you thinking?" I ask as I sit next to him. He shrugs his shoulders and continues his silent vigil. He seems disappointed to see me.

A little voice in my head shouts:

What are you doing still chasing after him? He's yours. Just take him.

No. I can't, I tell the voice. *He'll hate me.*

So? You gave him all that he wanted. A home, a career, fame, money and security and all you asked for in return is his unconditional love. Isn't that a fair deal?

Without a word, William stands up and leaves.

"Do you really hate me that much?" I ask, trying to hold in my tears of anger. I don't want him to think that they are tears of grief. I don't want to give him that satisfaction. "Will," I call after him, "Will. William," but he keeps walking away without responding. He is so cold and so distant from me.

I wipe my tears, and am surprised to see Phillip Stewart approaching me. He has that smile that used to rub me the wrong way, but Phillip and his rude mannerisms have started to grow on me. I'm not sure I want that.

Phillip sits next to me and says, "You should let him go."

"Why?"

"To be with me."

I laugh out loud. He looks at me the way I want William to do. He is so full of lust for me. It comforts me and restores my abused ego.

"And what can you offer me?"

"A life in which you can be yourself. A life without expectations," he says, and leans against me. "Let him go and be mine." He shoves one hand under my shirt, and the other slips between my thighs.

"No, wait. Not here," I pant, and gently push him away.

Phillip steps back to compose himself. He says, "I know the perfect spot where we can be alone." He smiles.

"No!" I snap. I try not to look flattered, excited or pleased. It's nice to be wanted so passionately. It has been so long since any man has wanted me the way Phillip does.

"Why not?"

"You and Maria. Me and William."

"There is no Maria and me. I broke off the engagement before we came to this island, and I broke off our relationship before she left the house. As for you and William," he nods his head towards one of the rooms behind me. I turn and see William talking to Selene.

"There is no more you two." He grabs my hand and pulls me closer to his chest. "There is only us." By the time he finishes his sentence I'm sitting on his lap. And I thought I was the master of making-out. I guess I was wrong. Phillip is THE Master. No wonder women can't stay away from him or keep their hands off him. The thought of his lean, muscular body being so close to mine, causes me to begin breathing heavily Phillip notices. He lifts me up and carries me to his room.

It's almost dusk and the weather hasn't improved yet. I grab my shirt from the floor and put it on.

"Where do you think you're going?" Phillip is watching me from the bed.

I feel confused about my actions, and regret what we did. I want to leave this place as soon as possible.

"I have to go," I mumble, and start to put my clothes on.

"No, you don't." He gets up and steps toward me. Childishly, I look away from his naked body.

What's wrong with me? I've never felt this way before and

it drives me nuts acting like a wallflower. It's not me. I'm strong, self-centered, and most of all, secure.

"You stay right here with me. In fact, I think you should move in with me," he smiles, and embraces me. I tremble and throw my hair back. I take two steps away from him.

"They're watching us," I tell him, and point at the cameras covered by the towels Phillip threw over them just after we entered his room.

"Not all the time." He kisses me on the lips.

"May I ask you something?"

"You may," he says, and moves over to the bed pulling me down with him.

"What are you going to do after the show? You know – you and Maria."

"I told you before. There is no Maria in my life. Only you," he smiles. "I might move to LA. I might be around you if – you – want me?" He states and my hearts begin to flutter like the hummingbird. I nod and say nothing.

"You don't have to give me an answer now," Phillip continues and pushes me down on the bed. We start to kiss me when the door opens.

"Have you seen…" The voice startles us. We find William standing before us.

Quickly, I button my shirt and zip up my pants.

"May I help you?" Phillips says in an amused tone of voice.

William smiles. He doesn't look angry or upset or disappointed. That hurts me. It's obvious he doesn't care about me anymore. I grab my shoes, shove William aside, and I walk out of the room.

"Carmen! Carmen!" I hear Phillip calling my name. I don't stop until I reach my room. I slam the door and lock it tight.

I start sobbing. It's a mixture of anger, disappointment, misery, and most of all, homesickness.

Phillip knocks at the door, "Please. Let me in." he pleads

with me for a few minutes, but when I don't open the door, he leaves.

The room turns quiet and I continue to sob. Angry and hurt, I decide to take Selene out. She will be my next victim. I always intended her to be, but Seth was in my way. Now that he's gone, no one can stop me.

I stick my hand beneath my mattress and pull my knife out. It is so beautiful, and the blade is nice and sharp. Perfect for cutting that little brat's throat.

"I don't think so," a voice whispers in my ear. Someone places a hand over my mouth and wraps an arm around my upper body.

Azazel, I think to myself, and hear him laughing.

"Hello, sister," he says. "Glad that you still remember me. Life as a human made you weak and pathetic." He kisses my cheek. My body begins to tremble in fear. I was sure he was dead. How is this possible?

"You thought I was dead," he smiles. "You became careless, much too human. It is quite sickening, and most disturbing of all, you fell in love with a hunter." He kisses the base of my neck. "It is time for you to go, and time for me to re-conquer what once was mine.

"Five little trespassers are having fun. One little trespasser is not," he says, and tears begin to fall down my face. My time is up. I don't want to leave. Who will protect my William? I wish I could tell him just one more time that I love him.

"And now there are five little trespassers left," he concludes and moves his hand away from my mouth and places it on my throat. My heart pounds furiously. "Bye – bye, sweetheart," he whispers in my ear and kisses me goodbye on my lips. Then he tightens his grip around my throat and…

Tony

What's this? I ask myself as I watch Phillip sneaking into the living room with Seth's chess piece. He seems tense and keeps glancing around him.

To my joy, he hasn't discovered me yet; I'm hidden behind a thick veil of shadows in the long, dark hallway.

I decide to follow him, and as I peek around the corner, I discover Phillip closing the secret door behind the painting.

I contemplate whether I should go after him or wait until he comes out. I decide to wait.

I walk out of the room, and at the bottom of the stairs I find William intently staring at me. He looks ready to pounce on me at any moment.

I nod to him as I walk past. He doesn't reply to my gesture, except to appear a notch angrier.

Yep, he is going to kill me, I say to myself. I keep walking. He knows I was responsible for yesterday's incident. He knows I was the one who convinced Carmen to slip his mother's ring into Selene's hand.

I see Carmen coming down the hall. She begins to study us. I watch her gaze move back and forth between us. Then she sits down next to him.

Quickly, I move away from them. I have an odd feeling that I'm in deep trouble, and I probably should steer clear of William.

In the kitchen I pour a glass of water and start to drink it when William's reflection on the window startles me.

I turn around. "You scared the….." and William grabs me by the throat and shoves me against the wall. I drop my glass, and it shatters on the floor.

"I thought I made it clear not to harm Selene," he snarls in my ear. His grip grows tighter around my neck. I didn't know William had such a dark side.

"I don't know what you're talking about," I gasp.

"Don't play stupid with me." He looks up at the cameras, suddenly remembering that we are not alone. The cameras are my only life line.

"It – was – Carmen's – idea."

"Don't worry about her. I'll take good care of her," he promises, and releases me. I drop to my knees and start to gasp for air. "I warned you to stay away from her," he tells me, and I stare at him like an idiot as he walks out.

"Damn it!!!" I shout, and pound my fist on the floor. I need her. How am I supposed to do my job without her? "Damn it. Damn it. Damn it!" I keep repeating over and over as I punch the floor in frustration.

Tired and sore, I decide to go look for Phillip. Soon I will figure out a way around William. No one will keep me from my goals – not even him. Who does he think he is?

I walk out of the kitchen hoping not to bump into William again. He is menacing, and I fear for my safety. Who knew William Hawthorn could turn out to be a threat to me?

Giggles and whispers interrupt my thoughts. I look up and see Phillip and Carmen climbing up the stairs hand in hand. I smile.

Satisfied and now certain to have enough time to explore the maze without being caught by Phillip or the others, I begin my investigation.

The search didn't last long. Phillip hid his chess piece in the first nook, and, to my surprise there were more chess pieces. I take one in my hand and read:

Priscilla

I take another one and read:

Jennifer

Then a piece of paper catches my attention. I bend over and read:

A C S E T O W K E H R

I stare at the paper for a few seconds, contemplating what it means, when one of the chess pieces catches my attention. A thick red letter T branded at its base stands out.

I smile.

"Well, well, well, Phillip," I whisper. "And I thought you were stupid, but you've just proven me wrong. You've just figured out where the clues are, but to my disappointment not the money or where the clues lead to." I start to collect the chess pieces and the piece of paper. I place them in my pockets and quickly run up to my room to hide them.

5 contenders remaining

Day Ten

Sunday, August 22, 2010

Yolanda

That's her. That's the woman I saw a few days ago. The one with the sheets wrapped around her neck. The one who tried to warn me about William or…

I look underneath the picture and read:

Kate Williams

William's mom. I gaze around Tony's room looking for more clues, and a thought comes to mind. What if she wasn't warning me about her son, but instead was asking me for help. Help for her son.

I flip through Kate Williams's files and find her cause of death. Suicide. She hung herself a few weeks after her son, William, was born. Pictures of the scene are tucked away at the back of the folder.

I go through them and notice dozens of porcelain dolls in the corner of her room. I recall Phillip's story. I put the files back and begin to search for him.

"Phillip," I call, seeing him bent over the coffee table writing something. He looks up at me. He seems nervous, anxious and a bit out of his mind.

"Yes?" he grunts.

"Show me where you met the woman," I tell him. He shakes his head in confusion. "The woman you and Raul met a few days ago," I specify.

"Why? What for?"

"I need to make sure this is only part of the show and nothing else," I lie to him. The fact is that I need to go there. My answer lies there. The spirits imprisoned here have been guiding me there from day one, and I was blind not to see it.

"I wouldn't go there if I were you."

"I have to," I assert.

Phillip nods and with a sour face draws me an accurate map to the whereabouts of the room.

I thank him, and without telling anyone where I'm headed, I grab some provisions and a flashlight, and run up to the fourth floor. It's time for me to stand up to my fears. I'm so sick and tired of being scared of my own shadow. I don't want to live like this. I want to enjoy life, and if this is what it takes, so be it.

It takes me an hour to find this hidden room, and it isn't a pleasant experience. The maze is filthy and windy. I'm covered with dust and cobwebs. I spent most of the time stomping insects rather than paying attention to the map Phillip drew. But I'm finally here.

The room is well hidden from the rest of the house. It looks more a playroom than a bedroom. It is filled with old toys, and there is a bed in the middle of the room.

I stroll around the area in hopes of finding something useful. In the furthest corner of the room, underneath a white cloth, something catches my attention.

I toss the flashlight and the backpack on the bed and walk over to the corner. I lift the cloth, and find a perfect replica of the castle. It contains five figurines sculpted exactly like the five of us.

On the first floor there's Phillip writing on a small coffee table in the living room, just like I left him. On the second floor I see Selene's figurine in Carmen's and Maria's room sitting on a bed. I'm wondering what she is doing in there. William's figurine is just outside the room, spying on Selene. Tony's figurine is in the dining room, sitting in front his laptop – as usual. And my figurine is…I look up to the fourth floor, and there it is, sitting on the floor in the exact room, and in the exact spot studying the toy castle as I'm doing right now.

Chills runs through my body. The figurines, the house. Everything is so accurate. I stand up and keep searching. I'm here now, there is no going back.

I open the closet door, drawers, and look underneath the bed. There I discover an old brown leather suitcase. I pull it out and toss it on the bed. Inside I find tons of pictures, paintings, and little knickknacks made by children.

A bracelet made out of paper attracts my attention. I take it and…

"It was made for me," a sweet girl's voice says.

I immediately drop the bracelet back into the suitcase and turn around. A little girl about age of ten with blue eyes and long fine blond hair is staring at me.

"Alice – is that you?" I ask hesitantly, not sure if it is. She nods. "What are you doing in here?"

"Should I not ask you the same question?" she replies. For an instant her pupils glow. I recoil from her. "What's wrong?"

"No – nothing," I reply, keeping my distance.

"You look a lot like your grandmother."

"You know my grandmother?" I ask, and stop moving.

"We've talked," she smiles. "She came here a few months ago with a small group of people. They wanted to see if this place was haunted, and that's when I met her. She is very nice and you look a lot like her."

"I know. Everyone says that."

"You don't sound too happy about it."

"Not only do I look like her, but I share her gift, and that's a lot of weight to carry around," I confess.

"She helped me finally leave this place."

"And now you're back," I state, half amused, knowing very well that she isn't Alice, but someone else.

"Have your fun at my expense, but in the end I'll be the one laughing," she says. I study her as she talks. Something about her feels wrong – strange.

"You're not Alice," I finally say. "You are not even related to William."

"Bravo!" She smiles and claps her hands.

"Who are you?" I ask, and right before my eyes she takes the form of a beautiful Creole woman. "What do you want?"

"Isn't it obvious? I want a body to own," she animatedly explains, and walks towards me. I continue to keep my distance from her. I'm afraid that mine might be the body she desires to have. "I want to feel the warmth of a man standing beside me. I want to taste and dance and touch everything. I want to live once more," she continues and my heart starts to race. "Don't worry," she smiles. "It's not your body I desire, but Selene Holloway's."

"Selene?" I repeat and she nods. "Why her?"

She bursts into laughter. "Haven't you figured it out by now? This show is a trap for Selene."

"What?" I gasp.

"The spirits in this house have been trying to warn you. They have been trying to tell you, but you were too blinded by Tony Roma." She continues to laugh.

"But why?"

"I can't let you or anyone else spoil what I've worked so hard for. The full moon is just two days away, and I'll have your little friend's body by then," she says. Before I can respond, the apparition disappears.

I grab my things and decide to run to Selene. I need to warn her. I need to tell her what I have found out. I need to help her, but suddenly the door slams and locks.

"Let me out of here!!!" I shout. I start to kick and pound on the door. "Help! Help!" I continue to scream, but no one answers. My only hope is Phillip.

Phillip

"Who is it...? Who is it...? Who is it...?" I keep murmuring to myself over and over.

There are only five of us and I can't believe that they're all losers, except for me and William, of course.

I never thought Tony, Yolanda and Selene would get this far. The show must be rigged. There is no way they could have lasted this long without outside help or without working for the show. The "Guest" must be one of them.

I was sure that William, Carmen, Seth, Maria and I would be the final five, but I guess that's not to be the case, unless…I stand up. I begin searching for a pen and piece of paper.

"Ah! There they are," I say, and walk to a small side table where a memo pad and pencil sit. I grab them and start to write our names on the pad:

William Selene Yolanda Tony Me

Then I stare at the names and notice the original groups have been split up and new ones have emerged. I quickly cross my name out. I know that I'm not the mole.

William Selene Yolanda Tony ~~Me~~

Now to the hard question. Who is the mole?

I start to consider each name, and absently chew on the pencil. An old habit of mine. It helps me relax and think.

"Phillip," someone calls my name. I look up and Yolanda is there.

"Yes?" I grunt. I turn my note pad over, not wanting her to see what I'm doing.

"Show me where you met the woman," she demands. I'm confused. What woman is she talking about? "The woman you and Raul met a few days ago," she explains. Now I'm even more confused than before.

"Why? What for?"

"I need to make sure this is only part of the show and nothing else," she says. I'm not sure if she's telling me the truth or not.

"I wouldn't go there if I were you."

"I have to," she asserts. At this particular moment I really don't care. I'm a bit busy, and I want keep working on my plan.

I tear a piece of paper from the pad and draw an accurate map to the room. I hand it to her. She thanks me and leaves.

Where was I again? Oh, yes. Right. I turn my notepad back over. I continue with William. He is a very quiet person and many people have warned me about quiet people.

"They are like ticking bombs," my old buddy back home, James, used to say every time he crossed paths with Ben, our weirdo at Mountain High. "They can go off at any moment." He was right. Three years ago he walked into our school, placed small bombs along the walls and detonated them.

Imagine the shock and joy we experience the next day when we went to school, and found large chunks of cement scattered throughout the building!

The police, fire department and TV Stations were all over the place, and for a whole week Allegan County was the talk of the world.

A month later Ben Bedeck was arrested, and convicted a year after that.

Sometimes I think if he hadn't blown up the school, I would have never met Maria, and my life would probably be much less stressful.

~William~ ~Selene~ Yolanda Tony Me

I cross out William's and Selene's names. I don't think either of them is the mole. William is quiet, but not strange like Ben, and Selene is both quiet and strange, but not as weird as Ben.

Now the others. They are quite vocal and pretty irritating to everyone else. I go over the events that happened since day one, and I'm convinced that the mole must have an accomplice. There is no way one individual could have done all this alone. And then a revelation hits me.

Yolanda's cousin disappeared on day three, and Tony's brother on day one. This would make it easy for the accomplice among us to distract everyone while the other collects us, one by one. My gut tells me that Tony is the mole. It must be him.

There is no way Raul would have been able to collect us. He is not strong enough. Tony has been on our backs from day one, brainwashing us about this place being haunted.

~~William~~ ~~Selene~~ ~~Yolanda~~ Tony Me

I cross Yolanda's name out and confidently believe Tony is the mole. To make sure my suspicions are correct, I sneak into Tony's room.

It is very clean and everything is neatly in place. I open his closet and find his clothes folded and tucked away.

I begin to search his room and discover something hidden beneath his clothes that take my breath away, a large plastic zipper bag filled with my chess pieces. The pieces I put so much effort into collecting.

"Holy Shhhh…" I shout, and then quickly shut my mouth. How did he find them?

And now what? Where should I hide them? Where? I continue trying to come up with the perfect hiding spot when my eyes stop on Matt's closet. I smile and conceal the figurines inside near the back of the lowest shelf.

Tony will never look for them here. As soon he finds out the chess pieces are missing, he'll search everywhere except for his own room.

If I don't win no one will win, and with that thought, I stroll into the living room. It is time for me to…

I stop as I discover Tony sitting on the couch with my notepad in his hands. He is reading it, and I start to realize that I forgot to rip out the page. What now?

"What's this?" Tony asks.

"What's what?" I pretend I don't know what he's talking about. I walk over and snatch the pad from his hand.

"Why did you circle these names and mine is the only one not crossed out?" he asks.

"I was trying to figure out who the mole is."

"Again with the mole?"

"Yes, and it's you," I confess. Tony starts to laugh.

"Me? How?" he asks. As I'm about to explain, Selene walks in. "Selene," Tony calls. "Have you heard the latest news?"

"No, what?"

"According to Phillip I'm the mole." He starts to laugh again.

"And?" she says seeming very indifferent.

"What do you mean, 'And?'" before Selene can answer, I start to explain why I suspect Tony. As I finished my account, Tony looks amused. Selene's face turns grave.

Tony stops laughing when he notices Selene's face.

"Selene," he says and smiles at her. But when she doesn't reply his face turns sour. "You can't tell me that you believe his bizarre story?"

Selene hesitates. "Why not?"

"What?" Tony glares at the both of us. "This is unreal. How can you believe him?" Selene shrugs. "Whatever!" Tony barks at her, and drops back onto the couch.

Tony

I can't believe she believes him! I thought for sure she would be on my side, but I was wrong. Then again, after what I did to her last night…Yolanda has stopped talking to me. She is avoiding me. I screwed up big time.

"Well," Phillip says as he stands up, "it was fun and all, but it's becoming a bit boring." He leaves the room.

"I can't believe you really believe his crazy accusations!" I utter as soon as Selene and I are alone.

"He has a good point," she answers, and looks around the room. "Have you seen Yolanda?"

"What?" I ask, raising my eyebrows. I notice how hard it is for her to talk to me.

"Have you seen Yolanda?" she repeats through clenched teeth.

"No, not since you and Carmen…" I stop, not wanting her to go after me the way Yolanda did. "I'm sorry," I tell her. "I apologized to Yolanda, to William and to you."

"Sorry is not good enough," she snaps. "You knew what you were doing and you had Carmen helping you. You knew it would hurt me, and not just physically."

"Yes, I did," I confess. Selene's eyes widen in disbelief. "Yolanda wouldn't help me. Just like you. I was desperate. I'm sorry."

Selene looks around the room, "Yolanda is right. You are a jerk." She snatches a book from the coffee table.

"She said that?" I ask, feeling a twinge of pain in my heart. How could she say something like that?

"I should have known you didn't really like her. You pretended to for your stupid book." She throws the book at me. I dodge it. "You are just like William!" She grabs at other objects lying around the room.

I run behind the couch and hope she'll stop soon, or someone will come to my rescue. But I doubt that anyone will help me. I've pretty much alienated everyone.

More objects fly toward me. I start to wonder if Selene's anger is more toward William than me. I don't know why I have to pay for his mistakes.

I become aware that Selene has stopped throwing things. I carefully peek out from behind the couch and see that I'm alone. The room is empty.

I stand up and look around for Selene. She's gone.

Suddenly the lights snap off, and I can hear a little girl's giggles.

"Four little trespassers are sitting in their rooms. One little trespasser is not," the voice whispers in my ear.

"I did what you asked me to do," I shout back and when I hear no reply I begin to run, but something stops me. My mouth and upper chest are wrapped in heavy, thick tape. I can't breathe, and I start to panic.

I try to fight back, but a small trap door opens beneath my feet, and I tumble into the blackness below.

"And now there are four little trespassers left," the girl sings.

Selene

Angry, frustrated and unable to calm myself, I stop throwing things before I hurt Tony. I'm angry, but not at him.

I'm in a horrible mood today. I couldn't sleep. I kept tossing in my bed, and, when I did manage to sleep, I had nightmares. I dreamt of Carmen feasting on my flesh, and William laughing at the sight of my dismembered body.

William showed me the most disturbing thing about his beloved Carmen. He did this on purpose. He wants my help, like I'm going to give it to him my help after he tried to feed me to that thing.

Demons. Who knew they really existed. I climb the stairs and begin to play with the cross my grandmother gave me before she died.

"Never take it off," she told me on her death bed. "And never leave home."

That was a promise I couldn't keep. I'm here. I left home and I hadn't regretted it, until now. What if she knew something – something bad?

William tried to show it to me, but I stopped him at the last moment. I was too afraid, and now I regret my action.

"That's enough," I tell myself. I'm tired of feeling sorry for myself, and march over to Carmen's room. I'm done running and weeping. It's time for me to stand up and stop depending on others.

I open the door, and to my delight, the room is empty. It appears that she never slept in her bed. On the nightstand, a gold bracelet with some kind of charms draws my attention.

I pick it up and study the object. I want to make sure it belongs to Carmen and not Maria. Inside there is an engraving. It says:

To my beloved Carmen - Love William

I smirk, and my heart shudders as I finish reading those words.

"Bastard!" I want to throw the bracelet against the wall, but I can't. I need it.

I take a deep breath, lock all the doors and pull the curtains shut. I'm now standing in darkness, and ready to begin.

I pull my gloves off and hold Carmen's bracelet in my hands.

Anger, solitude, hunger and jealousy take over my body. The feelings are powerful, and it is so hard to resist them. I need to concentrate. I can't have Carmen's emotions controlling me.

"It's nice to see you again," a masculine voice intrudes upon my thoughts. "How have you been?" Images begin forming around me.

I'm standing in an office surrounded by dark bookshelves filled with thick, old books, family picture frames and some decorative knickknacks. A large, heavy desk stands at one end of the room in front of a large window. A man with dark hair and blue eyes wearing a doctor's coat sits behind the desk on an imposing green leather chair. I move closer and see that the name Dr. Hawthorn is embroidered on his coat.

"I'm quite fine," says a female voice. I turn, and to the other side of the desk sits a younger version of Carmen, smiling at Dr. Hawthorn. "I'm quite pleased with your job," she says. I wonder what she's talking about.

"L.A. is full of easy prey, and my life is quite exquisite," Carmen continues. Dr. Hawthorn smiles and nods his head in agreement. "Congratulations on becoming a dad," she tells him. I can't get over the thought that a demon resides in that cute, little, innocent child's body. Or that a girl of just four years can be so mature. Then again, she is not a cute little human child, but a demon.

Unexpectedly, Carmen turns to me. "Please save William," she cries, and I take a step back. "Save him from my brother."

"What?" I gasp. This has never happened to me. I've never had an intrusion upon my vision, but then again, Carmen is no ordinary person. "Why should I," I snap at her. She appears weak and broken. I don't fear her anymore. "You and he tried to kill me. You wanted to feed on me."

"I'm no different than you," she says. I knit my brows at her bizarre response.

"Yeah, you are."

"You eat meat and I eat meat…"

"I do not eat human flesh," I protest.

Carmen smiles, "You humans are food to us. You are our livestock…"

"Excuse me," I retort. "I'm not cattle."

"To us you are, but I'm not here to defend or explain myself to someone like you." Carmen arises from her chair. "My brother is out, and he is after William and…" she begins walking over to

Dr. Hawthorn, who sits as immobile as a statue. She lifts a picture frame sitting on his desk and holds it up to me. "You."

"Me? What about me?" I ask. Carmen's lips start to move, but no sound comes from her mouth. She and the room fade from view.

I'm back to reality.

"No, no, no," I protest. I need to see more. I need to know more.

I begin to rub the bracelet. Nothing.

I move around the room and touch everything, but nothing happens.

I open the door and decide to sneak into William's room. I should be able to find something there. It has to work.

I step out the door and bump into something hard. I look up and find myself face to face with William.

"Will – iam," I gasp. "I'm – sorry."

"Good morning to you, too," he smiles, rubbing his chest.

"I'm sorry," I repeat. I can feel my heart going pitter-patter again. I didn't realize how much I liked him.

"Are you ok?"

"I'm fine. I'm great."

"You look pale and hot." He takes one step forward. I take a step back. "Are you still mad at me?" he asks. I don't answer, but stay silent. My mind screams, Jerk!!! Jerk!!! Jerk!!!

"I told you how sorry I was and how much I like you," he states, taking me in his arms. "Give me a second chance."

I nod. I just want to be left alone. I want him to go. I need to know more about him and Carmen.

"Will you give me a second chance?" he smiles. Once again I nod. "I won't let you down." He gently kisses my cheek. "Come. Let us go down."

"I – I have to use the bathroom," I lie. He studies my eyes. I smile wanly at him. "Badly," I add, feeling my face turn red.

"I'll wait."

"No. Don't. I'll meet you downstairs."

"All right then." He kisses me again and leaves.

I open my bedroom door as soon as I see him disappear around the corner, and sneak into his room. I begin to search for something very personal and quickly find it. His watch is lying on the nightstand.

Once again I shut the doors and the window. I sit on William's bed and after a few quick, deep breaths, I take my gloves off.

It doesn't take long for images to appear.

I'm standing on the third floor, watching William's sad and helpless face as I leave him. I remember this. It was yesterday, soon after I found out about Carmen wanting to feast on me.

William starts to kick, punch and throw objects around.

"I told you not to lie to her," a pretty little girl says to him. She must be the spirit Yolanda spoke of.

"Not now," he snaps at her.

"She'll forgive you," she continues. "She will. I know it."

He looks down at her. She smiles at him and William smiles back at her. "Here," she says, offering him a glass with some bluish liquid in it. "Drink it. I made it for you."

"I'm not in…" he says with hesitation.

"Please – for me," she begs.

"All right," he tells her and takes the glass from her hands. The girl looks ecstatic.

William places the glass to his lips, and something about that girl's smile sets me off.

"NO!!!" I yell, but he can't hear me. I can't help him.

William collapses to the ground.

"What's happening?" he gasps. The little girl bends over him.

"There, there," she whispers in his ear while gently caressing his face. "Everything will be fine."

I move closer.

"Master," she says and the room starts to vibrate. I look

231

around. "Accept my gift." William's body begins to rise.

"NO!!!" I scream. Once again I wake up, but this time I know what happened. I begin to cry with images of William holding onto his body – fighting for his life.

I open my eyes and my body begins to shake uncontrollably at the sight of William standing in front of me. I wait for him to attack me, to hurt me, or to kill me. Instead he just smiles.

William

Selene moves away from me and slides into the corner. Her eyes are wide open, and I can see the pulse in her neck pounding. She is frightened, and I can see it in her eyes.

"I won't hurt you," I tell her, and move closer to her. Selene tries to run away, but she is trapped. I place my hand on her cheek. "If I wanted to hurt you I would have done it a long time ago." I lift her face up by her chin. I kiss her.

She fights me and tries to push me away.

"Who – who are you? What – what are you?" she stutters as soon I remove my lips from hers.

I smile. "You already know what I am."

"Where's William?"

"He is well taken care of. I give you my word."

"Where is he?" she says and pushes me away.

"Be a good girl and stop fussing," I tell her. "It is most unwelcome."

"What do you want from me?" Selene shouts. I grab her hand and she quickly pulls it away. "Stay away from me."

"Always so stubborn. Always so fiery," I breathe. "I almost forgot how you Holloway women were."

"What?" she gasps. I notice her grandmother's cross peeking out of her shirt.

I smile. Like she can be helped by God, or by her grandmother. It's a bit too late for that.

"I see your grandmother raised you as a Christian," I smile. "Ironic, after all, that you are one of the children of Satan."

"No, I'm not!" she protests.

"Witches, or as you call them in today's society, 'Psychics,' are the devil's children. You have been given the devil's gift."

"I never asked for it. I never wanted it."

"Your ancestors wanted it, and that's why I'm here."

"What do you want from me?" she asks again, her face contorted with rage and disgust.

"I came to collect what is rightfully mine," I declare. "You."

"Me?" she cries in disbelief. I let her draw away. It's not like she can go anywhere. Now that I'm free, there's no place for her to hide.

"Your great-great-grandmother was an ambitious woman. She had a strong thirst for power and knowledge. She wanted it all.

"One night, she invoked me to ask for those gifts. I granted them, and in return she gave me one of her daughters. The seventh child.

"Catherine and her daughters tried to outsmart me by giving birth to only one child every generation. They hoped this would give them enough time to come up with an idea in breaking the contract they made with me. As you see, it didn't work," I smile.

"And – I'm the seventh child?" she asks trembling. What have they done to my queen? She is so weak – so frail. It displeases me.

"Yes," I state.

"I don't care. I'm not coming."

"Enough!!!" I shout, and Selene falls quiet. "Don't be mad at me, but at your ancestors. They knew the price and they knew I would come to collect you. Now, here I am." I smile and open my arms.

"No. I would rather die," she snaps. That fiery temper of the Holloways I came to love is rising. My siblings used to warn me about my devotion to the Holloway women. They said that one

233

day it would bring about my destruction, and it did once, but not this time. I came prepared.

"I know that," I smile, and grab her by her throat. She is so fragile. I could so easily snap her neck.

I start to kiss her face, and the blood vessel on her neck throbs violently. I can't resist her. Damn them all!!! They did this to me. I should kill her, but the thought of not being with her drives me insane. The thought of not touching, not kissing her, gives me pain.

I stop kissing her and, captivated, I begin to study her features.

"Are you going to kill me?" she asks.

"No. You are too important to me."

"What will you do with me?"

"I have big plans for you," I confess. "And I won't hurt you." I release her. "Come," I command and reach out to her.

Selene studies my hand. She is insecure. She would be wise to accept my generosity.

She puts her gloves on and takes my hand. She doesn't realize that her gift won't work on me. I gave it to her.

For now she is defeated, but my victory won't last long. She'll try to find a way out and I'll destroy her hopes, dreams and family if she tries to escape from me.

Back on the first floor, I discover Phillip huddled up in a corner. I walk slowly to him with Selene right behind me. I have her hand and don't intend to release her.

Phillip holds two more chess pieces in his hand. It looks like a rook and a knight.

"Who is it?" I ask, and Phillip jumps.

"Don't do that ever again," he snaps as he takes a few quick breaths.

"Did I scare you?"

"You think?" Phillip responds in a high pitched tone of

voice. He is shaking.

"Sorry," I tell him, but I'm not. "So, who are the latest victims?"

"Carmen," Phillip says. I feel Selene's hand jump.

"Carmen," she gasps and looks over at me.

"And Tony," Phillip concludes.

"Tony too?" Selene gasps one more time. I guess she isn't as excited as I am to be the last couple remaining.

"Yeah," Phillip says, and tries to hide the pieces away in his pocket.

"How? Why?" Selene asks. "Where is Yolanda?"

Phillip says nothing. He is angry, upset and miserable over the loss of Carmen. Who knew he liked her that much? She is not as warm and lovable as he thinks she is.

"Why her? She is great and beautiful and famous and has tons of fans," he says. "The show must be rigged."

"No way," I tell him. He is beginning to lose his temper, and the way he describes my sister is disturbing. She is not great or beautiful. She is pitiless and cold blooded. "She has an awful temper, and she doesn't have that many fans."

"Like you are any better," Phillip retorts. We begin swearing and threatening each other.

Selene tries to hold me back while simultaneously trying to calm us down.

"Screw you all," Phillip shouts at the end, and walks away.

"That was great," I announce and kiss Selene on the lips. "I didn't know I could already do it."

"Do what?"

"Instigate humans," I smile at her. "They are so easy and fun to manipulate."

"What did you do to Yolanda?"

"Nothing. I didn't touch her," I tell her. It's true, I didn't touch her.

"What about Carmen and the others?"

235

I pull Selene away from the hall. "Carmen is dead…"

"What?" she gasps, and stops following me. "How could you? She was your sister."

"What did you want me to do? She was about to kill you. I had to do something. I wouldn't let her hurt you."

"What about the others?"

"They are fine, as long you do what I tell you to."

"Like what?"

I smile, "Obey me." I take her hand and drag her into the living room. There is so much I want to know about this new century. There is so much I want to know about the new human race.

4 contenders remaining

Day Eleven

Monday, August 23, 2010

Yolanda

Restlessly, I look up at the ceiling and, hear the sweet laughter of a girl entering the room.

"All right, you had your fun. Let me out of here," I demand.

"I can't," she says with a sad smile.

"Why not?"

"You'll go to your friend and I can't allow that. I need her body." She walks around the room inspecting everything. "Do you know this was supposed to be the room of our child?"

I shake my head. "So, you are Dahlia?" I ask, and she nods. Then, right before my eyes, she takes the shape of the beautiful woman I saw the day before. "Is my cousin all right?"

"They are all fine," she replies with a kind smile. "They are unharmed and still believe this is part of the show."

"So, everyone is fine?"

She hesitates, "Except for Carmen."

"What happened?"

"My master took her life."

"What? Why?" I gasp. I feel my body quivering.

"I can't tell." She seems agitated. "Tony was the latest candidate to leave," she quickly adds, indicating that she wants to change the subject.

I'll go along with her – for now.

"I really don't care that much for him anymore. He used me," I protest, and lay back on the bed.

"Don't be angry at him. He is a very tenacious man. He wants to find out what had happened a few years ago."

"What did happen?" I ask.

Dahlia remains silent. She sits at the end of the bed, glaring at the floor.

"I tried to save her, but she wouldn't come to me."

"Who?"

"Alice," she says. "She found her mom's body dangling

from the ceiling of her room."

"Her mother hung herself in Alice's room."

"No, no, no," she scolds me. "Kate hung herself in her own room. In here. Up there," and points up.

I look up and discover a beam. "Visitors bring dolls for Kate. They think it might help her deal with the loss of her son, William. Some say that she is still wandering the castle, looking for her son."

"Is she?"

"You tell me. You're the psychic." I say nothing. I just nod my head. "One night, Alice snuck into her mother's room. She was worried about her. Alice hadn't seen her mother for days and she heard rumors that she was very sick. So she came up here and found her mother's body swinging back and forth, from the ceiling."

"Poor little thing," I gasp, and place my hand over my mouth. I can't imagine how she must have felt. It must have been so horrible for her.

"She lost her mind," Dahlia continues. "Alice walked into the kitchen and took a knife and…"

"She killed them." I whispered unable to believe the account.

Dahlia nods, "One by one. She had lost her brother, her mother, and she hated this place. Oh, How much she hated this place. She wanted to leave and, as you know, no one leaves from here, not even the dead."

"So, it was Alice. But why? How?"

"This place took everything from her. She wanted to punish them all for their sins and their wickedness."

"What did they do to her?"

"Horrible things. I can't mention them. It breaks my heart just to think about it. "

"It was you. You were behind the death of the staff and the disappearances of the children," I declare. She nods. "What did you do to the children?"

"I took them to a better place. To a place where they could be happy for eternity," she says. For some strange reason, I believe her. "I wanted to help Alice, but she wouldn't come. She wanted to stay here for her brother and mother, but when she lost them…"

"Where is she now?"

"She rests in peace beneath the castle. I gave her a proper burial. It was the least I could do for her."

"How – did she die?"

"She drowned. She tried to leave the island by swimming away, but it was too far for her and the current was too rough," she explains. A tear trickles from one of her eyes. "Two days later I found her little body on the beach," she concludes, wiping the tear from her cheek.

"And all this time I thought Carmen was behind everything."

"Carmen?" she smiles. "Not her. She is too self absorbed. She used my wrath as a diversion to escape from this island."

"What do you mean?" I ask, and once again she doesn't answer. She won't tell me. Fine. I'll try another way to find what I want to know. "So, what's your story?" I ask. Dahlia smiles.

"My story," she says and stands up. "I'm just a servant. I live to serve my Lord."

"Who is your Lord?"

"I can't tell you," she says and I'm tired of her game. I drop back on the bed. "I came to this island in love and I was four months pregnant when John's brother poisoned me, my husband and my unborn child," she continues, "Do you know what the craziest thing was?" I shake my head. "I wasn't afraid of dying. I remember how angry I was and how much I wanted to make them suffer for what they did to me, and then he came."

"Who?" I ask, raising my upper body in order to face her.

"My Lord," she smiles at me. "He told me that vengeance is engaging and he could help. I had to give myself to him and he would give himself to me."

"And?"

240

"And, I did. He gave me the power to destroy them one by one. Slowly and painfully, like the bastards they were."

"And you are happy to have given your soul to him."

"Yes," she confirms. "He gave me everything and more. He is now free."

"Yes, I know, with my help," I snap, and show her my hand. "And Selene's. Why did you need her blood?"

Dahlia smiles, "Her ancestress, Cut Throat Lilly, was responsible for my Lord's imprisonment on this island. I needed her blood to free him and I needed your body for the ritual.

"Psychics are very easy to manipulate. That's how I was able to leave the island and set up this trap for Selene, Carmen and William. I have to thank your grandmother for her unwilling help."

"Is she all right?" I raise my voice.

Dahlia smiles. "She's fine. Don't worry." I relax. I have to find a way out of here. I need to find Selene, and with her help we can stop them. "I know what you're thinking," Dahlia interrupts. "You won't be able to save your friend or stop my Master." She laughs and disappears.

I stand up and cross the room. I grab a chair and start to smash it against the door. I'm determined to escape and won't rest until I'm free. I'm not giving up. Tomorrow night is the full moon, and I have to do something, soon.

"Got it," I proudly shout as a large piece of the door breaks off. I drop the chair and start to kick at the small opening in an attempt to enlarge the gap. "Bingo!!!" I say aloud as another large chunk breaks loose. The opening is now big enough for me to climb through.

I grab my stuff and escape from the prison. Without looking back I begin running down the maze. There, at the end of the hall, I see light. Daring to hope, I pick up my speed.

"Three little trespassers are reflecting. One little trespasser is not." I hear Dahlia's voice whispering behind me.

I keep running. I cannot give up. Not now. Selene needs me. "And now there are three little trespassers left," and then, out of nowhere, she grabs my ankles. I drop to the floor and she begins to drag me away.

I sink my nails into the floor and try to fight her, but she is too strong.

"NO!" I yell. "Selene!!!"…

Selene

Yolanda has been missing since yesterday. I'm worried and hope William, or who ever that thing inside William's body is, can help me. I know he knows where she is, but I lack the courage to ask him what he's done with her.

I ask Phillip if he saw her or if has any clues to her whereabouts, but since Carmen's disappearance, Phillip has become unstable. He won't stop talking to himself or writing on his stupid notepad.

I know it may sound crazy, but at this moment I'd rather spend my time with the demon than with Phillip. He gives me the creeps.

"Come in," William says from the other side of his bedroom door. I put my hand on the knob and open the door.

William is half naked. He is by the window drying his hair.

"You've been outside my bedroom for quite a while," he smiles, and continues to dry his hair. "It is such a beautiful day." He turns around.

I didn't know he knew that I was outside, trying to force myself to talk to him, but than again, he is a demon.

I nod.

"I was wondering if – you – know where Yolanda is," I ask and stroll over to Raul's bed.

"I've told you before," he snaps. "I don't know where she is. What do you want me to say?"

"I don't believe you," I blurt out, and immediately regret it.

242

William's face turns angry.

"You'd better hold your tongue," he growls. "You're alive because of me."

"And I'm here because of you."

"NO!!!" he shouts. His pupils seem to lose their color. "You are here because of your grandmother. YOU WERE PROMISED TO ME!!!" My body stiffens. "You have two choices," he whispers in my ear, followed by a kiss at the base of my neck. "You choose to be part of my family, and you'll live, or you choose death, and your loved ones will share your fate." Slowly, I open my eyes. "Tell you what. If you decide to be with me – to be part of my family, I promise to give each of your friends, family, and everyone in this show a happy ending. A happy life.

"I feel generous today," he smiles, and turns his attention back to the horizon. "I'm finally free." I look back at Raul's bed. It has black candles, aromatic plants, a knife and jars on it. "It's for tomorrow. Either for your adoption, or your death," he explains. All I can think is, Great! "You know that I like you. You know that I want you and I would do anything to have you. I would give you anything if you stay with me, by my side, but if you decide not to, so be it. I won't stop you, but remember my irritation will hurt your family."

"Are you in love with me?" I ask, and William bursts into laughter. I blush and wish I could disappear. I'm so embarrassed.

"Why? Do you want me to be?" he asks, completely amused.

I look down at the floor and shake my head. I feel his arms wrapping around my shoulders.

"I'm sorry to disappoint you," he says. "To me you are a very expensive investment." I lift my head up and stare into his beautiful eyes, although they are not his, but William's. "A very pretty investment," he states, and kisses my lips.

"How do you do that?"

"Do what?"

"Kiss me. Touch me. I feel nothing. Is it because you are…"

"A demon?"

I nod.

"No," he smiles and releases me. He walks over to his bed and lies down on it. "It's because I gave something of mine to your family with the promise of getting it back. As I told you before, you are a very expensive investment."

I swallow. I want to know more, but I'm afraid. He is like a ticking bomb, or my mother going through menopause. One moment he is happy and the next he is fuming. I don't know how to get along with him.

I take a deep breath, collect what courage I have and ask, "Investment how?"

He smiles and places his hands behind his head. "I was a soul dealer," he says. "One of the best, and in a very short time I became the Lord of District 69. Scotland to you humans." He lifts his head. "Come. Sit next to me," he commands, and I obey. "Being a soul dealer is an honorable job. It is the best job and I was good at it. I was one of the best and gained respect and power. As you know, power and respect bring you a lot of enemies. My twin sister, Lillith, was one of them. She made a deal with a hunter family."

"Hunter – family?" I ask confused. I images of humans with guns and hunting dogs, chasing demons down the valley forms in my mind.

William looks amused. I guess he must have read my thoughts. "They're not the kind of hunters you think they are. They are bred to hunt us down. You and me," he explains. Then he places his hand under my chin and his expression turns dark. "Don't think they'll spare your life just because you are made of flesh and warm blood. You are a psychic – a descendant of the devil. Do you understand?" I nod. "Good." He kisses my forehead.

"What exactly does a soul dealer do?"

"A soul dealer lures humans into accepting a wish or desire in return for their souls," he proudly explains.

"Is this – what my grandmother did?"

"She was a witch, a white witch. The harmless and innocent kind, but not to hunters. They hunted her down and captured her. That's when she called me forward and asked me for help and power.

"So I helped her. I gave her a fraction of myself with the promise of collecting her seventh daughter."

"What did you give her?"

"A piece of my soul."

"I didn't know you had a soul."

He smiles. "You have no idea what we are," he replies. His voice sounds almost sad.

"Why the seventh daughter and not the second or fifth or whatever?" I ask. I realize that my voice is rising. I stop and take a deep breath.

"The number seven represent perfect completion," he explains. "I had to let my investment grow and prosper," he quickly adds with a smile, making me feel more like a savings account or a piece of produce than a person.

"So, you made me what I am?"

"Yes," he states without remorse or regret. It angers me. He has no idea how difficult life has been for me. "Don't look at me like that. What I gave you – it made you very special."

"To whom?" I raise my voice and move away from him.

"Don't be like that, Lene…"

"Don't you call me that!!!" I snap at him. "Only my family calls me Lene. You are not family."

He says nothing. He does nothing. He just sits on the bed, smirking at me.

Angry and frustrated, I turn around and place my hand on the door knob. I'm about to open the door when suddenly William is beside me. He holds the door shut.

"I understand that you are angry at me but it wasn't, and still isn't, my fault," he says softly in my ear.

"Please," I mutter. "Let me go."

"I will, and make sure to choose well. You know what I want. Be sure you give it to me. It won't be wise for you or your family if you refuse. I've invested too much into you."

I nod, and he walks away from the door.

I open the door and run into my bedroom, where I intend to stay beneath my blankets for a very long time.

William

"Don't you call me that!!!" she snaps at me. She stands up and walks away. "Only my family calls me Lene. You are not family." She raises her voice.

How dare she to talk to me that way. She is alive because of me. Her brother and parents are alive because of my generosity. I could have had them killed at any time just like I did my sister.

We glare at each other. Neither of us is willing to surrender.

Selene turns around and is about to leave. I jump to the door and hold it shut. I don't want her to leave. I want her to stay here with me.

I hate him and hate what he made me. I can hear her thoughts screaming in my mind. I want to go back home.

"I understand that you are angry at me, but it wasn't, and still isn't, my fault," I tell her and her hatred toward me continues to scream in my head.

"Please," she begs. "Let me go."

"I will and make sure to choose well. You know what I want. Be sure to give it to me. It won't be wise for you or your family if you refuse. I invested too much in you."

I don't want to go with you. I want to go back home to my mom and dad and – Seth, she thinks. I start to get angrier. I better let her go before she sees my true colors. I need her to come with me, and I can't forcefully take her. It was the loophole that Katherine was able to slip into our deal.

She nods and I walk away from her. She is free to go – for the moment.

She opens the door and runs away. I can hear her foot steps echoing down the hall.

"You only have to deal with her until tomorrow night," my faithful follower says in my ear. I smile as her cold hands slowly and passionately wrap around my upper chest. "I can't wait for the moment you and I are able to lie in bed together, as humans do. I can't wait for the moment I am able to feel your warm body next to mine, and lay my head upon your chest, and hear the beating of your heart."

I take a deep breath. I'm agonized. I don't know how to tell her that I've changed my mind. I want to keep Selene the way she is. I need her. I've invested too much effort into her.

I take her hand and kiss it. "I can't wait to make love to you as demons do," I lie to her.

Dahlia smiles at me and kisses the base of my neck. "Me too."

We stay silent, holding each other, watching the horizon.

"Yolanda is out," she says after a while.

"I thought you wanted to get rid of Phillip?"

"She escaped and wanted to stop us. I'm not about to lose my body. I've waited too long and risked too much," Dahlia states. The world has changed so much. I don't know how I'll be able to walk among humans who have developed so quickly. Once my kind was hunted, and now humans worship us out in the open without any consequences. They want to be part of us. How strange the world has become.

"Is everything all right?" Dahlia asks. I take her hand and kiss it one more time. I nod. "You should rest. You've been locked beneath the ground for decades. And you are not used to the body."

"I'm fine," I smile at her and turn around. I hold her face. "You worry too much."

"You are my Lord. You saved me and gave me all I've asked

for and more," she tells me. Her words are comforting.

Maybe I should kill Selene, and give her body to Dahlia. She'll be loyal to me, unlike Selene. She carries the Holloway's blood.

"Are you sure you are fine?"

"Yes, why?"

"You're so tense and agonized."

"I'm fine," I smile at her. "I'm great." I move over to the bed and lie down, feeling a bit unsteady. "You're right. The body does drain a lot of my energy."

"It's nothing that you can't deal with," she says, and lies beside me.

In the background, I hear Selene playing her violin.

"She's quite good," Dahlia confesses. "I hope to keep her talent."

"Why?"

"So I can play the instrument for you every night."

"I won't be home all the time. You know I have to reclaim my kingdom and power."

"I know, but I hoped we would remain together. To be like…"

"Humans." I stop her. "I'm not human and neither are you – not anymore. We can't be like them, and don't forget, they exist only to feed our needs."

"I know. I'm sorry," she whispers. "I'd better leave you alone." She goes without giving me a smile or a kiss.

My comment hurt her. I know what she wanted to be. I know what she wanted us to be. I can't give it to her. To be honest, I detest humans. They smell and their attitude is most repulsive. I don't know what Lucinda saw in them.

It's late in the day, and I must have fallen asleep. I walk out of the room. The hall is dark and cold. It feels empty, and a deep surge of loneliness fills my body. One of the side effects of occupying a body that doesn't belong to me. It will take a few months before this one will be fully mine and rid of all these useless human emotions and weaknesses.

A door opens and Selene steps out. She immediately drops her gaze to the floor. She looks uncomfortable.

"Hey!" she says. I take her hand and pull her closer to my chest.

"Hey," I whisper in her ear and kiss her on her head. I can't stay away from her. I'm so addicted to her. I condemn them all, all the Holloway's, so beautiful and powerful. They made me one of their hostages.

Another door opens and Selene and I turn around. It's Phillip.

"Ready to go down?" He asks with some hesitation in his voice. He is tired and has lost all sense of reason. I expect him to blow up at any minute.

Selene and I nod and walk hand-in-hand into the dining room, where another chess piece is waiting for us on the table.

Phillip approaches the object and grabs it.

"Yolanda," he says and Selene's hand jumps in mine. "Damn it!" he snaps, and throws the chess piece on the ground. "It has to be one of you two," he mutters.

"You're crazy," I tell him. "It's not me or Selene. It must be you."

Phillip glares at the two of us. He looks confused.

A thought enters my head. I decide to have some fun with him and begin talking telepathically to him.

Phillip!!! I call his name and watch his body start. Is this still a game? Was Tony right? Is someone after us? Who? Why? And who will be next?

I smile internally watching Phillip struggle to control himself. I pull Selene closer to me, keeping my eyes fixed on him.

"If you want to live, you better stay away from me." Phillip storms into the kitchen.

I hear doors opening and closing, and after a minute or two, he walks out with food in hand.

"Do not come after me," he grunts, flashing a butcher knife at us.

Selene's hands grasp my arm and, I don't budge from my position.

Phillip and I stare at each other for a few seconds, and then he leaves.

"What now?" Selene asks.

"Nothing," I smile at her, and walk into the kitchen.

"What do you mean nothing?" Selene follows me. "We have a lunatic on the loose."

"And?"

"What do mean and?" she says, sounding hysterical.

"I'm not afraid of someone like him and you shouldn't be either." I toss her some cookies. "Now – eat."

"What?" She stares at the food I just gave her.

"You need to eat something. You need to be strong for tomorrow."

"OH!" She looks demoralized.

"Do you want me to send my hounds after him?"

"NO!" she yells. "I'm fine. I'm not afraid anymore. I'm here with you. I know you'll take care of me. I know you'll make sure nothing happens to me."

I smile. Her words invigorate me.

At least until tomorrow night. I hear her thought finishing in my mind. I continue to smile.

"Have you come to a decision?"

Selene nods.

"I have no other choice but to offer myself to you. To be loyal to you."

I walk to her and take her in my arms. She feels so good, so warm, and at this moment, I understand Dahlia's desire to be human. I start to panic. I realize that I'm beginning to fall in love with Selene, and it scares me. Damn them all. Damn the Holloway's who made me a sick human wanting love and adoration from her.

Phillip

"Damn it!!!" I yell as I read her name. "It has to be one of you two."

William's body stiffens in anger and, offended, he shouts, "You're crazy. It's not me or Selene. It's you."

I glare at the two of them and keep thinking over and over: Who is the mole? Who is the mole? Who is the mole?

Phillip!!! Suddenly a voice in my head calls my name, startling me. Is this still a game? Was Tony right? Is someone after us? Who? Why? And who will be next?

I watch William pulling Selene closer to him while keeping his eyes fixed on me.

It must be one of them, but which?

Selene is quieter than normal, and seems more dependent on William than ever before. The energy in her eyes appears to be gone, concealed by darkness.

William's pompous attitude is gone, and his eyes, once filled with arrogance, are now intense and vigilant. He seems ready to attack anyone who would come between him and Selene.

And I, no longer with my head in the clouds over women, am now alert to any sound and strange movement. My confident personality is now in a deplorable condition. I can't sleep and it's starting to show. My hands won't stop trembling. I need to get out of here.

"If you want to live you better stay away from me," I threaten and storm into the kitchen.

I'm determined to get away from them. I grab food and water, and decide to hide somewhere in the house where neither of them can find me. I already know where to hide.

With provisions in a backpack and a kick ass knife in my hand, I walk out of the kitchen and growl, "Don't come after me," flashing my knife at them.

Selene's hands grasps William's arm, and he puffs up his

chest like a rooster, ready to come after me.

We glare at each other for a few seconds, and then I decide that it is time to leave. I can't, and don't want to, stay here any longer. I give William a quick glance. He smirks at me. I jerk. His expression is so cold, his features so hard, and his attitude is very menacing.

I'm out of here, I tell myself, and hastily stride into the leaving room. I enter the hidden maze and don't stop until I reach Selene's room.

I start to set up my headquarters in the crawl space I discovered with Warren and Seth while searching for Priscilla. I'll have full view of their movements. I know William very well. He'll probably lock himself and Selene in this room and when one of them makes a move, I'll be watching. I won't be caught by surprise. I'll be the one who'll survive.

After an hour or so, I hear footsteps, scuffling noises, and whispers. I peer through the peep hole and observe the two of them walking through the door, placing food on the floor, and then shoving the closet in front of the bedroom door.

Ah!!!! William, William, you are so predictable, I laugh internally.

"This should be fine for the moment." William smiles gleefully and jumps onto Selene's bed. He motions for her to lie next to him. With some hesitation, she does. She places her head on his chest and they remain silent.

I sigh. I was hoping for some action between the two of them but – I guess – Selene is one of those good girls and William is a perfect gentleman (with her). I have to smile, because I know William. He is just like me. We take what we want, and we don't dance around little girls' feelings. But I guess he must be in love, and with that in mind, I start to think of Carmen.

I smile once again. I think I was overcome with love. I miss her and her awful temper very much. I wish she could be here with me. We would certainly spend our time better then those two lying arm in arm. How boring.

I see doubt and fright in Selene's eyes. She seems scared and none too happy about being with William.

I begin to study him. I can't imagine why, but his presence makes me nervous and troubled.

William looks at the clock and his face turns grave.

Then he glances in my direction. His pupils turn pure white. Astonished, I look away.

What was that?

3 contenders remaining

Day Twelve

Tuesday, August 24, 2010

Phillip

I open my eyes, but there is nothing but darkness. I must have fallen asleep while I was watching the two of them.

Selene now appears to be very nervous. It took her a long time to fall asleep. William was awake all night and talking to himself. He is losing it. Too bad for him.

My plan for the day is to sit here and keep an eye on them.

One more day, Phillip. One more day, I tell to myself over and over again. I look through the peephole and find William sitting next to Selene. He is caressing her head and whispering something in her ear.

Selene doesn't react. She is still, almost lifeless.

William starts to hum a lullaby to her, and my body begins to shake uncontrollably. Something is wrong, but what?

Then, unexpectedly, William turns his eyes on me. My heart leaps into my throat and I feel paralyzed. I'm unable to look away from him or move away from this spot.

He smiles at me and that's when…

"Two little trespassers are blissfully together. One little trespasser is not," I hear the voice of a little girl singing nearby.

I turn and glance to my side. A Creole woman smiles at me and draws nearer.

"And now there are two little trespassers left," she says in a childish voice.

I try to stand up or move but I can't.

I open my mouth in an attempt to scream for help, but no sound comes from my lips and then…

Selene

"Good morning," William, or whatever that thing is, says to me. He gently kisses me on my forehead and places something in my hand. I sit upright and open my palm. Another chess piece. It's

255

Phillip. He's gone, leaving me alone with William. "Get dressed," he smiles at me. He is in a fantastic mood. "I'll meet you downstairs in the kitchen."

Without a word of protest, I obey his wish. I'm left with no other choice. My life, my dreams and everything dear to me, are at his feet to do whatever he likes with in order for me to obey his laws. I don't care much about my life or dreams but my family...

I feel a giant knot building up in my throat. I need to calm down. He doesn't like it when I'm upset or miserable. He says that my horrible mood rubs off on him.

I wipe the tears from my face and march into the bathroom where I begin my usual morning routine.

Finished and ready, I descend the stairs. The aroma of fresh bacon, scrambled eggs, coffee, and warm waffles reaches my nostrils.

"Morning," I shyly smile at him as I enter the kitchen. I try to appear happy so as not to displease him.

"There you are..." he starts, and when he lifts his eyes to look at me, he stops. He seems displeased at my taste in clothes. "Before I bring you home, I'll have Victoria buy you some new clothes."

"Victoria?" I ask half confused. I look down at my boots, pair of blue jeans and white shirt. I see nothing wrong with what I'm wearing, but I don't protest. I'm walking on thin ice that can break at any moment. He can kill me just as easily as he did his sister. I'm just a pawn in his game.

"I won't hurt you," he whispers in my ear. I jump. He is extremely fast and powerful. "Victoria is my assistant. Now sit and eat."

I nod and take a seat in the kitchen breakfast nook. William starts serving me several different foods that he cooked. I'm not hungry. My stomach has shrunk during the last few days, but I must eat. I need my energy and can't offend him after he prepared this meal for me.

I take a fork in hand and sink it into the scrambled eggs. I stop and look up at him. He is sitting on the opposite side of the table smiling and watching me.

Then he winks and starts to eat. "This is sooo good," he says. "I haven't eaten for so long, and while this body remains human I'll try to eat everything I see. Your civilization has changed so much. I see everything and try to learn as much as I can."

"What do you mean 'as long this body remains human?" I ask him.

William places his fork on the plate. "This body won't remain the same for long. In the next few days, weeks and months you'll see changes – physical changes. Once the body is completely finished adapting to my needs, I won't be able to eat or drink anything humans do," he concludes, and picks up his fork.

"What will you eat then?" I ask, and notice his grip tighten around his fork.

"You'll see when the time comes," he says in a cold voice. He doesn't look at me.

"Will – I – change too?"

William drops his fork and glares at me. "I have a present for you," he says and takes something from beneath the table.

"A cat," I utter in confusion, wondering at the same time where he found a cat on this island.

"It's yours." He places the cat on my lap. It is pure black and has bright, warm, blue eyes. He is frail and extremely thin. "Does he remind you of someone you know?" he asks. I study the cat's wide eyes. A silver collar with a silver bell is around its neck. I take the bell in my hand and see a name engraved on it. It reads:

William

My heart jumps.

"Why?" I ask him, trying to hold back my tears.

With a smile he says, "What did you want me to do? He is

my enemy. I just made sure he wouldn't interfere with my plans."

"He was no threat to you," I interrupt. I see loathing and desire for me in his eyes. He hates me for causing him so much pain. I'm death to him, as he is to me. We are bound together. "Will I, one day, also share the same fate and hatred you give your enemies?"

"Never," he replies and his face softens. He moves forward wanting to kiss me, but in the last moment he stops. "I could never hurt you. You are so precious to me," he whispers in my ear.

"My Lord," a female voice calls.

William stiffens, "Dahlia, my love." he smiles and takes a pretty young woman into his arms. They kiss, and I look down at the cat. I start to pet him, telling myself that I'll find a way to rescue him. I pray that I will be able to keep that promise.

William, the cat, starts purring and rubs his head gently against my hand.

"Tonight, I'll be yours," Dahlia smiles. I'm not quite sure what she is talking about.

William and Dahlia look at me. "Change of plans," William tells her. I see Dahlia's body tense.

"What change of plans?"

He steps over to me and places his hand on my shoulder. "I've decided to welcome her into my clan. I'll make her my heir."

Now Dahlia glares at me and I feel threatened. "What? Are you insane?" She shouts, turning back to William. "Do you know what this means? What she'll be?"

William's eyes turn completely white. His face becomes an ugly mask. He turns around.

"I'm sorry," whispers Dahlia. "Please forgive me." There is a submissive tone to her voice.

My heart is beating wildly. I'm afraid for her life. I grab the cat and clutch him to my chest. Like the coward I am, I look away.

"I suggest you learn your place," he growls at her.

"Yes, my Lord. I'm sorry. Forgive me," Dahlia pleads. "I

just thought you wanted me. I'm sorry. Never mind."

I feel his breath closer to my face. He places one of his hands under my chin and lifts my head up. "You can have Carmen's body…"

"Lillith's body?"

"Go ahead. It's yours." Dahlia gives me a very cold glare. I need to watch my back with her. "Take that as a piece of good advice. Her fate could be yours if you displease me again. And make sure nothing happens to Selene." He kisses my cheek. "I'll hold you responsible for her well-being as long we are on this island."

Dahlia's body tenses and her eyes flash. "I thought it would be just you and me."

"And it will," he smiles, winking at me as if to say, 'Not'. I see Dahlia as a woman full of love, and completely devoted to him. "I thought you weren't too happy about having her body. According to you, she is too dull, innocent and unoriginal," he declares. My ego is hurt. I always knew I wasn't a knockout, but dull and unoriginal – that's mean. William laughs lightly and presses his lips to my ear. "Not that I find you that way," he whispers, "I find you quite interesting."

Interesting. Is that a good thing? Is that something a girl wants to hear from a guy? What do I care? He's a demon. His opinion shouldn't matter to me.

"You'll keep me busy," he says in a very amused tone of voice. He looks up at Dahlia. "Take Carmen's body. It's yours to have. Do what you want. Now, leave us." With a wave of his hand, Dahlia is gone.

William picks up my fork and takes a bite of scrambled eggs. "It tastes pretty good. I'm not a bad chef," he smiles at me. I don't understand the new William. One moment he's angry and the next he's happy. "It's not poisoned," he continues, and moves the fork closer to my mouth.

Embarrassed and feeling silly, I try to take the fork away

from him, but he won't let go. Finally I open my mouth and take a bite. "So?" He asks.

"Good," I nod, and grab the fork from his hand. I force myself to eat, not wanting him to feed me again.

He chuckles and caresses my hair. I feel like I'm his pet.

"William," I call, and the cat looks up.

"Lukas. Call me Lukas."

"Is that your real name?"

"My human name."

"And your demon name?"

"That is not for you to know," he says. He no longer seems angry or irritated. "Now, what did you want to ask me?"

"Is – is my family ok? Will they be safe?"

Lukas moves his upper body closer to mine. "Only if you obey me and my laws. I promise to be kind to you and to your love ones, but if you don't do what I say…" He grabs William by the shoulders and lifts him off my lap. The cat starts growling, meowing and hissing.

"Please. Don't!!!" I cry out, and try to get him to release his grip. "Please, Lukas."

He stops as I call his name. "You really care for this thing." He hands the cat back to me. I pull him close to my chest. I can feel his fragile body shaking. "Don't cross me or your loved ones and everyone you came into contact with will share a fate much worse than his. Come to think of it, I'm not finished with him yet. He'll pay for what he and my sister did to me."

I look away from Lukas. I'm unable to meet his eyes. He scares me so much and the thought of spending my entire life with him is terrifying.

"I put a dress on your bed. I want you to wear it tonight," he says. "I'll see you later."

I watch him leave the room, and as soon as he is out of sight, I drop to my knees with William in my arms. I start to cry.

Lukas

The moon is full. Perfect for a union. Two enemies coming together under a bond – a contract between two people, but this time I won't be the fool I was centuries ago. I found a method that might help me fight the curse the Holloway's gave me centuries ago.

"She's coming," Dahlia calls. I turn around and my heart leaps with joy. She is so beautiful and innocent, a trademark of the Holloway women. "Are you sure you want to do this?" asks Dahlia.

Dahlia wants me to kill her. Truth be told, it would be the wisest path, but the thought of not having her around pains me terribly.

"Yes," I state, watching her walk closer to me. "Ready?" I smile at her.

"You promise me, if I become part of your family, you'll leave my family alone."

"I promise. I give you my word," I assure her, tracing my finger over my heart.

Selene nods. "I'm ready."

Dahlia, my dark priestess, begins our union. I trust her. I always have. Not once has she disappointed me or given me any reason to distrust her, unlike the Holloways. Beautiful and cruel, both at the same time.

Dahlia starts chanting in her old language, a remnant of an ancient civilization long since vanished from the earth.

I remember the first time she called me out of the holy confinement set upon me by the Holloway's. She asked for my help and I asked for my freedom. A perfect union between men and demons.

Dahlia and I are friends, family and lovers. My blood runs in hers, and hers in mine. Within the next few minutes, another will join me. The thought of tasting Selene's blood arouses me. The thought of Selene being by my side for eternity brings me joy. I'm reborn once again.

Dahlia is ready to cut our palm. I look at my new alliance and see a very frightened little girl. She is shaking, and her skin seems so pale in the moonlight. Saliva is accumulating in my mouth. She is so mouthwatering, and I can't wait for the moment to taste her blood.

Selene looks up at me. She seems to be reading my mind or, to be more correct, my facial expression. Her face is turning paler, and her pulse is accelerating.

I wipe the saliva off my lips and eye Dahlia. She isn't too happy with me at the moment, and she knows exactly what I'm thinking. Our minds are connected.

Dahlia grabs Selene's palm and slices it with a knife. She is troubled. She hopes that I will change my mind, but I won't. Then Dahlia cuts open my palm as well. Together, Selene and

I pour our blood into a golden bowl. Dahlia lifts the bowl up and prays to the gods for Selene's acceptance into my family.

"Drink," Dahlia says to Selene.

Selene looks uneasily at the bowl and turns her gaze to me. I smile at her and motion for her to continue the ritual.

She takes a deep breath, and with her eyes closed sips from the bowl.

I take the bowl and lift it up. "Bless our union and bring us fortune and glory," I say, and drink the remaining contents. It tastes so good. I hadn't drunk blood for decades, and I've forgotten how delicious it can be.

I turn to Selene and wipe away a trickle of blood from her lips. "From today you shall be know as Selene Crowell. Humans shall know you as my adoptive sister, and our kind shall know you as my heir," I say. Dahlia's body stiffens and I feel a strong wave of resentment. "You'll obey only me and only my laws."

Selene bows, "I shall obey only you and your laws. You are my Lord," she declares. My love and devotion for her becomes stronger than before. I never desired anything as much as I do her.

I kiss her forehead, restraining myself from kissing her lips. "You can go. Enjoy your last few hours in the world you used to know and love." I tell her. "Tomorrow night, when the doors and windows will be unlocked, your life will be completely changed. You'll be mine."

"Yes, my Lord," she says, with a bow she leaves.

I watch her walk away and I want her in my arms. I desire her company and love.

"How could you make her your heir?" Dahlia interrupts. I shake my head. "You love her don't you?"

"Yes. I do love her," I answer.

"It can't be. You love me and not her!" Dahlia's eyes blaze.

"I want to make her my queen."

"You told me you wanted me as your queen," she cries. She slowly vanishes, leaving me alone in my misery.

2 contenders remaining

Day Thirteen

Wednesday, August 25, 2010

Selene

On my last day, I find myself standing alone in the house. Lukas has left me with the task of deciding who should win the money.

After all we are still playing a game. Hahaha.

At least that's what Lukas wrote to me in a note.

I'm torn between several people. My brother, of course, Yolanda, and the Johnson sisters. Among the four of them the Johnsons deserve the money the most, but I want to give it to Seth as my goodbye gift to him. I want to make sure he and my parents will be safe and happy.

I look up and examine a box on the other side of the dining room table. I open it and find sixteen chess pieces inside. I take one of them and turn it upside down. There is a letter W on the base. I grab another piece and turn it over. A letter T is engraved on the base.

Excited, I run to the living room and find a piece of paper and pen. I sit down on the table and write down each letter. I switch the letters around, trying to make something sensible.

Finally, after an hour or so, I'm able to come up with:

Search west tower

Ecstatic, I run to the west tower only to find it completely empty.

"Oh, well," I sigh. "It's not like I have to be anywhere soon." I begin searching the area.

Inch by inch, I knock on the walls, stomp on the floor, and in the end I find nothing. Discouraged, I sit down by the chimney. I begin stare at my hands, and in that moment I realize what I have to do.

I take a quick breath and pull my gloves off. I start moving my hands all along the cold, massive chimney.

Images of Jay Owen and Dahlia form before my eyes. Mr. Owen is walking across the room with a confident, smile holding a small black suitcase in his right hand.

"What are you doing?" Dahlia snaps at him as she tries to keep up with his swift pace.

"Hiding the money – of course," he replies in a superior tone of voice. I watch him place the case inside the chimney.

"What for? You know they won't make it to the end. Azazel has to feed..."

"HE WILL NOT," Mr. Owen yells at her. At this moment a new side of Jay has been revealed. His face transform into a snarling dog, extremely demon-like. He glares at her, but with a twitch of his neck and a deep sigh, he composes himself, and reverts back into the calm person I have come to known.

Dahlia takes one or two steps back as Jay steps away from the chimney. Dahlia's eyes and mouth are wide open. She didn't expect him to lose his temper. Neither did I. He seemed to be the type of person who always has his emotions under control. I guess I was wrong about that.

"He'll need to feed on something. He is weak," Dahlia says in a most respectful manner.

"He'll find something else to chew on. I'm sure you'll make certain of that. My guests are not part of our arrangement. I worked very hard to get where I am today, and I like show business. Azazel and I go way back, but I won't put his desires before my own happiness."

"You promised us the Holloway girl."

"And you'll have her as I promised," he confirms. "But let me warn you. They are trouble for you, me and most of all Azazel."

"What do you know about them?" Dahlia asks and I sense tension in her voice.

Jay casts his gaze at the floor. A minute passes by. "They are strong, smart and very conniving. Azazel is like clay in their hands. He is their puppet, and if you want my opinion, Azazel should not be freed, not by the hands of a Holloway. They mean trouble for all our kind."

"But you promised – you promised to help him."

"Yes, I did. But let me warn you, watch your back with her. She is not to be trusted."

And with that, their images dissolve and I'm back in the present.

I put my gloves back on with a sour taste in my mouth. The last words of Jay Owen, 'watch your back with her. She is not to be trusted,' ring in my head, not to mention Lukas's real name. It sounds old and powerful. For some reason his name keeps ringing in my head and it drives me insane, because I've heard of him before.

My new home won't be pleasant at all, and definitely not safe. I'll have to be cautions.

I kneel down and peek into of the chimney. Something large is blocking the flue. I reach in and give it a good yank. The suitcase drops to the hearth in front of me.

Thrilled, I place it on my lap and try to open it, but it is locked. Something occurs to me. The last chess piece, the king, didn't have a letter. What if...

I snatch the bag and run down to the dining room.

There, I seize the chess piece and examine it. I twist the base, and a small key drops out.

With key in hand, I open the bag, and find packets and packets of cash. I let out a whoop and jump up. I've found the money!

I grab a piece of paper and write the winner's name down. I place the paper inside the bag and, satisfied, leave the room. I decide to walk into each of the other contestants' rooms. It is a way for me to say goodbye to my old life.

I save my brother's room for last. As I sort through his stuff, a giant knot forms in my throat. I can't imagine a life without my parents or my brother. I just hope they'll be happy.

At four fifty-nine in the afternoon I stand in front of the entrance door and wait to be released from this place.

The clock starts to chime. It's now five p.m., and the doors and windows unbolt themselves. I place my hand on the doorknob, turn it, open the door, and take a step outside.

Bright lights and cheering greet me. I close my eyes and when I open them again I find myself in a group, all of whom are clapping their hands. I look up and see Joanna walk out of the house with a victorious smile, holding the aloft.

"I thought you would choose your brother," a voice whispers in my ear. I turn to my side and Lukas is smiling at me.

"She's the best choice," I whisper back at him. "Besides, without me, my family doesn't need any money, because they never left the life they loved so much." My voice quivers.

He agrees with me, "Shall we congratulate her?"

I nod, and we walk together to the happy Joanna.

Back on the boat, the scene is surreal. Lukas is sitting next to me talking to Yolanda and Raul as if nothing had ever happened. All is as it should be. Straight ahead, where William Hawthorn once sat next to Carmen is now Phillip. He finally found his place in life. Carmen, AKA Dahlia, is watching me, and when Lukas places his hand on mine, she glares angrily. She loathes me and I know why. Behind me, I hear Seth and Maria planning to move in together. I'm happy for them. I think, and hope, she'll make him happy. With the thought of no longer being a part of my brother's life, I pace the deck. The land is rapidly approaching, and I'm frightened.

"Are you ok?" Lukas asks.

"Yes, just a bit melancholy."

"For you or your family?"

"Both." I confess. "I'm going to miss them all."

"They're happy. They'll be safe. I promised you that." He pats my hand. "Your parents are back in Seattle. Your father has his clinic and your mom is teaching once again. In a few years Seth will marry Maria and a few years after that they'll adopt two children."

"Adopt?"

"You are, and will be, the last of your family. I made sure of that," he states.

"What about Carmen?"

"You mean Dahlia?" he asks and I nod. "She'll have the life she always wanted, full of fame and glamour."

"Except she won't have you," I interrupt. "I have you."

Lukas moves closer to me and whispers in my ear, "Yes, you have me and I have you, for eternity."

1 contender remaining

<u>Part Three</u>

The Reunion

Reunion

Saturday, October 30, 2010

Wayne

"Welcome! Welcome!" Jay Owen seems overjoyed to see us, not on Black Bird Island this time, but in a studio filled with fans and loved ones. "It has been almost two months since the last time we saw each other," he continues. I look over to my brother who is holding Priscilla's hand. They appear happy and comfortable with one another. "So, Wayne," Owen calls to me. "How has your life changed since the end of the show?"

I smile. "It's been great," I reply, and hear the crowd cheer. "I moved to Hollywood and decided to enter show biz…"

"And it has been very successful," Jay Owen jumps in as the audience begins to cheer once again. Ah! How much I love to be admired.

"Yes," I smile. "I was selected to play a short role in 'Blue Vein'." More cheers come my way.

Warren

Wayne is enjoying the attention – maybe a bit too much, but he deserves it.

"What about you two?" Mr. Owen puts his arms around Priscilla and me.

"We're in love," I reply, and kiss Priscilla's hand. Sighs echo through the studio.

"How adorable," Wayne mocks me.

Priscilla blushes.

"Shut up!" I bark back and shove him.

Jay Owen ignores our confrontation.

"What's new?" He asks.

"The four of us moved to L.A. at the same time," I say, pointing at Priscilla, Ivy and Wayne. "We became quite comfortable with one another."

Priscilla

"Yep, we are," I add. "Wayne and I are searching for fame, success and glory."

"While Ivy and I discovered we share the same passion," Warren smiles, and winks at Ivy.

"And what's that?" Mr. Owen asks.

"They opened a bakery. It's called, 'Sweet Jewels from the South'," I declare.

"We have to thank our family, friends and fans for our success," Warren states, pointing toward the audience.

Everyone stands and claps.

"We love you," I shout, and give each of them an air kiss.

Ivy

"I've heard it's doing pretty well."

"It's doing great, fantastic even," I reply to Mr. Owen. "As Warren said before, we couldn't have done it without the help, support and love of families, friends, and fans," I restate and the audience begins to cheer again.

"How did you react once you found out that the Jones brother are rich – I mean, very rich?" Jay Owen asks. Priscilla and I stare at each other and begin to giggle. "What's so funny?" He asks.

"We knew it from day one," Priscilla says. "Their hands were professionally manicured and both wore Harmon, a $300 perfume."

"I told you," Wayne snaps at his brother.

"Whatever," Warren answers.

"What about the disappearances of your personal belongings?"

Wayne and Warren startle. They had hoped this part would have been forgotten.

"They reimbursed us," I state with a smile.

Jennifer

"They didn't reimburse all of us," I snap.

"You don't seem happy," Jay Owen states.

"Not at all," I continue to complain. "They destroyed a very important piece of jewelry. It was from my ex-boyfriend. I really, really liked that necklace."

"We told you how sorry we are," Wayne shouts from the other side of the stage. I'm not buying it. He knew what he was doing.

"I'm not going to forgive you," I declare and look away from the two of them. I'm on the verge of crying out of anger and frustration.

"How did your life change since you won the show?" Jay Owen asks my sister. I guess he must have felt my anger and frustration.

Joanna

"It's great," I smile. "More than great."

I glance over at my sister and grab her hand. I see how angry Jennifer is and how hard it is for her to forgive the two brothers. The necklace was very dear to her. "I paid our parents debt off and had some money left over."

"She bought a small two bedroom apartment," Jennifer interrupts me. "Joanna and I are now living together."

"The show reunited us. We are now not only sisters, but best friends," I confess and Jennifer embraces me.

The audience begins to cheer for us.

"I love you."

"I love you too," I tell her and we begin to tear up like idiots.

The audience cheers wildly, and I can see our parents standing proudly, clapping for Jennifer and me. Tears stream down their cheeks.

I watch my mom's lips forming the sentence, "I love you."

"I love you too," I tell her back.

Yolanda

Watching all the candidates, something feels so wrong. The picture doesn't look right to me.

A day after the show ended my grandmother called me. She asked me what had happened, and I told her that nothing did. She, of course, protested. The cards told her something else.

"Like what?" I asked her.

"Something has escaped from the island," she explained. "And death was there too."

"Nothing happened. No one died. We are all fine," I kept telling her, trying to calm her fears.

"Watch for the Crowell siblings. They are not what you think they are."

Those were her last words.

The next day my mom called us, informing us that my grandmother died, and on that same day, Raul won the lottery. He is $ 250,000,000 richer.

How ironic.

Raul

"And now to our millionaire," Mr. Owen introduces me. Everyone looks around the stage, not knowing who he is talking about. "Raul Ramirez won the lottery a few weeks ago. He is a very rich person."

The room becomes silent, and all attention is turned to me. I feel uncomfortable.

"Any plans with the money?" Seth asks me.

"Yolanda and I will travel around the world for a year or two and after that we'll attend college," I declare. The audience claps, and I can hear some of the contenders congratulating me.

Phillip

"I have to tell you," Jay starts smiling at me. "You were right all along."

"About Tony and Matt working for the show?" I ask. He nods his head joyfully. "Dahlia and I knew it from the beginning. We don't believe in ghosts or haunting or whatever people think is out there."

Matt

"But we had you fooled for a while," I step in. "Some of you were on the verge."

"Not me," Dahlia states with a click of her tongue. "I knew all along that it was one of you two. The constant ghoulish stories Tony came up with everyday. They made no sense to me."

"Whatever," I tell her. "I know we had you fooled for a while."

"Why did you do it?" Yolanda asks.

"For our book," I honestly state. "We were willing to do anything to onto on Black Bird, Island and the station knew it. They approached us." I stop as I look around and feel a bit uncomfortable. I think Tony and I may have gone a bit too far.

Tony

"For us to be in the show we had to scare the hell out of you," I step in. I see my brother becoming nervous.

"And day by day take one or two of you out of the show," Matt continues.

"I hope it was worth it," Yolanda snaps. She really can't stand me anymore after finding out what my brother and I did.

It does hurt me that she won't talk to me, but it was all worth it for our book. I would do it all again, without hesitation.

"Yes, it was," Matt snaps back at her. "Black Bird Island" will be out in bookstores this summer."

The audience and contestants begin to clap, all except for Yolanda.

"How did you choose your victims?" Raul asks.

"The American public," Matt replies. "Every day they voted for their favorite candidates and the person with the least votes got booted out. Simple as that."

"It would have been nice if someone had informed us," Ivy snaps.

"Then the show wouldn't have been so amusing," Mr. Owen smiles.

He turns over to Dahlia.

Dahlia

"And how has life changed for you?" Jay asks me. I smile.

"Never better," I tell him. "Our career has skyrocketed." I take Phillip's hand, even though, deep inside I wish it were Lukas's.

"Yes, it did," and Phillip kisses my cheek.

I glance over to Lukas. He is totally mesmerized by Selene and it breaks my heart. I wanted to be the one standing by his side. I would have made a much better choice than her. I would have made him happy and he could have trusted me.

Maria

"And how has your life changed?" Jay Owen smiles at me.

I grab Seth's hand and with a large smile answer. "My life has changed for the better too. Seth and I are living together."

The audience claps and I blush.

Unexpectedly, Seth kisses my lips.

Seth

"She transferred over to Seattle University, and I'm very happy," I declare, embracing her.

"So," Jay Owen continues, "A happy ending after all."

"Yes. We had our problems at the beginning of the show, but as it continued we were forced to confront them, and I'm happy to say that we resolved our differences. We've begun a new life together."

Selene

I don't know if I should be more unhappy about not being able to see my family anymore, or the fact that they seem much happier without me. They don't even miss me.

I know that since I walked out of the asylum I'm no longer their child, but still...The recollection of them ever having given birth to a second child is wiped from of their memory. I'm no longer my Dad's little girl who he taught to hunt. I'm no longer my Mom's little lady, who she taught how to bargain for deals. I'm no longer my brother's little shadow who followed him every where. I admired him and hoped to be just like him.

I take a deep breath and look down at Seth. He seems so happy and in love with Maria.

I shift my eyes over to my parents. They're sitting in the audience, and look so much happier than when they were living in Montana. Dad has his clinic in Seattle and Mom is still teaching kindergartners.

Lukas puts his hand on my lap. I jump, and he gives me a quick smile. I smile back at him and glance at to my new mom, Victoria, Lukas's partner.

Victoria is not the typical mother figure, or someone who even wants to be a mom. She is all business and has no time for anybody but Lukas.

Lukas loves her, but not in the same way he loved Dahlia, or loves me, but in a friendly and respectable manner. According to Victoria, Lukas saved her once, and raised her as his own daughter.

Victoria did the best she could to keep Lukas's name and fortune alive, but without him, she couldn't hold his empire together.

Now that he is back, Lukas will attempt to reclaim his estate, with Victoria's help, of course.

"I can't wait to be back home," Lukas whispers.

I stay silent. I can, I think to myself. Victoria is typing like a crazy on her E-Phone. She is probably checking on her soul quota. It's a brutal business, I think half amused and half disconsolate.

Lukas

Selene is not happy. She is upset seeing her family so happy without her. Seeing them not miss her even a bit.

I miss them so much, I hear her thoughts.

I move closer to her. "They are not your family anymore," I tell her. "You have to let go of them. I promised you a happy ending for everyone you knew in return for your loyalty."

"I know," she says through clenched teeth, "and you have it."

"They are not part of your new life. Let them go and you'll be free," I conclude. Selene pushes my hand away from her lap. She is angry and hurt.

"And what about you two?" my old friend Jay Owen asks. I'm grateful to him and Dahlia for the help they gave me. "Have you become closer?"

"Yes, we have," I tell him and signal with my eyes to be careful and not go too far with me.

"What about you Selene? Do you like your new home?"

"Y-yes," she stutters. "Devil's Creek is beautiful, and I've already made friends."

279

I raise my brow in disappointment. I hate that place. It is so isolated from civilization. Packed with supernaturals, and the handful of humans actually living there are so dull.

Selene loves it. I don't understand her, nor do I agree with her choice of friends. Selene and the sheriff's daughter, Carly Carlton, became quite close, and this could impede my work. It forced me to send Selene away.

"Hey, Carly," she smiles and waves to the cameras.

"One last question," Jay smiles and the look on his face alarms me. "Most of the viewers are wondering if there is any romance between the two of you."

I jump. Selene's head droops, and Dahlia looks over to me, waiting for an answer.

"No, No, No! Lukas and I are siblings." Selene adds and her comment rubs me the wrong way.

"You were adopted," Jay quickly adds. "You are actually not related."

"True – but no. We are not in love, nor will be," she declares, and I can feel anger exploding within me.

"I do have to say that we are all a bit disappointed. We had hoped for another happy love story," Jay continues. Now he is going too far, friend or no friend. "Did you at least get to know each other better? After all, you entered the show for that reason. To learn more about one another.

"Yes, we did learn about one another and we came to love and respect each other even more," I declare. Selene seems very unhappy with my answer. I don't care. She had better learn that she belongs to me, and I decide if and when we should be a couple or not.

I turn my attention back to Selene and watch her close her eyes. A tear runs down her face. The images of her family become visible in my head. I feel her pain, sorrow and mourning.

Good-bye, I hear Selene's voice whisper in my head, and the images of her family slowly disappear.

She is releasing her old life. I should feel badly, but I don't. She is now truly mine.

"Selene," I softly call her name. She opens her eyes. "How do you feel about spending a weekend in New Orleans?"

Breinigsville, PA USA
03 February 2011
254707BV00001B/1/P